By Gayle Callen

The Wrong Bride
Redemption of the Duke
Surrender to the Earl
Return of the Viscount
Every Scandalous Secret
A Most Scandalous Engagement
In Pursuit of a Scandalous Lady
Never Marry a Stranger
Never Dare a Duke
Never Trust a Scoundrel
The Viscount in Her Bedroom
The Duke in Disguise
The Lord Next Door
A Woman's Innocence
The Beauty and the Spy
No Ordinary Groom
His Bride
His Scandal
His Betrothed
My Lady's Guardian
A Knight's Vow
The Darkest Knight

THE WRONG BRIDE

Highland Weddings

GAYLE CALLEN

AVONBOOKS

An Imprint of HarperCollins*Publishers*

This is a work of fiction. Names, characters, places, and incidents are products of the author's imagination or are used fictitiously and are not to be construed as real. Any resemblance to actual events, locales, organizations, or persons, living or dead, is entirely coincidental.

AVON BOOKS
An Imprint of HarperCollins*Publishers*
195 Broadway
New York, New York 10007

Copyright © 2015 by Gayle Kloecker Callen
ISBN 978-0-06-226798-6
www.avonromance.com

First Avon Books mass market printing: November 2015

Avon Trademark Reg. U.S. Pat. Off. and in Other Countries, Marca Registrada, Hecho en U.S.A.
HarperCollins® is a registered trademark of HarperCollins Publishers.

Printed in the U.S.A.

10 9 8 7 6 5 4 3 2 1

I'd like to dedicate this book to the pets who enrich our lives and bring such joy. To my sweet dog, Apollo, for giving me your beseeching, soulful look whenever I think I'm too tired to walk, for pressing all seventy-five pounds of you against my side on cold winter evenings, and for great hikes in the woods where you run with blissful abandon. Watching you sleep with your paws straight up in the air always makes me laugh.

THE
WRONG
BRIDE

CHAPTER 1

Great Britain, 1727

Riona Duff was startled out of a deep sleep, groggy and uneasy. For a moment she didn't know where she was. A single candle burned in its holder on the bed table, so she could see the wavering glow of light illuminate the canopied bed and part of the door.

This wasn't her room. Where was she?

And then she remembered—she wasn't in London anymore, the city where she'd spent the majority of her life. She'd gone north to York with her uncle's family while her own parents and sister traveled to the south of France to improve her sister's fragile health.

Something creaked, and she froze, for it sounded like a door. The one beside her was firmly closed, so that meant—

A large, male hand suddenly covered her mouth.

Riona's eyes went wide and she screamed, but the sound was muffled. She smelled horses and sweat and her own fear. Though she tried to buck and slide away, she was hampered by the bedclothes, and then the man's other arm across her body, pinning her down. Her heart seemed to be dancing in her chest, racing with terror and making her light-headed.

"I'll not harm ye," he said softly, gruffly.

He spoke with the Scottish accent that still lingered in her father's speech even after so many years in England.

"Just do as I say," he continued, "and I'll free your mouth if ye promise not to scream."

Her eyes darted frantically about, and though she could see the outline of his shaggy head, the candle was behind him and his face was a mass of shadows. He loomed over her like a mountain, a stranger who'd dared breach her bedroom from the balcony. He could want—anything.

He gave her a little shake that made her squeak with fright.

"Do I have your word, lass?"

Having no choice, she nodded. The hand slid away, but the arm across her body did not, a heavy, threatening weight that made her feel fragile.

"What do you want?" she choked out, her voice trembling. "I've nothing of value. They'll catch you if—"

"Silence." Though soft, his voice was deep and full of a threatening growl. "Ye're coming with me."

He took her by the arm and pulled her upright, her arm like a twig in his massive fist.

"But—where are you taking me?" she demanded, aghast.

Drawing her closer, he gave her another shake. "I'll answer all your questions later. But not another word from ye until we're away."

He raised her to her feet, hands on both her arms, like she was a stuffed doll. And that made her realize how truly large he was, towering well above her, the width of his body an impenetrable blackness. She was trembling so badly she swayed. Her only hope now was that someone came to rescue her, but her attacker had made little sound, and she knew no one would be checking on her. She was only a niece, tolerated out of family duty and little else. Her cousin Cat would have cared, but she was away in the countryside with friends.

"I've brought ye clothes," he said, shoving a bundle against her stomach. "Put them on."

Her mouth sagged in horror, and then she closed it with a snap and tried to make herself sound braver than she felt. "I will not disrobe in front of you."

"Och, I'm not asking ye to. Keep your nightshift on then, and wear the gown over it. I even brought ye a petticoat, since I ken ladies need them."

"My own garments—"

"—are too fine and will draw attention to us. Hurry, unless ye want my help."

She held her breath for a suspended moment, then let it out when he dropped his hands from her. Snatching the bundle from him, she turned away, dropping it on the bed. There were no stays, which would make her a very loose woman, but she could not bring herself to ask about their absence. She stepped into the rough linen petticoat and tied it above her hips. There were no hoops stitched in place, as she had inside her own petticoats. Her face felt hot at knowing this man, this stranger, stood behind her and watched such an intimate act. Her maid would have gently lowered the garments over her head. She wasn't used to dressing alone.

She had to hurry, or he might go through with his threat to help her.

She could feel that the gown was made of plain wool with a square décolletage. No open front or stomacher to pin into place. His choice was practical. As she settled the gown over her petticoat, she was surprised to feel his hands tugging at the lacing at her back. Gritting her chattering teeth, she felt forced to allow this intimacy.

When he was done, he put both hands on her shoulders and pushed her toward the French doors leading to the balcony. She took two steps, and suddenly images flashed in front of her eyes, of being kidnapped, assaulted, her body degraded—her body never found. Ransom might be asked from her uncle, who didn't care about her, and her parents, too far away to respond. Did the man even have a weapon? She hadn't seen one, and that knowledge made her suddenly bold.

Riona flung herself sideways, startling him enough that he let go. She stepped on the edge of her skirt trying to straighten up and run for the door, only to have the man grab her around the waist and lift her off the ground, her back to his chest. She kicked backward with her legs, even as his other hand covered her mouth again.

"That's enough," he said sternly into her ear.

He carried her to the glass door. All she could do was swing her legs at him, but *his* legs felt as unaffected as the trunk of a tree kicked by a bird. She reached behind to grab at his hair with her free hand. Though he swore, he didn't stop his inexorable stride out into the cool summer air on the balcony. She was used to the sounds of London, carriages at all hours of the night, the calls of street vendors and their customers even before dawn. But away from the town center, York was as silent as the moors, as if they were the only people left in the world. She felt an ache of desperate loneliness.

When her captor went right to the edge and leaned over it, she gasped as the half moon illuminated a steep drop into the shadows of the garden.

Her head reeled with dizziness. He couldn't possibly have forced her to dress only to push her to her death.

And then she saw the flash of a lantern signaling them from below before being quickly shuttered, followed by the dark, boxy outline of a coach. Two black horses pulled it forward into the moonlight, away from the building, and then the well-trained animals went utterly still.

"I'm going to lower ye to the coachman," the man said in her ear. "If ye fight, ye might fall, and we don't want that. Do ye understand?"

She nodded, but when he removed his hand from her mouth, she spoke hoarsely, quickly. "Why are you doing this? I'm not worth anything to you. A ransom—"

"I want no ransom. Quiet."

The first tears spilled down her cheeks as he pulled up a rope affixed to the stone balustrade. Had he climbed up that way? She couldn't possibly do the same!

"There's a loop at the bottom. Ye'll stand in it and I'll lower ye. Now up on the balustrade."

She gasped when he put both large hands about her waist, then lifted her until she was forced to stand on the narrow stone or risk tumbling and breaking her neck. With a groan, she closed her eyes, swayed, and was actually grateful the man kept a firm hold of her hips.

"None of that," he ordered sternly. Then he sighed. "This won't work, I see that now."

"Then let me go and I won't tell anyone what happened here!"

She opened her eyes, then reeled as the shadowy walled garden seemed to expand into darkness, and the wind picked up. She felt dazed with shock and disbelief.

"I'm not letting ye go. Ye're my future, lass."

His future? But she didn't have time to even guess what he meant when he suddenly vaulted onto the balustrade beside her, his movements cat-like for a big man.

"I'll just have to carry ye then. Now don't move, or ye'll kill us both."

Horrified, she began, "Carry me—"

Then he tossed her over his shoulder like a sack of grain, and she landed with an "oomph" that surely bruised her stomach. She was hanging upside-down, the world spinning around her, the rough wool of his coat against her mouth, his arm across the back of her thighs as he bent to grip the rope.

"Hold on, lass, or it'll end badly for ye."

For the first time, he sounded truly menacing, as if he didn't want her antics to send him hurtling down with her to an ugly death. She could feel the muscles of his chest and back tense with strain as he began to lower himself down the side of the bal-

cony, using his feet to brace himself, and then only
his arms as the rope swayed in mid-air.

She closed her eyes and clutched his coat with
both hands, too terrified to do anything other than
pray. And then it was over, and she thanked God for
solid ground. Not that she felt it with her own feet,
because she was suddenly tossed into the interior
of the coach, where she landed hard on a leather-
covered bench. As she scrambled to sit upright, her
captor looked through the doorway, his shoulders
blocking the meager moonlight.

"Be a good lass and keep quiet if ye don't want
company tonight," he warned in a hard voice.

Then he slammed the door shut. There was no
lantern lit, and both windows had a curtain drawn
down over them. She was in absolute blackness.
Hands fumbling, she found the door handle, but
somehow it was jammed from the outside. She
shook it in frustration, then sank back and just
hugged herself. The coach lurched into motion, the
wheels clattering repetitively on the cobblestone
street outside her uncle's town house.

She was too numb and disbelieving for tears
now. She was the prisoner of two men, and didn't
have any idea what they might do to her. Unless
someone had seen what had happened—and there
was no sound of pursuit—she was alone against
these strangers. She could sit here and wallow in
fear—or she could find a way to free herself.

The first thing she did was try the door again, but even the leather curtain had somehow been fastened shut. She explored by touch, finding blankets, cushions, and candles in the storage compartments beneath the benches, even a selection of garments, but no weapons or tinderbox. They must not want her setting the coach afire, she thought grimly.

She found a corked bottle of cider, some cheese, and something like bread that she nibbled on. Did it have the taste of . . . oats? She suddenly remembered her father talking about the food that had comprised much of a clansman's diet: oatcakes.

Why had a Scotsman kidnapped her? She wanted to fling the food aside in her anger, but knew she needed nourishment to stay strong, because there were *two* of them, and only one of her. Her eyes stung again with alternating fury and helplessness. Just for good measure, she slammed herself against the door, as she'd seen a servant do when a door was stuck, but all she got for that was a sore shoulder. And she could have gone headfirst out into the road . . .

For a while, she kept herself fully alert, ready to leap outside the moment the door opened. She stamped her feet, rubbed her arms, shook her head when her eyelids felt heavy. But the coach journeyed on and on, the roads getting bumpier. At last, her head drooped and bounced with the motion, and her eyes closed in a fitful doze.

She came awake with a start when the coach lurched to a stop, then perched near the door, ready to jump out and run. The faint light of dawn was a gray line around the leather window curtain. The fertile Yorkshire valley would be full of farms; surely she could reach one. She squeezed her eyes shut, trying to concentrate on the present and not the terrifying fear that made her heart pound and her breath come fast.

The door opened; she launched herself out, then rammed hard into a broad male chest. He caught her arms before she could tumble to the ground.

"Whoa!" said her captor, sounding more tolerant than angry. "Ye're a she-devil. I like that in my women."

"I am not your woman!" she cried, struggling to free herself. "Help!" she screamed.

Her voice practically disappeared into the vast countryside. The sun had just crept over the horizon, illuminating broad swaths of rolling hills enclosed with half walls of stone in a checked pattern as far as the eye could see. The occasional stone barn stood solitarily in the middle of a green field, but the only living creatures in sight were sheep and cattle enclosed within their broad pastures. Green grains swayed in the early morning breeze, ripening their way toward the autumn harvest.

She sagged with dismay in her captor's hold and he gave her another little shake, the kind she was already growing tired of. She struggled, but he didn't release her, and she felt each of his fingers against her flesh.

"I'll let ye go if ye promise to stand still. If I have to chase ye before breakfast . . ." He let the words trail off.

Mutely, she raised her gaze to his—and stared at her first view of the man who held her prisoner. His hair was black as the inside of the coach, thick with waves that would have reached his shoulders, if he hadn't pulled it back in a queue. His face was arresting, not pretty in the manner of some of the men in London with their face powder and beauty patches, but rugged and masculine, with heavy brows above gray eyes that in a trick of the light seemed to shine silver. His cheekbones could have been carved like stone on a windswept moor; his mouth was a thin line that looked incapable of smiling.

Blinking, she stiffened and asked herself why she would ever care if he smiled. She focused on the scar cut into his chin like a cleft, proof that he was a scoundrel. For more proof, she stared at the pistol in the waistband of his breeches, and the sword belt slung over one shoulder and across his chest.

He was studying her just as intently.

From behind, another man spoke, his tone polite. "Ye want her to stand still? Ye keep asking the lass to promise things she doesn't want to give."

Riona took a step back, though it brought her up

against the coach, the better to keep both men in sight. The second man, the coachman, regarded her with interested brown eyes in a plain face. The hair beneath his cap made him unique, bright red curls that looked barely tamed by his queue.

Her captor eyed the coachman. "If she doesn't promise, I'll be forced to tie her up."

"I won't stand for such treatment," she said, though her voice sounded hollow. "I demand to know why you have abducted me, and what nefarious deeds you have planned!"

His dark brow arched, but otherwise his expression remained impassive. "Lady Catriona, I am chief of the Clan McCallum. Our fathers betrothed us in marriage many years ago. I've come to take ye to wife."

CHAPTER 2

Hugh McCallum stared at his betrothed in the early morning light, and her beauty . . . glowed. Her hair had come out of the simple braid she'd worn, and now the many-hued golden strands looked as unkempt as if she'd just gotten out of his bed. Her green eyes were full of sparks, as if she wanted to set him afire. Her face betrayed her every emotion, from full lips that trembled, to the spots of color high on her creamy cheekbones, to her wide eyes that betrayed stunned shock. The gown, chosen to give her the appearance of a plain farmwife, only served to emphasize how elegant she truly was, with a woman's slim yet alluring curves. By candle-light just a few hours before, he'd glimpsed those curves poorly hidden within her fine linen night-shirt, and he'd been stunned.

She was a bonny lass—and she would be his.

He was surprised that his father's cold bargain

with their enemy, the chief of the Duffs and also styled the Earl of Aberfoyle, made long ago when Catriona was a baby, had granted Hugh such a beautiful bride.

Her mouth formed breathless words. "Wh-what d-did you say?"

"We are betrothed. Ye did not know?"

Samuel made an abortive cough, but Hugh only eyed his bodyguard with unspoken warning. Samuel raised both hands, then left to tend the horses.

"You are lying," she finally said, in a voice that was regaining its strength.

At least she wasn't about to swoon at his feet. He liked to see the strength in her, even when she was fighting against him. He crossed his arms over his chest and spoke patiently. "I do not lie."

"My father would have told me," she insisted, small fists on her hips.

The gesture only made his gaze focus there for a brief moment. He stirred himself to resume their discussion. "You are Catriona Duff. I visited your home this afternoon to speak with your father and he behaved dishonorably."

Her complexion suddenly flushed. "I'm not the only one who is confused. You have got the wrong bride!"

He hadn't expected anything else from her. She was desperate to escape the truth, and it was obvious that her parents had hid that from her. Hugh couldn't be surprised that they would have tried to break the contract and refuse to pay the tocher after they'd won twenty-two years of shared rights to the finest McCallum land just by signing.

"Ye may deny it all ye'd like, but 'twill not work with me."

She flung her arms wide. "I am telling the truth."

"Ye're Catriona Duff."

"Yes, but there are *two* of us. My cousin and I share the same family name because neither of our fathers would give in to the other. We call her Cat and myself Riona."

He ignored her ridiculous attempts to dissuade him. He knew the duplicity her family was capable of—there were centuries of evidence, including cattle raids during a time of peace. "Riona fits ye well. Womanly."

He took a step toward his betrothed, feeling the need to touch her. When she darted to the side, he told himself he could be patient. Too much was at stake within his own clan. The money from her tocher would increase their prosperity. And he needed a peaceable, willing bride on his return home after so long away, to cement the clan's respect and dull their memories of his foolish youth.

Knowing he could outrun Riona, he waited to see what she would do. She hesitated, and her tense shoulders gradually slumped as she gazed solemnly at the vast expanse of the valley, the dales rising in the northwest, the moors to the northeast. Their long journey would take them up the center between them. She was as cautious as a butterfly, waiting to see which way the wind would blow her. At last she faced him again.

"Laird McCallum," she said.

She was now trying to sound reasonable, although the trembling gave her away. One eyebrow raised, he simply waited to see what she'd do next.

"Take me back," she insisted. "Surely we cannot be that far from York. My uncle will explain everything. Cat was in the country yesterday, but she was to return today." She briefly closed her eyes. "Goodness, Cat doesn't know about this betrothal. When she finds out . . ."

Hugh appreciated her determination, if nothing else. He was not offended that she tried so hard to deny their upcoming marriage. It had obviously taken her by surprise. Though his own father had been a poor specimen of a man, drunk more than sober, at least he'd informed Hugh of the commitment when he'd been old enough to understand. Not that Hugh had accepted his fate with good grace . . .

And then his father had taken to the whisky even more, until Hugh's mother had taken him and his sister to live with her family.

"I can't marry you!" she cried. "I'm—I'm already betrothed."

He shrugged. "Whatever actions ye committed because your father did not have the honor to tell ye the truth have no bearing on the agreement between our families. Your family agreed to this contract at your birth, and from that time on, they have shared the wealth of our best land. Now 'tis time for my own family to benefit—with the tocher."

She blinked at him. "Tocher?"

"The bride price. The dowry."

"So it's money you want," she said disdainfully.

He eyed her. "Is not money involved in every marriage among the privileged? But 'tis not only the money. My clan has dealt honorably with your father, giving up full control of the purest springs, the finest peat, the best barley, all that we use for our whisky. This product supports my people. The contract was a great sacrifice my father made to ensure peace between our clans with only the promise of future honor on your side. We mean to see the bargain met."

She stared at him for a moment, then gave an abortive laugh that held no amusement. "Cat's life and freedom were a tradable commodity to promote *whisky*?"

He frowned. "Do not ever let my people hear such disdain in your voice for that which promotes our clan and provides coin, something there is little of in the Highlands, thanks to the Sassenachs." He practically spat the last word.

Her forehead knit with confusion. "Sass . . . what?"

"Englishmen, outlander. Did your family have so little pride as to neglect your Gaelic?"

She drew herself up. "My mother is English."

He turned away, saying over his shoulder. " 'Tis not true. Your falsehoods will not change your circumstances, Lady Catriona. Like every woman, ye knew ye had to marry and that the choosing of your husband would not be in your own hands."

"Well I wouldn't have chosen you! And neither would my cousin Cat. If you don't take me back, you'll have no hope to win her. Our family will consider this act of treachery an insult and—and a reason to break the contract."

And then he found himself looming over her, watching her shrink back against the coach. "Do not speak to me of treachery after the way your father coldly tried to negate the contract yesterday, claiming he could not in good conscience allow his daughter to be 'hauled off to the McCallums'— his words. I saw a man—if he can be called one— looking for a way to break the contract. My father is now dead, and the responsibility of Clan McCallum is mine. The earl will live up to his bargain when he sees he has no choice. *He* is the reason you were stolen from your rooms instead of presented to me with honor. I came with gifts suitable for the joining of our clans. Our meeting should have been celebrated as the promise of the future."

"I—I—"

To his surprise, she pushed at his chest. He didn't move, although this display of spirit improved his mood. It wasn't her fault she'd been brought up poorly. He grasped her soft, delicate hands and kept them on his chest. "Examining the goods, my lady?"

She gasped and pulled away, and he let her. He almost smiled, but he would not let her think him her friend, or a man who could be convinced to change his mind. He was none of those things. He was her future husband, her laird. She had to understand that she would now be ruled by his word alone, not by her treacherous father.

"Now fetch the food I left inside the coach," he said. "Unless ye mean to starve."

Her green eyes narrowed mutinously, and he almost hoped she'd defy him, so their sparring could continue. Then she lifted her chin and turned to climb inside the coach.

Hugh met Samuel's gaze and found himself nodding with satisfaction. Samuel's smile was tinged with worry, and he shook his head. Hugh thought his bodyguard's concerns unfounded. They'd come to York and done what they'd had to. But he could admit to himself that he, too, had been worried about the kind of wife he'd be saddled with. True, she might still be a shrew, but he hoped he could settle her eventually.

She appeared in the doorway of the coach, the cloth sack in one hand. He reached to assist her down, but she thrust the sack into his hands and descended on her own.

Not meeting his eyes, she said stiffly, "I need a moment of privacy."

He crossed his arms over his chest and spoke firmly. "If ye try to run, I will be forced to bring ye to ground. There's no one here who can help ye."

"I'm not blind. But the countryside will not always be so desolate."

"Ye've not been to the Highlands lately, have ye?"

"We're not there yet," she returned heatedly. "I assume you're both gentlemen. Please remain here while I'm behind the coach."

"My patience is not endless. If ye don't reappear in a suitable time—"

Exasperated, she said, "Then I will call out and tell you my plans moment by moment. Does that suit you?"

She didn't wait for an answer, just huffed, walked around the large wheels of the coach, and disappeared behind.

WHEN she'd finished, Riona lingered for just a moment by the half wall of rock that seemed piled almost haphazardly, yet was overgrown with moss and weeds as if it had weathered centuries. She gazed with despair across the pastoral scene and prayed there would be a shepherd she could wave to for help.

But what would a poor shepherd do against two large Highlanders, one of whom called himself chief of the McCallums? How could she bring innocent lives into her dilemma, perhaps getting them killed? She didn't even know if he'd told her the truth. Except . . . she recognized the clan name he'd used, enemies of the Duffs, her father's clan. They shared a contentious border. But that didn't mean this man was telling the truth. He could have kidnapped her for her dowry, as if the Dark Ages were still upon them. He might be lying about everything, and she'd end up in a hovel doing his bidding.

She might end up that way even if he were the chief, she thought with a shudder. She'd heard stories of the wretched Highlands from her father, who'd fled to England in his youth. How often he'd said he was lucky to be the son of an earl, with the ability and opportunity to escape his native country. He'd never understood the clansmen who'd worshipped his father, and now his brother, as if they were gods. Highlanders were a savage lot, according to him, and he'd told her stories of senseless raids back and forth on rival clan's cattle, of feuds so bloody that entire clans were demolished.

She'd never felt so helpless. She'd thought she'd had little control in her life up until now, told to remain closeted with her sister most of the time, left behind when the rest of her family had gone to the Continent. But now, she couldn't even have a moment of privacy without her captor's permission.

She hugged herself and rubbed her arms, though the sun was warm in the vale. It wouldn't stay warm for long. In the Highlands it was rainy and cold more often than not. Bleak and forbidding, that's what her father had called it. Full of savages who had to plow through rock to survive. She took a deep breath. She wasn't in Scotland yet, and perhaps she could find a way to change her captor's mind—or escape. They had to travel through a village *sometime*. Surely they'd need supplies.

"Lady Catriona!"

Her captor's voice was a bark that made her jump. She gave one last look at the rolling pastures and then walked slowly to the other side of the coach. The two men were speaking to each other in Gaelic, and they didn't even look at her as they chewed their oatcakes and cheese, washing it down with the dubious contents of another bottle they must have stored in the coachman's box.

Silently, Laird McCallum pointed to the coach.

She winced. "I cannot even see outside this prison."

"When ye've proven to me ye can be trusted, I will give ye a window. Until then—"

With his strong fingers, he pulled two of the

nails free and tacked several inches of the leather curtain.

"Thank you so much," she said with sarcasm.

She climbed up inside, but instead of folding in the stairs and shutting the door, Laird McCallum followed her and sat down on the bench at her side.

She slid into the corner, then thought better of it and fled to the opposite bench. "What are you doing?" she demanded, trying to keep the thread of fear from her voice.

"Getting some sleep."

"But—but—"

Her mouth sagged open in dismay, even as he stretched out his legs until they could go no farther. His broad torso seemed to take up his half of the coach. She was intimately alone with this man—this kidnapper—and totally under his power. She swallowed, but the lump remained in her throat, and she braced herself into the corner as if awaiting an attack.

"Samuel and I will be taking turns riding with ye," he said. "Surely ye cannot expect us to get no sleep on a journey of ten days or more."

"Ten days!"

"We're from the southern Highlands. It could have been worse." He eyed her coldly. "Have ye no memories of such a journey? Did your father think so little of his heritage that he denied ye your birthright?"

"My childhood is none of your business." It

stung that he was right, but she would not give him the satisfaction of letting him see that.

"Everything about ye is my business. Ye're to be my wife."

"I will not marry you and you can't force me to. Cat—the woman you say you were betrothed to— she won't marry you either."

His narrowed, wintry eyes seemed to trap her.

"Mark my words, Lady Riona—ye *will* marry me."

The intimate family name on his lips was chilling. He folded his arms across his chest and closed his eyes as if that ended the conversation. And it did—what could she do but rail against him and make him angry enough to—what? She shivered. If he thought himself her betrothed, thought that gave him the right to do whatever he wanted . . . She stared at the sword and pistol he hadn't bothered to remove.

"I can feel your trembling from over here. Fetch a blanket if ye're cold, lass, but let a man sleep."

She wasn't cold; the coach was stifling with two bodies breathing and taking up space. But she was terrified and trying not to cry, and wondering when help would come. But she'd had a horrible thought in the night, one that hadn't borne examination then, because she couldn't imagine it. But now . . . now, by the light of day through the crack he'd given her in the window, her bad thoughts surfaced. She tried to beat them back by telling herself that once her uncle knew she'd disappeared, he'd gather people to look for her.

But another part of her whispered doubts she hadn't wanted to face. She and her uncle had never been close. The earl was a cold man focused on his own wealth and prestige. When her parents had taken her sister to the Continent and left Riona behind, he'd only reluctantly taken her in when her cousin Cat had insisted that Riona couldn't stay alone with only the servants.

And now, if McCallum was to be believed, he'd talked with the earl yesterday—just before Cat discovered her parents were sending her to friends in the country. Cat had been surprised, but not displeased at the idea, although the speed of packing had seemed strange. She'd wanted Riona to go with her, but her parents had insisted there was no room at the house party. But . . . had all this been deliberate, sending Cat away after McCallum's appearance? Had the earl regretted the contract so much, he'd gotten his daughter out of harm's way?

And the most damning part, the part she couldn't get out of her mind, was that at dinner, her aunt had seemed pale and withdrawn, eyes downcast when the earl brusquely told Riona she should sleep in Cat's bedroom, since hers had to be cleaned and painted. It had seemed so strange—why not wait to paint until they'd departed for London?

But now, it made much more sense, and her stom-

ach twisted with betrayal and grief. Had the earl
put her in Cat's room because he'd anticipated the
savage Scot trying to make off with Cat, and was
looking for a legal reason to break off the betrothal
altogether? The earl could have stationed guards
there and caught McCallum in the act. It seemed
unbelievable for just that reason, yet . . . She swallowed and tried not to think the worst. If she let
her terror overwhelm her, she'd never find a way to
escape the man who now rested with eyes closed
and chin on his chest, his broad legs taking up all
the room in the coach, forcing her to press deeper
into the corner to avoid touching him.

He spent two hours sleeping, barely moving, as
he if he was long used to sleeping quietly and expe-
diently. She couldn't sleep at all, for fear he'd wake
up and try something wicked. When he finally did
awaken, he eyed her impassively, and without a
word knocked on the roof of the coach. It came to
a stop, he got out, and then Samuel took his place.

When the coach began to move, Samuel looked
around, and then out the narrowed window, seeming to try to settle himself without meeting her
gaze. Now was her chance.

"We haven't been properly introduced, sir,"
Riona said.

His skin was freckled and fair beneath his bright
hair, and he reddened almost to match it. "Samuel
McCallum, my lady."

"Of course you're related," she said, feeling defeat encroaching, but not ready to let it claim victory.

"Distant cousins," he said, a small smile of sympathy growing. "Ye'll find a lot of McCallums where we're going."

She wasn't ready to give up. "Surely you see what he's doing is wrong."

Samuel's expression remained pleasant and even understanding, but he shook his head. "Nay, my lady, I don't see that at all. Ye're his betrothed."

"But I'm not!"

"Ye're Catriona Duff, are ye not?"

"I am, but so is my cousin!"

"Sorry though I be, I cannot help ye. A contract was signed between your families, and we take that seriously."

"I know nothing about any contract," she grumbled, folding her arms beneath her breasts and narrowing her eyes at him.

"That is the fault of your father. I've been Hugh's man a long time, and he's known about the betrothal since he was a lad. Believe me, it's interfered with his life more than once." He seemed to break off even as he looked away.

"Interfered how?" she demanded.

"That's none of your business, my lady. Now do let a man sleep."

He closed his eyes and dropped his chin, just as his chief had done.

"But wait, would money change your mind? I don't have much, but if you help me . . ." She trailed off.

He didn't even open his eyes as he spoke. "Your coin cannot buy the loyalty earned through generations, my lady. And your coin cannot make me forget the treachery of the Duffs through that same time. Now hush."

She blanched. Treachery by her ancestors? A marriage between their clans was supposed to make up for that? Any Duff married to a McCallum would never be at ease, it seemed, if such grievances were never forgotten. She'd heard stories of the feuding when her uncle and father were in their cups, reminiscing with anger and pride. No wonder they stayed away from Scotland, she thought, leaving their factors and tacksmen to manage their estates.

But this feud had become intensely personal, and she wasn't about to meekly accept what was happening to her. She was still in England, where people would help her against the Scots. When they stopped for the midday meal, she'd look for her first opportunity to escape. If that didn't work, she'd come up with something else.

CHAPTER 3

Hugh knew Lady Riona wasn't going to give up her attempts to escape. Her moods alternated from anger to frustration, although her fear seemed to be easing away. He wasn't certain that was a good thing.

They were taking their midday break in a woodland copse near a burn, hiding the coach away from the road itself. The hobbled horses could drink while they grazed on the grassy banks. They were surrounded by trees; a rare and more remote spot could not be imagined.

Lady Riona asked for a moment's privacy behind the coach, and he allowed it, remaining stretched out on his side near their small fire, where oatcakes cooked on a flat iron girdle.

"We'll be needing supplies soon," Samuel said.

"The fowl I've shot not good enough for ye?" Hugh asked.

"These are almost the last of our oats. And I'm feeling the need for an egg or two." Samuel looked to the west. "And a storm is coming, the first droplets to hit us soon. We might be needing an inn this night."

"Nay, not this far south in Yorkshire. We'll find a protective copse like this one, and we'll all sleep inside the coach if we have to."

"Her ladyship will find that cozy enough," Samuel said dryly.

Hugh made a disinterested sound deep in his throat.

"She's been asking for my help, of course," Samuel continued.

"She's got spirit, that one." Then he lifted his head. "Shouldn't she be back by now?" He raised his voice. "Lady Riona?"

Nothing answered but the call of birds flying overhead.

"I'll be back in but a moment," Hugh said with resignation, leaving his weapons near Samuel.

"Easy on the lass, Hugh. If it were us, we'd try to escape, as well."

"I would not try to escape from my duty to my family."

"Sanctimonious, aren't ye?" Samuel teased.

Ignoring him, Hugh jogged beyond the coach. It was easy enough to track Lady Riona, whose wide skirts trampled grasses and broke twigs. To her credit, she'd circled back the way they'd come, though the nearest village was several hours' journey behind.

He heard her before he saw her, crashing through undergrowth as she tried to remain hidden by following the main road without actually being on it. He could have called to her, using simple reasoning to force her to see that it was useless to make such foolish attempts, but . . . she needed to temporarily fear him, and the lesson had to be memorable.

He approached soundlessly from the rear, which was easy, because, thinking herself safe, she'd begun to make too much noise, and even grumbled aloud a time or two, which he found amusing. She marched with determination, her strides hampered by the overgrown weeds tugging at her skirts.

In two strides, Hugh came out of hiding to grab her around the waist with one arm and lift her right off the ground.

THE sudden assault was so startling that Riona screamed until his hand covered her mouth. It was like a repeat of last night all over again. She would never be free of him, and frustration and despair made her struggle though it was useless against his strength.

"I could have been a highwayman," he said angrily, his lips against her ear. "Ye've put yourself in danger."

She kicked at him even as he turned to take her farther from civilization, farther from rescue. Their legs entwined, her skirt trapped his foot, and suddenly they were falling. To her surprise, he twisted and landed first, then let out an "oomph" when her elbow caught him in the gut. She didn't feel bad about that, but her gloating faded when he rolled and pinned her beneath him, rocks digging into her back. Though she squirmed to buck him off, he used the weight of his body to subdue her. When she tried to slap him, he took each wrist and held them to the ground over her head. Arched uncomfortably, she was gasping for breath, furious, still fighting, but it began to dawn on her that Samuel was not there to act as a buffer against McCallum's need to dominate her. Though fear could cripple her, she felt it surge anew.

"Stop it," he said firmly.

Her struggles only made him sink between her legs, which, along with her skirt, finally trapped her in place. She was breathing hard, gasping, and for the first time felt a man's body against hers, and went still. Something seemed to shift between them at such intimate contact, and she remembered too late how little control she truly had in the grasp of this big Highlander. There was no one around to help her—even his coachman could not act as a buffer. She'd put herself at his mercy.

"Please . . ." she whispered, hating how weak

and trembling her voice sounded, but helpless to stop. "Let me up."

"So ye can run again?" he demanded.

His voice was full of anger, but his gaze . . . his gaze was on her mouth, and there was a heat in their formerly winter depths that made her think of molten silver.

"Stop—stop looking at me like that," she whispered, unable to look away, as if he'd pounce given half the chance. "I'm not some little . . . morsel for a vulture."

When he spoke, his voice was husky. "Vulture? I don't eat innocent creatures. I'm just a man. But lying together like this makes me think of our wedding night."

Aghast, she sputtered ill-conceived words. "Y-you mean because you'll have to hold me down?"

For just a moment, she could have sworn a corner of his mouth twitched with the beginnings of a smile, but that wasn't possible, not for a man so bent on clan revenge and false justice that he'd steal a woman against her will. He released her hands at last, and she pushed at his massive shoulders, but he didn't get up right away. His hips were braced between hers, and she'd never felt such pressure. It was uncomfortable and awkward and . . . strange.

She shoved at him again. "I can't breathe."

He sat up, but only leaned back on his heels,

knees still pressed to either side of her hips. He folded his arms across his chest and just looked down at her. "I can't have this again."

"*You* can't have this?" She felt pinned to the earth by the hips. Pushing him away would mean touching his thighs. "And you would meekly go along with your captor were our situations reversed?"

He cocked his head. "They're not."

"But if they were."

"I would honor the commitment made between our families, regardless of whether I agreed with it or not."

"So even though you've never met Cat, you will marry her, even if she is . . . unattractive." She had to find a way to convince him of the truth, even if she had to bring his mistake up every moment they spoke.

He didn't flinch. "There is no mysterious 'Cat' of which ye speak, Riona. There is only you and me. And we will be married. Running away is simply childish."

"Childish?" she echoed, furious. He hadn't called her Lady Riona, and much as the honorific was not hers to use, it kept a sort of . . . distance between them. "I am Miss Duff to you, and it is hardly childish to run when a man accosts a woman, kidnaps her away from her family, and carries her off to be—molested!"

"I have not molested ye."

She pointed wildly at him. "What do you call this? The gentlemanly way to treat a lady?"

And then he bent over her and braced his hands on either side of her head. "I call this showing ye who has the power here, *Riona*."

He emphasized the intimacy of her Christian name, and she found her breathing shallow again as he loomed above her, his face too close to hers, his gaze once more smoldering as it focused on her mouth.

"If you kiss me, I will bite you!" she hissed.

He arched a brow, but didn't move.

"You are not my husband, not yet."

He sat up slowly. "Ye have it right. And I will not force myself upon ye before marriage." He rose to his feet, then bent to offer her a hand. "But ye'll suffer the consequences if ye try to escape again."

"You would harm a woman you insist will be your wife?" she demanded, pulling away from his firm, warm hand as soon as she got to her feet. She knew he could crush her fingers if he held on, but he didn't.

"I will try not to. But as for those ye ask for help—I cannot guarantee what will happen to them."

He was deadly serious, and she knew that. Her shoulders sagged, and when he took her by the arm, she didn't protest. But inside, resentment and anger still simmered along with the fear. She would find a way to escape without hurting anyone else.

But until then . . . she could make herself incredibly annoying. Maybe she'd make him change his mind about marrying her after all.

It was strange to feel wanted, she mused, having rarely felt so in her life, except by her cousin Cat. Her parents had needed her, used her, as both a nurse and companion to her sister, Bronwyn. And though she'd known her sister needed her, Riona had resented the constant dependence, and how her family had never given her respite. She'd only been called to give of herself, over and over, but seldom had anyone cared enough to return the favor.

But "wanted"? She knew even McCallum didn't truly want *her*, but a wife who would fulfill this marriage contract that was so important to his clan. She was just . . . a substitute, and at some point he would be faced with the truth of his misdeeds. And then what would happen to her?

She felt a chill go through her, and barely noticed McCallum guiding her through the brush that tugged at her dress. Her reputation would be ruined, she realized. It was one thing to go for walks in public with a man, but travel with him? Even though it was against her will, it wouldn't matter. She might never find a husband, and then she'd be forced to continue as nursemaid to Bronwyn, then nursemaid to her parents.

All because this—this *man* snatched the wrong woman, she thought angrily, then bleakness set in as she remembered the chance that her uncle had put her in harm's way.

"Picking up your feet would help," McCallum said, maneuvering her past another overgrown bush.

Silently, she did as he asked.

HUGH simply wanted to sleep late in the afternoon. The storm was moving closer, and who knew what the night would bring. But he entered the coach warily, not sure about Riona's mood. After he'd recaptured her, she'd been strangely quiet, and he hoped that meant she'd surrendered to her destiny, and would make the journey easier on all of them. As he opened the door, he bitterly wondered why she would make it easier.

As he sank onto the uncomfortable bench, and the coach began to rumble forward, he eyed her. She was staring out the small crack in the window, which only showed endless farm fields and sheep pastures, the occasional thatched-roof cottage far in the distance. But they'd be going through a village soon, and he wondered if she'd try another escape. He suspected she was not yet thoroughly cowed. She probably planned to annoy him, but he'd slept on mountainsides and through storms. He closed his eyes, content.

"McCallum, I cannot continue to wear this same dirty gown every single day."

He didn't open his eyes. "If ye hadn't tried to run, it wouldn't be dirty."

"But it is. And I need to wash . . . items."

Opening one eye to look at her, he remembered the sight of her in her thin nightshift, the silkiness of the garment rubbing along her arms when he'd held her still. The candle had made her skin glow, and he'd felt momentarily relieved at his good fortune and intrigued to see more. Though he had her clothe herself in plain garments, thinking to hide her beauty, nothing could hide her regal bearing and the golden fall of her hair. She would make a fine wife to a clan chief.

She was still wearing that nightshift, he mused.

"McCallum?"

She said his name again as if he were daft.

With obvious exasperation, she said, "You could answer me instead of just staring like I'm speaking gibberish."

"The English tongue is rather harsh compared to the Gaelic, but gibberish? Nay." He closed his eye again, knowing it was best not to think of her nightshift.

"I need clothing," she insisted. "And hot water for washing. I feel unclean."

"When it's safe, I'll consider it."

"Safe? You can't mean to make me wait until we're in Scotland! Didn't you say that was *days* away?"

"Your behavior could influence my decision, of course."

"You mean if I remain meek and cowed and subservient."

"Your words, not mine. I'd take respectful."

She gasped, and he withheld a smile.

"Why you—you—savage!"

Though he knew she was just repeating words others had used, her slur stung. In London, he'd been looked down upon for the land of his birth, his words often discounted. Everywhere people assumed he was an uneducated crofter. The months each year he'd had to reside there were full of frustration and regret for the outrageous money he'd had to spend to support himself, all for so little benefit.

"If I am a savage, my lady, then so are you, as we're both Highlanders." He folded his arms and kept his eyes closed, although his jaw was clenched.

"You're even more a savage if you keep a lady imprisoned with nothing to distract her. I need a book or needlework—something. Surely there's a grocer or bookshop in the next village—"

"I can think of ways to distract ye," he said in a low voice, then opened his eyes and stared hard at her.

She swallowed and thrust out her chin in a defiant gesture, although he saw the way she clasped her hands to hide their trembling.

"You said you would not force yourself on me."

She sounded so prim he wished he could laugh. "I won't need force. One touch, one kiss, and ye'll fall under my spell."

To his surprise, she didn't look away.

"I consider that as using force. I don't wish those things from you. I keep telling you, I'm not your betrothed."

"And I keep telling ye that lying will not help your plight."

They stared at each other for a long silent moment, and he rather enjoyed the contest of wills. Rain began to fall softly on the coach roof.

He sighed. "Ye'll not get your chance to experience my kisses today. The rain looks to get worse, and Samuel has orders to find shelter for the horses and join us inside."

She folded her arms across her chest and looked away at last. He closed his eyes again, hoping for peace.

"No one is following us, are they?" she asked, her quiet voice touched with sadness.

He should be angry that she kept disturbing him, but, in some ways, he pitied her for the way her family treated her. "Men with horses would have caught us by now," he said. "Your father has seen the wisdom in honoring the contract."

"You mean my uncle has happily abandoned me in my cousin's place. He means to wreck your precious contract, you know."

He gave a loud sigh. "I will gag ye if I must."

She was quiet for a few minutes, but soon she again interrupted the beginning of his doze.

"How did you know in which room to find me?"

He let out a long breath. "I bribed a kitchen boy."

"They put me in Cat's room, perhaps on purpose, to ruin the contract."

He ignored that. "Your family did not share their plans for your marriage. Ye'll not miss such people. After all, what kind of man abandons his clan?"

"Neither my uncle nor my father abandoned Clan Duff. They employ factors and tacksmen to oversee and care for the land and its tenants. They simply prefer the civilization here in England."

"Such civilized men treated ye well, did they?"

She bit her lip, and it was her turn to remain quiet.

"I won't pity ye. I see my people scraping a living off barren soil. I see cattle starving through bad winters. My father did the proper thing contracting marriage with the daughter of a powerful earl."

"Are you trying to talk yourself into believing that?" she demanded. "People should be able to marry for love."

He snorted. "Now I know ye're lying to yourself. No woman of your station expects to marry for love, not even in England."

They both felt the coach rumble over uneven ground, then come to a halt. The rain came down harder, drumming on the roof of the coach.

"Samuel has found shelter off the road. I'm going to help him with the horses. I will bar the door, since this conversation doesn't inspire my trust in ye."

"I don't need you to trust me," she shot back. "I need you to believe that I won't marry you. Even in Scotland, I doubt a woman can be forced to marry against her will."

"Ye'll see the wisdom in marriage, my lady."

"Go ahead and say it—you think I *have* to marry you, because no man will have me now."

"Nay, I think ye need to marry me to honor your family's word. Regardless of your behavior, ye seem far more honorable and innocent than the rest of the Duffs."

Bending low, he left the coach and firmly shut the door behind him. By the time he and Samuel returned from seeing to the horses, their clothes damp and rain running from their bonnets and into the collars of their coats, Riona was pale and emotionless once more. She blanched further when they stowed their pistols in the compartment beneath their bench.

She slid to the center of her bench. "You both can keep to one side. Gentlemen wouldn't allow a lady's garments to dampen."

"So now we're gentlemen and not savages," Hugh said with sarcasm, even as he tossed his bonnet into the corner of her bench.

But he and Samuel squeezed side by side opposite her, and he saw the satisfaction she couldn't hide. That satisfaction faded when she seemed to realize their legs took up a lot of room, forcing her into the center between them, where she tried to tuck her skirts around her legs to keep them from getting wet.

Both men folded their arms over their chests, and Samuel closed his eyes.

"We're going to wait out the storm?" she asked. "Should we not go to an inn?"

"Ye've not proven yourself capable of restraint, lass," Hugh said.

"I've never slept overnight in a coach," she protested.

"Ye did last night, and ye're about to do it again," he said with a sigh. "Ye're dry and sheltered. Be grateful. I'll try to keep to my side of the coach and not be overcome by lust for ye."

"Warn me so I can keep my eyes closed," Samuel said.

Hugh kept his expression impassive, although it was difficult. He was wet and chilly and tired. Riona had done her best to annoy him all afternoon, and she could certainly continue by forcing him to stay awake.

"There are blankets beneath my bench," she said stiffly. "I'm cold."

"Then fetch them," he said with exasperation.

And that was an error in judgment on both

their parts. She was forced to stand, turn her back to them, and bend over. Without hoops, her skirts fell gently along the curve of her hips. Swallowing, Hugh glanced at Samuel, who pointedly turned and stared out the window as darkness descended.

Right in front of him, Riona's hips swayed as she rummaged in the compartment. Hugh could have put his hands on them and—

She straightened up, dropped the bench, and sank back on it. Clutching several blankets to her, she eyed the men skeptically, as if they would take them from her.

Hugh was too busy trying to forget that she would be his wife in but a few weeks; he was supposed to have patience. Instead he watched as she moved about and tried to get comfortable, feeling reluctantly aroused and frustrated.

"I don't like leaving my post," Samuel said at last, squinting through the narrow slit of the window. "We're unprotected like this."

"The spot ye've chosen to hide is well concealed," Hugh answered. "We can afford to sleep a bit until the rain ebbs. No highwayman will risk getting his powder wet. Then we'll start a fire and warm up."

Samuel looked unconvinced, but Hugh forced his eyes closed, determined not to think of Riona. He'd just met her, and already she exercised far too much control over his thoughts. She was spirited and defiant, exasperating and sympathetic, and she was far too alluring for his peace of mind. But it wasn't just a surface beauty. There was something about her that made it obvious she undervalued herself. It was rare that a beautiful woman did not know and use her powers over men, but he suspected Riona incapable of that.

He was not a man given to rushing to judgment, so he silently warned himself to take a step away and remain objective.

From beneath his lashes, he studied her hungrily again. He wanted her for his own—he wanted her to want *him* in return, but didn't know how to make it happen. He suspected being forced to kidnap her might be hard to overcome . . .

CHAPTER 4

Riona awoke and for a moment, didn't know where she was. She was lying cramped across something hard, where she couldn't stretch her legs. She wasn't cold, for a rough wool blanket covered her, and another was pillowed beneath her head.

With a gasp, she sat up, remembering everything. Her kidnapping, her aborted escape, having to try to sleep with two large Highlanders snoring mere feet away from her.

But she was alone now, although the coach wasn't moving. Light filtered in the slit of a window, and she tried the door handle with little hope. To her surprise it opened easily, and she distinguished muted voices outside. She ducked her head out, and they saw her at once. Both men were sitting on logs before the fire, dressed in only their shirtsleeves and breeches. Their stockings and coats were spread across other logs, steaming damply in the heat.

"Lady Riona," McCallum said, coming to his feet. "Samuel has made porridge for breakfast."

"I smell . . . ham," she said with hesitation.

"I rode to a nearby farmer and bought more provisions. We have eggs, too."

"Eggs," Samuel repeated with satisfaction, looking at the griddle where several fried.

"Come out, Lady Riona," McCallum said, "as long as ye promise not to run."

"I promise not to run during breakfast," she amended, stepping down from the coach.

He eyed her, and again, she thought his mouth quirked in a smile—or she could be imagining it. Hugh McCallum didn't smile. He believed the weight of the world, or at least his clan, was upon his shoulders, and he would do anything he wanted in the name of that clan. If any of this entire story were even true. Maybe it was an elaborate scheme to get her dowry. She was too hungry to debate the notion for long.

Soon, they were on their way north again, and this time McCallum drove first, and Samuel sat across from her in the coach. Though the sun occasionally peeked out from behind clouds, the road was far worse after the rain, and occasionally the wheels caught in the mud, or McCallum was forced to drive along the rough edge of the road to avoid the holes. Riona often found herself holding on to the bench with whitened fingers to keep from being flung to the ground. Good thing she had a strong stomach, or she'd have lost her breakfast. But always, they continued the slow, steady progression, the coach climbing higher by slight degrees.

By late morning, she thought she'd go out of her mind with boredom, and was trying to think of irritating ways to annoy McCallum with requests, when the coach slowed down.

Samuel stiffened. "He said he'd drive until midday."

"Stand and deliver!" cried a man's unfamiliar voice.

Riona gasped. "Highwaymen!"

She pressed back into the seat as Samuel drew his pistol and cocked it. The man who'd seemed shy and malleable compared to McCallum now had the demeanor of a deadly soldier, eyes hard, mouth pressed into a grim line.

"Whatever happens, stay here," he told her in a low voice, looking through the small opening in the window.

"If you go out there, that highwayman might shoot you!" she said with urgency. "He's probably not working alone."

"Odds are, they won't hit Himself and me both," he said, as if indifferent.

Riona began to wonder if this robbery attempt might be her salvation. Highwaymen were focused on coin and jewelry; surely she would be worth more coin than they could imagine, if they ransomed her to her family. It was a wild, dangerous idea, but wasn't it better to risk that than to end up a Highlander's wife forever?

To distract Samuel, she said, "Don't you have a purse to give? My father carries two, his own and a small one for highwaymen."

"Quiet," he insisted, leaning toward the window to hear.

She did the same.

"Stay in the box," the same highwayman ordered McCallum, then added, "Keep an eye on him," as if to someone else.

"He has partners," Riona whispered.

Samuel ignored her, head cocked as he listened intently.

They heard the crunch of boots approaching on gravel.

"Ho there, inside the coach. We have pistols on your driver and will use 'em if we have to."

Riona let loose with a shriek, and Samuel gaped at her.

"I've been kidnapped! Free me and I'm worth a great ransom!"

Samuel dove to cover her mouth, and she had no choice but to let him. Then the carriage rocked, as if McCallum had jumped from it. A gunshot echoed.

"Ballocks," Samuel muttered. He flung himself at the door and slammed it open, vaulting out.

Riona followed him to the door and held on to the frame. The same stone half walls and fields greeted her, but the land rose in long flat waves to the sides, and patches of forested land covered the hillside. Not a barn or cottage was in sight—perfectly remote for two fugitive Highlanders to take her, perfect for highwaymen to avoid exposure. She imagined that they weren't used to their victims fighting back, but McCallum had obviously been more of a challenge.

One of those highwaymen was already struggling to mount his horse, his leg covered in blood and difficult to maneuver. Had the gunshot come from McCallum's pistol? The clan chief was grappling with another man, and Samuel was charging at a third, sword and pistol drawn, as the retreating man ran for his horse. She was startled when Samuel let loose a bloodthirsty shout.

The last man fighting saw his men in retreat, and it was obvious that McCallum was toying with him at sword point. The man dodged a thrust, then ran for his own horse. Not bothering with a chase, McCallum stood triumphant, sword point resting in the ground, barely breathing hard.

"Cowards!" he shouted as the horses galloped away.

Riona's plan had failed, and she wondered what her punishment would be. But for the moment, McCallum and Samuel seemed to have forgotten her scream and simply grinned at each other like boys who'd just won a horse race. She hadn't seen McCallum smile before, and she was surprised at how it lightened the cragginess of his features, made him actually appear . . . handsome, in a rugged way.

But that smile died when he turned and focused his narrowed gray eyes on her. His hair had come loose from its queue, and the dark waves settled to his shoulders. He looked like a wild Highlander, and she'd just gone against him. She tensed in the doorway, knowing it was too late to flee.

"What did ye think of my plan?" Samuel called, as he slid his sword back into its sheath. "Lady Riona's screaming, I mean."

She stiffened and tried to mask her shock.

"That was a plan?" asked McCallum skeptically.

"I was certain they'd want the chance to ransom a highborn lady," Samuel continued. "Their hesitation was all ye needed to attack. Ye got two of them with one jump. Impressive."

She swallowed heavily, attempting to appear confident, while inside she was stunned that Samuel would defend her. She wasn't certain why he'd do such a thing, and it made her feel both indebted and worried about his motives.

"You have my thanks, because it worked," McCallum said. "That piercing scream distracted them like nothing else." He glanced at Riona, then spoke with a trace of reluctance. "Well done."

She nodded, surprised to feel vaguely guilty. Why should she feel that way when she was but their prisoner? "I don't suppose you'll be better prepared next time."

One dark brow arched, but he seemed in too good a mood to respond in kind. "We'll not have to fash about that in Scotland. The pickings are too poor for highwaymen."

Samuel laughed but she didn't see what was funny.

"I'll drive until midday," McCallum said. "Let's put some distance between us and these brigands before they get their courage up again."

Silently, Riona climbed into the coach and felt it dip behind her as Samuel followed. He seated himself across from her, and she simply stared at him in confusion. The coach jerked into motion, even as Samuel closed his eyes.

"Why did you lie for me?" she asked hesitantly.

He opened his eyes and regarded her with a sympathy that felt foreign to her.

"Ye're a frightened, desperate lass. And I understand ye, so I helped ye this time. But he's my chief—my friend. I won't help ye again, so don't make a foolish mistake."

She swallowed but her words still sounded hoarse and full of pain, even to her own ears. "Is it foolish to want to go home?"

"'Tis foolish to wish to change what cannot be

changed. This was decided long ago, my lady," he said kindly.

"But not for *me*!" she whispered fiercely. "You've got the wrong woman."

He shook his head and closed his eyes again, and Riona angrily wiped away a tear. Crying was useless and would get her nowhere with these men.

THEY crossed the River Sark and into Scotland two days later, and it was like a little part of Riona died, along with her hope of rescue. She could only depend on herself now.

They stopped to refresh themselves and the horses in the river, and it was as if McCallum and his coachman thought the water tasted better on this side of the border, they were so glad to be back. The water ran fast and high due to the rain that had plagued them the last day, and the bank was muddy and overgrown with weeds. Riona tried to wash her face and ended up sliding down the embankment and up to her thighs in icy water. McCallum reached her first and hauled her to safety, where she stumbled and landed on her backside, her skirts a sodden mess. She desperately wanted to cry, felt filthy and smelly, and now her gown was ruined. Shoulders slumped, she covered her face with her hands and took a deep, shuddering breath.

"We should stop at an inn tonight," Samuel said. "We need fresh clothes."

She kept her head bowed, knowing if she looked too hopeful, McCallum might deny the request.

"Aye, we'll stop in Gretna Green," McCallum said, "at a good Scottish inn."

Where no one will help a Sassenach, Riona thought despondently. Of course, part of her was Scottish, but a lot of good that would do against a clan chief. Yet to be clean and dry seemed the height of luxury five days into their journey, so she'd hold off complaining until tomorrow.

Not that McCallum had seemed all that bothered when she'd tried to annoy him into abandoning his plan to marry her. He'd simply ridden in the coaching box with Samuel, leaving her all alone for hours on end. Samuel had slipped her a pack of cards the day before, and she sometimes occupied herself by making random patterns, because she knew no games to be played alone. But it was something to do with her hands.

Often, she stared out the slit in the leather curtain for hours, watching for the changes that would mark Scotland, but there was nothing very different about the Lowlands.

They reached the small village of Gretna Green, where several roads converged around a triangular green. There were a collection of thatched-roof, whitewashed cottages, a blacksmith shop, a church, and little else. If there was a "good Scottish inn" here, she was baffled. Frankly, she didn't care where they stopped, if only she could be free of this coach for a night.

The "inn" ended up being two rooms above a tavern, only one of which was private. She was exceedingly grateful when McCallum led her up the cramped rear stairs from the stable yard, rather than through the front hall where she'd be gawked at. She knew he was probably trying to avoid curious stares, but she didn't care.

The private room was small; only a bed, a table with two chairs, a washstand, and pegs on the wall for her clothing. Inns in England were luxurious compared to this. Or the ones her parents frequented were, she amended to herself.

"Please tell me you were able to ask for a hot bath," she said, keeping her voice polite.

McCallum eyed her. "The innkeeper wasn't happy, but he'll oblige us."

"Us?" she echoed, feeling a new stirring of unease.

"There's a bed for Samuel in the dormitory, but of course, a man and his wife can share one."

She stared at him in growing anger. "Y-you told him we were married?"

"Ye've not proven yourself trustworthy, Lady Riona. I cannot allow ye to be alone for a night, and I cannot name ye my mistress, can I?"

Her mouth moved, but nothing came out.

"If it helps, the innkeeper's wife was very gracious about your river accident, and promised fresh clothing and will have yours cleaned."

Fresh clothing—it sounded like heaven. Just days ago, she'd taken such things as baths and clothing for granted. No more. And hadn't she slept in the coach with McCallum—how was this different?

But it *was* different, and she knew it. "We will not be sharing that bed," she told him, hating how her voice trembled. Every choice was being taken away from her—she had to stand up for herself.

"We will," he answered, as if he expected his word to be law. "And I will hold to our agreement that I will not take ye before we're wed."

Her face heated, even though her limbs still shivered with the wet and cold.

He eyed her. "I can't have ye sick with the ague. Where is that bath?"

He went into the hall to call for a maidservant, and Riona tried not to panic. How was she supposed to bathe? If she were smart, she'd try to escape right now, but . . . who would help her in this tiny village against the chief of the McCallums? Where would she go?

She was just as trapped here as she'd been in the coach. Her feelings of hope and perseverance were slowly draining away. Nothing she'd said had convinced this man he was wrong. She would keep trying, of course, along with denying him her consent to marriage. She wasn't sure what would happen after that, but she could see no easy choices.

McCallum opened the door and held it open for two male servants carrying a bathing tub between them. Soon buckets of hot water were carried in a slow procession, until the heat steamed from the tub. The towels were rough, but clean, and the soft soap in a pot didn't smell terrible.

The innkeeper's plump wife tsked when she saw Riona. "How dare yer man lose yer trunk," she said, shaking her head.

Riona knew not to expose the lie, or McCallum would take her back to the cold, wet coach. He eyed her with confidence, as if he knew just what she was thinking.

The woman laid out a chemise, petticoats, an open gown laced at the bodice, a nightshift, a man's breeches and shirt, and stockings for them both. "He paid me handsomely for these," she said with satisfaction. "I'll be back to collect yer own garments," she added, eyeing them with both distaste and sympathy. "How ever did ye fall into the Sark?"

"The bank was muddy and I slipped," Riona said absently, eyeing the tub with longing.

"Och, listen to me blather. Shall I empty the tub later and refill for ye, Laird McCallum?" She seemed weary but resigned to the necessity.

McCallum faced the woman, looking like an immovable mountain dwarfing the furniture—and absorbing all the heat of the fire, Riona thought crossly.

"Nay, I'll use the tub when my wife is done," he said. "No need to make more work for ye, mistress."

She gave him a grateful smile. "Then I'll leave and let ye use it before the heat is gone."

The woman bustled out, and the room was suddenly as silent as a church funeral service, but for the flickering flames of the peat fire. Pungent smoke hung heavily in the air, but it wasn't unpleasant.

McCallum pointedly bolted the door.

"You need to wait in the corridor," Riona insisted, relieved that at least her voice didn't tremble.

He only rolled his eyes then headed for the hearth, removing his coat to lay it across the back of a chair before the fire. His waistcoat came next and he pulled his shirt out of his breeches before unbuttoning those.

"What are you doing?" she demanded sharply.

"Drying my garments. The shirt is long enough for your modesty, have no fear."

And then he pulled his stockings, breeches, and drawers off and laid them out, too. His shirt came down to his mid-thighs, and she hastily looked away even as he sat down before the fire with a deep, satisfied sigh. He was naked but for that shirt. The sight of his bare, muscular, hairy legs felt permanently imbedded in her mind.

How was she supposed to bathe like this, right beneath his knowing gaze?

As if reading her mind, he said, "I'll keep my back turned, but do be quick about it, my lady. I'd like my bath to be middling warm."

She was too dazed for words—and then she realized she could not unlace her gown alone. "I need to call a maidservant," she said, heading for the door.

For a big man, he moved with speed. He reached the door before she could.

"None of that," he said.

"But—"

He turned her about like she was a child's doll and started unlacing. It seemed to take too long, and soon he began to grumble.

"Damned wet laces."

She bit her lip, saying nothing, feeling every tug as if he stroked her skin. She'd never felt like this before, so aware of someone so close to her. No man ever had been. She knew she was not ugly, but Cat was vivacious and cast a long shadow that hid other women when she was about. And then there was Riona's constant care of Bronwyn, nights when her cousin attended a soiree alone since Riona had to attend her sister.

But now . . . this *Highlander* thought he would marry her. He thought he had the right to put his hands on her, to undress her. Everything inside her wanted to rebel, but it was useless, and tears burned her eyes. The moment her laces loosened, she fled across the room, holding the bodice in place.

He watched her, hair loose about his shoulders, eyes as smoldering as the peat fire. Bare legs, big strong feet, and callused hands meant for war. He could do anything he wanted to do to her—would she really make things easy by disrobing in front of him?

For a long moment their gazes held, and something hot seemed to uncurl down in the pit of her belly. She couldn't breathe deeply, couldn't blink, and only when he turned away did she take a deep breath.

He went to the hearth and sank down in a chair, and without turning his head, said, "Aye, we'll have a good marriage, my lady. I can already feel what's between us."

"Between us," she echoed with disdain. "You are mistaken. There is hatred and anger inside me, nothing else."

His head turned now, and she caught his profile, the heavy brows, the strong nose, the firm mouth.

"Your anger lights your eyes with a green fire that I find enthralling. I can mold that fire, my lady, see if I don't."

And he turned away again.

She wanted to scream at him, to deny everything he said, but he *wanted* that kind of emotion from her, and she wouldn't give him the satisfaction.

Keeping her gaze on his every move, she pulled off her gown and left it in a heap, followed by her petticoats and then her chemise. By now she was trembling, although the room was warm enough. Practically tripping in her haste, she stepped over the edge and sat in the tub, cursing that the water barely covered her breasts, no matter how deeply she sank.

She was naked in the same room with a man who was nearly so, a man who intended to force her into marriage. She grabbed a facecloth, lathered a poor amount of strange-smelling soap, and began to rub her skin. The feel of being warm and clean was glorious—if only she could revel in it. But she felt like a rabbit tiptoeing past a wolf, desperate to finish before she was noticed.

Not caring that she'd already made the water foul with just her skin, she dipped her head back to wet her hair, then began to soap it as well. If given a choice, she'd wash it over and over, but she had no time. Luckily, the maidservants had left one pail of clean water, and she used that to sluice through her hair. When water splashed on the floor, McCallum turned his head, not quite looking her way.

"Waste not the water, lass," he ordered. "I do plan to use it."

She winced and could only be grateful he'd allowed her to go first.

At last she felt as clean as possible. At home, her

lady's maid would be standing there with warm, thick towels to wrap her in. It never occurred to her that she'd have to fetch them herself. The towels were on the table, and she'd have to cross the floor, dripping water, to reach them. She huddled in the tub, feeling like the worst kind of fool, frozen with indecision.

His head turned again when she made no more sloshing sounds, and she saw when he focused on the table—and the towels.

"Why didn't ye say ye needed help," he grumbled, rising to his feet.

The soap left some bubbles floating on the surface, but not enough to hide her. She drew her knees to her chest, a meager protection, hoping he'd bring her the towels with his eyes averted, like a gentleman.

But he wasn't a gentleman. He stood above her, towels in hand, and stared down at her. His gray eyes, normally so cold and impassive, seemed to glitter by candlelight.

"I've known about ye for a long time, lass," he said, his voice low and husky. "I did some foolish things in rebellion against our shared fate. There were times I railed against my father for fixing my future without my consent. I was never free to give more of myself to a woman. But now that I've met ye . . . I am satisfied with the bargain between our families. More than satisfied. Ye have spirit and intelligence, Lady Riona, things I value highly in a bride. I look forward to our wedding and our future, but right now"—his voice became even deeper, rough—"I most look forward to our wedding night."

Riona hugged her knees even tighter, feeling a strange mixture of emotion churning inside her, frustration, worry, and a new one, flattery. That last one—how could she feel flattered by the praise and attentions of the man who'd kidnapped her and dragged her north against her will?

But he thought she was his bride, and he was pleased by that. She felt foolish, knowing her confusion was because she'd been allowed so little experience with men. A little flattery, and her insides softened.

"I will not marry you, McCallum," she insisted, trying to forget she was naked. "I keep telling you, you've got the wrong bride, and at some point, you'll accept the truth."

For a long moment, he continued staring at her, his expression unreadable, until at last one side of his mouth tilted up. "I should have said ye're stubborn, too."

He put the towels on a stool beside her and turned away. Shivering, she wrapped one around her hair, then stood up. She dried her upper body in haste, hopped out, and finished, sliding on the nightshift so quickly it clung to the damp spots she'd missed.

But at least she had something to cover her naked-ness. If only she had a dressing gown, too.

"I'm finished," she said, approaching the fire.

He rose up, and she was reminded once again how small and defenseless she was next to him. She wanted to scurry away like a frightened mouse, but didn't. He'd promised not to force himself upon her until marriage—and she was going to try her best to make sure that never happened. He brushed past her, and she took his place at the fire, taking down her wet hair and beginning to comb it out with her fingers. She didn't look behind her as she heard the splash of water, and then his groan of satisfaction. That sound made her shiver, but it wasn't from fear. It was as if her body reacted to him in ways she had no control over, and no understanding either.

He said nothing for a long time, and she found herself almost dozing as the warmth and fresh clothing worked their magic. And then her stomach growled loudly, making her wince.

"Supper will be sent up," McCallum said.

She nodded.

"Looks like 'tis my turn to forget a towel," he added.

She could have sworn she heard a smirk of laughter in his voice, but when she turned around, his expression was as impassive as always. She was tempted to throw the towel at him, but he'd done her too many favors this night for her to risk rousing his wrath. She took the last towel off the table and brought it to him, keeping her eyes averted as much as possible. But unless she was going to trip over the tub and land on him, she was forced to see something of his big body crowded into the little tub. His chest and arms boasted the muscles of an active man, and more than one scar to match the one on his chin. He didn't keep his knees to his chest as she had, but thank goodness soap bubbles obscured what was beneath the surface. She might be ignorant, but something inside her seemed to respond pleasurably to his form—and she didn't like feeling that she had no control over parts of herself that should be private.

He took the towel. "My thanks, lass. I might need ye to dry my back."

She didn't dignify that with a response, only went back to the fire to continue drying her hair amid his damp clothing. When there was a knock at the door, she cringed when he answered it wearing only the long, clean shirt. Dismissing the servant, he brought a tray of food to the table, and she watched the steaming mutton chops with appreciation.

Spinning her chair around, she found herself across a table from McCallum, as if they were two normal people. Was she supposed to serve him, as so many men of her acquaintance would expect from their women? But he gave them each a plateful of turnips and carrots with the mutton chop, and to her surprise, waited politely until she'd had her first taste.

When he continued watching her closely, she frowned and asked, "Is something wrong?"

"'Tis fine mutton. Do ye like it?"

"It's tolerable." Although to be honest, it tasted heavenly after five days eating cold food or something scorched over a fire.

"Ye'll see the difference when you have what Mrs. Wallace prepares. She was the cook at Larig, but now I believe she might be the housekeeper."

Riona said nothing—she didn't plan to be at Larig for long. McCallum *had* to believe the truth eventually. For several minutes, they ate in silence, and she simply absorbed the heat of the fire and of feeling clean. And then she thought of having him alone, where she could learn something that might help her sway him. But it was difficult to be civil, to be accommodating, after everything he'd done to her.

"You said," she began slowly, "that you've known about the marriage contract for much of your life. You didn't fight it?"

He swallowed another bite of his food and regarded her. "I had only reached the age of thirteen when Father told me what my future would be. I did not take it gracefully."

"What did you do?"

"Everything I could to make my family miserable." He turned and stared into the fire, where shadows made his eyes hooded beneath his brows. "I acted out, I was defiant, I did the opposite of what my father wanted me to do. And since half the time he was drunk as a tosspot, it didn't affect him as much as it did the reputation of my mother and sister."

"You have a sister?"

"Maggie." Though he didn't smile, his tone softened. "She's suffered more than I ever did, but that is her story to tell."

"Your mother didn't suffer, being married to a drunkard?"

His cold gaze returned to her. "I didn't say that. What happened behind closed doors she never said. But she was a coward where my father was concerned, and her children suffered for it."

Riona stiffened. "I do not know your family, but from what you've said about your father, a powerful chief who could make life or death decisions for his clan, what was your mother supposed to do against him?"

"Do not mistake me. She finally did do one thing, and that was to take Maggie and me away from Larig when I had fifteen years, to live with her family in Edinburgh. Saved me from making a bigger fool of myself than I already had."

"Sounds to me like she saved you from a drunken father."

"She could have saved much more than my youth—but it no longer matters."

"It sounds like it still does, to you. You hold a grudge."

He said nothing, only continued to eat as if he was unaffected. But Riona saw a weakness about him now, a man affected by emotions toward his family, a man with some guilt about the behavior of his youth. Not that she had any idea how to use these things against him.

"How long did you remain with your mother's family?"

"Three years. Until the Rising made me stand on my own feet as a man."

She inhaled in dismay. "You were with the Jacobites during the rebellion?"

"Rebellion?" he scoffed. "Now ye truly sound like a Sassenach using that word."

That made her hot with embarrassment, but she said nothing.

"But I ken ye've been living in England, and ye cannot be blamed for what your father made ye do. England must accept that we won't forget our true and rightful king. The King Over the Water deserves our support."

"He will never be king of Great Britain, McCallum—or so my father says."

"Your father, the one who can be trusted to keep a contract?" he sneered.

"That is my *uncle,* as I've told you over and over again."

He snorted.

"My father is his younger brother. But regardless, they speak often of the futility of going against the Crown. James Stuart can never be king—he's Catholic. He won't be accepted now that his cousin George is on the throne."

"That means nothing. It's been obvious since the Act of Union that England only meant to keep us subservient to them. Scottish noblemen were denied a place in the House of Lords, though they'd been promised it. Our taxes went up, our privy council was abolished—we were betrayed."

"But you cannot raise a large enough army—didn't Sheriffmuir and the failed march into northern England make you see that?"

"The Earl of Mar was a poor leader. We were twelve thousand strong in Perth, ready to march south, and instead he delayed. And delayed. Men deserted over the lack of discipline. We had superior numbers at Sheriffmuir when we met the Duke of Argyll and his supporters. And we were victorious."

"Didn't Argyll claim victory, too? I heard there were many casualties on both sides, and nothing was decided." He opened his mouth angrily, but she rushed on, "You were so young—were you hurt?"

He ignored that. "I may have been young, but I

knew our victory could have been conclusive if Mar would have risked the whole army, but he wouldn't, and victory was hollow when nothing came of it. I couldn't march into England for the battle at Preston that ended in surrender. Even when our true king came to our shores, it was too late to matter."

"I heard the man was ill and left within the month."

McCallum said nothing, just tore a piece of bread apart like he was taking apart the enemy.

"If you didn't march into England, were you wounded? If so, you were lucky. You might have been captured."

"Not so lucky. I had to spend the spring recovering at Larig. I thought I could alter my relationship with my father, but everything became worse."

He stared into the fire, and the shadows flickering over his face looked harsh and menacing, as if his memories of that summer were terrible. She could not press her luck, not this night.

"So you only stayed with your father the first half of the year after the Rising? What did you do then?"

Those gray eyes focused sharply on her again. "For someone trying to convince me ye're not involved in my plans for the clan, ye ask many questions."

The food seemed to settle hard in her stomach, and she sat back in her chair, no longer hungry. "I am only curious and trying to pass the time. Would you rather I sit here silently?"

"At least then I would ken your purpose." He pushed his plate away. "Enough of this. We have to get an early start in the morn. Let us retire to bed."

She'd known this was coming—perhaps part of her desperation to learn something about him was just to put off the inevitable. She glanced at the bed, trying to hide her fear. Fear only showed her vulnerability.

"I already made ye a vow that I would never force ye into what ye're not ready for," McCallum said coldly. "I don't break my vows."

She had no answer to that. His vow had led him to take her captive—she didn't trust the strength of his supposed vows. But she couldn't tell him that. "I will sleep in front of the fire."

"Ye'll not. Ye need a good night's sleep as much as I do. Get into that bed."

She stood up to face him, gritting her teeth. She wanted to refuse, to fight, but he only had to toss her onto the bed and hold her down and maybe . . . no, she couldn't let that happen. So she whirled and marched to the bed, climbed in and pulled the counterpane up to her chin. She wished she could protest that there was no room for him, that his big body would crowd her out.

He went to the fire, laid another piece of peat across it, and rearranged his drying garments once again. After blowing out the candle on the table, he came to her, a vast shadow against the light of the fire. Riona's heart was pounding so loudly that surely he could hear it. She wondered if she should have insisted that Samuel share the room with them. She needed a buffer, but there was no one. If she screamed, Samuel would hear her, but . . . would he go against his chief?

McCallum sat on the edge of the bed, and it dipped toward him. She braced herself with a hand, even as he lay down on his side, facing away from her. She hovered there, waiting, looking at the width of his shoulders, and the counterpane he only caught beneath his arm.

"Are ye going to lie down," McCallum asked with obvious exasperation, "or sit up all night?"

Very slowly, she lay back on her pillow, tense, as if she needed to spring up at a moment's notice. But nothing happened except that his breathing deepened. Would he really leave her alone?

CHAPTER 5

It took Hugh a long time to fall asleep, though he knew he'd successfully convinced Riona otherwise. Her lithe body had barely dented the mattress, but he felt the fight finally go out of her as she slipped into sleep, and some of his own tension eased. Listening to her even breathing, he imagined the future, when the worst of this marriage battle was behind him. Would he feel at peace when he lawfully lay beside her? Would he ever find a way to convince her that he would make an honorable husband? Or would his past come between them in the end?

It had been strange to discuss the things he'd done in his youth with another person, especially the one who would be his wife. He'd kept some of it to himself, which could be a mistake, considering what she might hear from his clansmen. But he didn't want to scare her off any more than he already had.

But somehow he must have slept—and slept deeply, a rarity for him—because he came awake to the sensation of soft warmth along his side and the silkiness of bare, feminine legs entwined with his. Without moving, he opened his eyes to see that somehow in the night, Riona had pressed herself along his side, pillowed her head on his shoulder. Her hair was like another blanket along his chest and arm, and she must have unconsciously felt the same heat, for the bedclothes were lowered around both of their waists.

He hadn't been able to get much of a glimpse of her nightshift, not with the way her gaze had been shooting daggers at him. He'd spent the evening avoiding looking below her neck; her face was captivating enough.

But now he could look his fill, at least of her breasts, so, being but a man, he did. He could feel the soft roundness of them against his own chest, the gentle pressure as her breathing deepened and then let out. The nightshift was caught beneath her, pulling the fabric tight so that he could see the vague outline of her nipple. He ached to touch and caress and give her the pleasure that he knew would make her see that they would have a good marriage.

But she wouldn't see such an intrusion that way. So he fisted one hand in the counterpane to control his urges. He lay still, listening to the sounds of the birds beginning to awaken before dawn, then dozed briefly, more content and relaxed than he'd been in a long, long time.

He felt her stir before he heard her. She arched slowly against him, and he squeezed his eyes shut to keep from pulling her beneath him, from settling between her legs where he wanted to be. Those legs moved against his, bare skin on bare skin, her thigh creeping up along his. Her soft, sleepy moan made him regret the months that had passed since he'd last known a woman's bed.

And then she went all stiff with awareness. He closed his eyes and feigned sleep, although it was difficult to lie still when he could feel her breathing increase with agitation, and that only made her breasts seem as if to caress him.

She raised herself up slowly on one elbow, her hair sliding against him like the fan of a flirtatious woman. He regretted the loss of her touch acutely, but she didn't move completely away. What was she doing?

And at last he opened his eyes and saw that she studied him with suspicion, even as her eyes slowly widened.

"Ye can't get enough of me, lass?" he asked with satisfaction, knowing it would be the wrong thing to say, but unable to help himself.

With a groan she tried to push away from him. "How dare you! Let me go! I shall scream!"

He caught her flailing arms. "Enough. I did not do this. I seem to remember sleeping apart from ye. Surely it was your body that betrayed ye."

When she groaned, he let her go, then swung his legs over the side and stood up. He arched and stretched, feeling well-rested for the first time in days. Glancing over his shoulder, he found her once again with the counterpane pulled to her chin, glaring at him.

"I need some privacy," she insisted.

"And when Samuel arrives, I'll give ye some. Until then, be patient."

He opened the door, found a pile of cleaned clothing, and brought it inside to dress. Just as he finished, someone knocked, and he called entrance.

"McCallum!" Riona cried, outraged, even as she yanked the counterpane to her nose.

He ignored her.

Samuel stepped inside, and his eyes went wide at the pretty image Riona made in bed. "Uh . . . good morning. Breakfast will be brought up soon."

"Good," Hugh said. "Can ye remain outside the door while I see to our departure and Riona dresses?"

"Of course."

Samuel seemed eager to be away from them, and Hugh shook his head. When he stepped into the corridor himself, he heard something hit the door behind him.

Samuel eyed him. "Did ye bed her?"

"Nay, but I wasn't about to sleep on the floor. I slept well, and I think she did, too, which is part of the reason she's upset."

"I saw a tub . . ."

"I turned my back while she bathed, like a gentleman. And when it was my turn, 'twas refreshing."

"I bet that went well."

" 'Twas . . . enlightening."

GETTING back into the coach was as dreadful as Riona knew it would be. Her bruises from the rough ride seemed magnified, and would only get worse, because the roads certainly were, even here in the Lowlands. The innkeeper had kindly given her a frame, cloth, and thread for needlework, but it was often too bumpy for her to sew. McCallum had opened her window more, so at least she could see the countryside. For several days, they followed a river valley and on either side, hills rolled in the distance, some of them brown and bare of trees along the summit. At night the men slept on bedrolls by a fire, and she slept within the coach, uncomfortable, but dry.

Coaches were few and far between now; they often had to pull aside for a string of laden packhorses being led south toward the markets in England, and once a herd of shaggy black cattle meandered on the path, reluctant to move.

When McCallum rode inside the coach with her, he tried to arouse her interest about the countryside, telling her of the heated, healing waters at Moffat, or the Roman ruins at Abington. And though part of her was interested in learning about her own country, she concentrated hard on seeming indifferent. She was still so appalled at how she'd relaxed in her sleep, cozied right up against McCallum as if he wasn't her kidnapper. Her body had betrayed her, and she was so afraid it would happen again that she didn't even ask to find an inn, though it rained on and off, and the men took turns getting damp as they drove her ever northward.

She found herself so bored that she kept flashing back to memories of that intimate night together, his bare legs against hers, how safe she'd felt in his arms when she'd first awoken and couldn't remember everything. Safe? Someone was supposed to be keeping her safe from the likes of *him*. But no one was rescuing her—she'd given up hope for that. She could only rely on herself now, and her powers of persuasion. Somehow she would make him believe the truth.

They reached Glasgow, a port burgh that McCallum reminded her proudly had had a university as far back at the fifteenth century. It was now a hub of trade with the American colonies and the rest of Europe. There were more people here—foreigners and Sassenachs—but McCallum was no fool, and did not allow her to spend a night there.

"Ye'd have worked your wiles on those poor men," McCallum told her as she stared out the window sadly at the dwindling buildings behind them.

At least they'd stopped for provisions, although he would not allow the time for clothes to be laundered. She could see he was growing more and more alert as he looked to the north, toward home.

It should be her home, too. Their clan lands bordered each other. But her parents had made sure it was not home, and she couldn't overcome that feeling of . . . intruder, outlander, Sassenach.

They took a drovers' road northeast of Glasgow toward Stirling, where the land seemed bare yet captivating, miles of rolling farmlands giving way to higher bare ground of moors and bogs, bleak and brown, but full of a strange beauty that intrigued Riona. This was the land of her people, and she'd always been told how wild and savage it was— wild, yes, but magnificent in its own way. McCallum once again talked of the history, of the second wall built nearby by the Romans, just like the one on the English border, only this was to keep the men of the Highlands out. More than once she saw the ruin of a castle on distant hills. The poor horses strained to pull the coach ever higher, and the going was slow until they reached the low summit, with the valley spread out below toward Stirling. And then she was forced to listen to McCallum's pride in the burgh.

"Armies of old aimed to hold Stirling if they wanted to encroach the Highlands. One of the royal castles of the kings of Scotland is there. And 'tis where I keep a private stable."

That jolted her from her dazed stare out the window. "What?"

"We'll be able to go no farther in the coach, so I house it there."

His home was so remote a coach couldn't travel there. She groaned and closed her eyes, feeling as if she were going to the end of the world.

"I had a letter from a friend in Inverness," McCallum continued in a wry voice. "The first chaise made it there only last year. He said the whole town came out to see it."

Riona could only stare at him in horror. What kind of place *was* this?

As they approached the town, Stirling Castle rose high above the surrounding valley, up on a rocky promontory, and Riona saw McCallum's expression cloud. She knew enough of her history to know that the Jacobite forces had tried to take the castle during the Rising, and had been unsuccessful. Had he been there, too, trying to take back the Scottish castle of his king from the English? But all she could focus on was what lay beyond Stirling, the daunting line of mountains to the northwest, where they were headed.

There was no inn that night, much as she might have wished it. McCallum kept a room above his stables roughly furnished with beds and trunks and a table. Samuel shared the room with them, though he seemed embarrassed by it. Riona almost didn't care by that point. She was exhausted in both mind and body. No wonder her parents had never brought her to the Highlands.

To her surprise, McCallum remained in Stirling a second night, so that he could purchase supplies for the journey. Samuel was with her constantly, though she spent much of the day dozing on her bed. McCallum seemed concerned about her that night, and she insisted she wasn't sick, simply appreciative that the furniture wasn't rocking furiously under her. More than once in the coach, she'd been thrown to the floor.

Then at dawn, she found herself riding a mare across the valley floor, toward the bleak mountain range that rose up as if in warning. The drovers' road was barely a path, overgrown with heather and gorse, with only the occasional beech or pine trees in the lower foothills. The two men positioned her horse between theirs, leading a packhorse behind. She had no choice but to follow Samuel along the narrow dirt path that wound its way ever deeper into the Highlands. Why did it feel so permanent, like she'd never leave again?

AFTER a day of slow travel, occasionally following the River Teith through the rising hills, they made camp outside the village of Callandar on a cool summer night. The next day, their journey took them along Loch Lubnaig, where pine forests came almost to the water's edge, and the bare mountaintops seemed like the uneven backs of lumpy animals. Riona thought they would climb the snow-topped heights of Ben Ledi itself, but to her relief, their path turned and edged the loch, then another river before heading west into a glen that eventually broadened into Loch Voil, another beauteous lake nestled within mountains.

It was late afternoon when Riona wanted to rest, but McCallum insisted they push forward, along the lake and past the next rising mountain. She wasn't all that anxious to see the place where she'd live temporarily. The few villages they'd passed, thatched-roof huts with stone walls, had not gotten her hopes up. Perhaps McCallum wouldn't allow the cow to occupy a room in the cottage, like some did.

She was just about to insist they make camp when they took a turn, and to her surprise, the first square tower rose above the trees, with guards standing watch on battlements. They rode farther, up to a low hilltop where a large castle had been built, overlooking the hills. The fortress was long and broad, with walls of stone keeping intruders out, but for a guarded gatehouse. Several square towers rose higher than the walls.

McCallum was watching her now, his expression one of amused condescension, as if he'd known the bleak cottage she'd been imagining. She lifted her chin and said nothing, but she was impressed nonetheless.

All around them on the hillsides, black, shaggy cattle roamed, and below them in the distance, small farm fields clustered around another village in the glen. But the castle, which had been hidden from below by a curve in the hillside, dominated the skyline and rivaled the mountains themselves for grandeur.

As they came closer to the gatehouse, guards dressed in black and red plaid, their legs bare, moved to take up a position to stop them. Surprised, Riona looked to McCallum, whose expression remained neutral even as he began to speak in Gaelic. She thought she heard him say his own name, which shocked her. Was he having to introduce himself to his own people? Or had he been lying to her about his identity all along?

But Samuel only waited patiently, as if he had no concerns. And true enough, the guards seemed to come to attention, doffing their bonnets and look-

ing abashed. One led their small party through
the gatehouse, and Riona looked up at the sharply
pointed portcullis that would drop through the
ceiling and bar the entrance from invaders. She felt
like an invader right along with McCallum, but she
was truly a captive of war, the war that had been
going on between McCallum and Duff for centuries.

Within the courtyard, dozens of people moved
with purpose from the grand towerhouse rising
four stories, to the other halls and barracks built
into the thick castle walls. Chickens and ducks
seemed to have free rein, chased by children, who
barely spared a glance for travel-stained visitors.
She could see an arched opening that led into another courtyard.

The guards must have passed the word to others
about McCallum's identity, because they gathered
together now within the courtyard, waiting. Some
came running from the other courtyard, still carrying claymores and shields, as if they'd been at
training.

She tried to ask Samuel what was going on, but
he hushed her. Then a large wooden double door
opened in the first floor of the towerhouse, and a
man emerged, causing voices to drop to murmurs.

"The tanist, Dermot McCallum, Hugh's cousin,"
Samuel said in a low voice. "He was nominated as
the man next of blood to the chief when Hugh was

selected, the one who will succeed him if Hugh dies without heirs. He's been in charge since Hugh's father died a few months ago."

The man came down the stairs, tall, thin, but Riona suspected his build was deceptive. Though she'd seen men wearing wigs in Scotland, his brown hair was bare and tied back. His plaid was belted meticulously about his waist and the end draped up over his shoulder, where a brooch gleamed. He approached McCallum, who still sat atop his horse, as if he ranked above all the clansmen gathered before him. And he did.

Dermot patted the horse's neck nonchalantly, eyeing McCallum, who said something else in Gaelic, then gestured toward Riona and switched into English.

"I am home with my betrothed, come to stay and take up my rightful place within the clan. Ye've done well, Dermot, and I appreciate the care ye've given my people."

"*Our* people," Dermot said coolly. "We are all McCallums at heart, are we not?"

Someone briefly cheered, but it died away when no one joined in. Riona's spirits rose a bit. McCallum was not the invincible chief he'd portrayed to her. Dermot obviously disapproved of a laird who'd been gone for so long. But she wouldn't make the mistake of screaming that she'd been kidnapped. There was a long history among the clans of healing feuds with the help of an unwilling bride. If she tried to win the support of the McCallums, she'd be doing nothing but ensuring that the clan would rally around its chief.

With a little patience and persuasion, perhaps there was a way she could win her freedom, she thought, eyeing Dermot.

CHAPTER 6

Hugh followed Dermot up the stairs to the great hall, holding on to his patience by the narrowest rope. He'd been elected chief after his father died, even though he hadn't been at Larig Castle. He'd corresponded with Dermot, had assumed all would be well, but his uncertain reception today irritated him. Had his cousin thought he'd have free rein over the clan for months or years?

The great hall was as he remembered it, and he turned to see Riona's eyes widen as she took in the high beamed ceiling, the clan armor and weapons on the walls, and the ancient tapestries displaying the stories of the McCallums. Preparations were under way for supper, since the trestle tables were being set up by servants.

Hugh remembered how his father would enter this room like a king, taking his place at the dais and waiting for his gentlemen to beg his favor or to give their reports. But Hugh wasn't going to be his father—he would earn his command by earning the respect of his gentlemen and household, not their fear.

The men gathered around him, and though Dermot's smile was perfunctory, many of the younger men wore grins of welcome. Upon spying Riona at his side, they asked eager questions in English of how things were in London and Edinburgh these many years. He could practically see Riona's ears perk up, and knew everything about today had increased her curiosity.

He raised his hands for quiet. "Enough, enough, we've time for this at supper. My betrothed needs to refresh herself, as do Samuel and I."

"Your rooms have been ready for days, Laird McCallum," said Mrs. Wallace hurrying toward him and wearing a broad grin and twinkling eyes beneath her lace cap. " 'Twill be fine to have ye home for good."

But Hugh was aware of the murmurs in the hall from the men not crowding as close. The older clansmen remembered the childish behavior of his youth, and would have reservations about his ability to lead. And as for the events that had transpired when he'd been recovering from wounds sustained at Sheriffmuir? That wouldn't have been forgotten either, though the young woman had been dead almost ten years.

Mrs. Wallace turned to Riona expectantly, and if she had any concerns about a Duff making herself at home at Larig Castle, she didn't show it.

"Mrs. Wallace," Hugh said formally, "may I present Lady Catriona Duff, soon to be my wife."

The housekeeper bobbed a little curtsy. Riona nodded her head hesitantly, but to Hugh's relief, she didn't make any protest. He'd wondered if Riona would bring up the kidnapping when they arrived, but so far, she'd been circumspect. He hoped that meant that at last she was accepting their inevitable marriage. Perhaps it had begun when they'd woken up together at the inn, after so naturally turning to each other in their sleep.

But by looking into Riona's lovely face, he couldn't tell one way or another what she was thinking.

"Come, Laird McCallum, Lady Catriona," Mrs. Wallace said, leading the way. "'Twill be your first time in the chief's rooms," she added over her shoulder to Hugh.

They followed her up the curving staircase built into the square tower just outside the great hall. On the second floor, a central corridor ran along a series of bedrooms. The last one took up one end of the towerhouse, several rooms overlooking the courtyard and gardens below, and beyond, the whole Balquhidder Glen in which Loch Voil nestled. He stood at the window and remembered thinking that when the sun shone, the loch looked like a jewel.

Behind him, Mrs. Wallace gestured to the dark wood wainscoting that covered the walls, as in most of the family rooms, talking to Riona about the Scottish landscapes hung there, but Hugh only paid half a mind. The large four-poster occupied its place of prominence against one wall, its curtains woven of the McCallum tartan. A massive wardrobe for hanging garments resided next to a chest of drawers, while several chests with lids lined a wall. At a writing bureau near the window, his father had done much of his correspondence, and the old man's wig stand still rested on the dressing table. Hugh grimaced. He was not a man made for hot, uncomfortable wigs, regardless that they were the fashion.

Mrs. Wallace led Riona through the dressing room where his parents had once entertained close friends, and then into the mistress's bedroom. Hugh followed and stood leaning against the door frame, watching Riona's expressive face as she took in the lightly colored wainscoted walls, the delicate furniture in a French style. Instead of a four-poster, this room had a box-bed built into the far wall, with tartan curtains to enclose the bed in privacy. There was an elegant writing desk, and on the dressing table rested a swivel mirror. Nothing but the best for his mother, he thought, repressing the usual surge of bitterness. At least this would not be his mother's room again.

Riona put a hand on the bathing tub that already

rested before the fire. Her expression looked . . . relieved.

"I'll leave ye to your bath and Mrs. Wallace's excellent care," Hugh said.

Riona gave him a long look, but only nodded.

"If ye need anything, ye know where to find me."

Riona watched as the door closed, saying nothing, wondering if he would really give her the privacy she hadn't known for two weeks. Mrs. Wallace eyed her curiously for a moment, then bustled to the wardrobe and opened it.

"Ye'll find plenty of things to wear in here, Lady Catriona," Mrs. Wallace said. "Some will have to be taken in, I'm sure, but ye know the lacin' on others will do wonders to adjust to yer fine figure."

"You've noticed I've come with no garments of my own," Riona said with a trace of bitterness.

"I ken 'tis a long journey from England, my lady," Mrs. Wallace said gently. "Ye did not remember how remote we are here in the Highlands?"

"I don't remember Scotland at all," Riona confessed. "My parents took me away when I was but a child."

"And educated in the ways of England, I can tell by yer accent." Mrs. Wallace sniffed disapprovingly, though her smile returned. "But that isn't yer fault, my lady. Ye're back now, and ye'll come to realize ye're simply one of us."

"I—I'm not one of you," she whispered.

But before she could say more, someone knocked on the door and a line of servants entered with buckets of steaming water. Mrs. Wallace wanted to stay and help her bathe, but it had been so long since Riona was alone, she excused the house-keeper, who seemed to understand.

In the blessed silence, Riona heaved a sigh and went to the window. Below her, she could see the crowded courtyard, but beyond the curtain wall, Loch Voil glimmered with hushed beauty, serene, peaceful. There might have been a time that she would have enjoyed such a view, but now? She was a prisoner, and the lovely scenery might as well be a landscape painting, for all she'd be able to enjoy it. If she wasn't locked inside her bedroom, she might as well be. She could go nowhere without assis-tance of some kind, and she had no one to rely on. Chief McCallum was the rule of law in these hills, the sheriff, the judge. To speak against him was to risk . . . everything.

But Mrs. Wallace had been so kind that Riona had almost made the mistake of talking to her about what McCallum had done—and would that have been the wisest thing? Mrs. Wallace had ob-viously been here since at least McCallum's youth. She, and everyone else, would be *with* the McCal-lum and *against* a Duff. Goodness, the woman most likely *was* a McCallum from somewhere in her parentage.

Riona was an outsider, practically a Sassenach, according to McCallum. She would have to be smart and bide her time. Dermot McCallum—he didn't seem all that happy to see his cousin. Perhaps *his* disapproval would help convince McCallum that he was in the wrong. She would have to find out more about Dermot, see if he was the sort of man who could objectively listen to her story and confront McCallum at her side.

Feeling more at peace with a plan, however tenuous, Riona began to unlace the bodice of her gown, pull out the stomacher that covered her chemise, and let the gown sag off her shoulders and onto the floor. It was so travel-stained that she didn't want it to contaminate the upholstered chairs or the bedding. The petticoats came next and at last the chemise. She sank into the tub with a groan of delight. No one was going to use the water after her; no one was there to hurry her along, stare at her, or make her feel all flustered and overly warm.

She washed slowly and leisurely, eyes half closed, letting the steam as much as the soap cleanse her skin.

"I had no idea I'd be a lucky man again."

She let out a gasp and dropped the cloth; the

splash caught her in the face and she sputtered. McCallum stood leaning in the doorway, his narrowed eyes full of satisfaction.

"You—you—this is my bedroom! If Mrs. Wallace finds you here—"

"And what will my housekeeper do if she finds me in my own suite of rooms?"

And what could Riona do about that except feel furious, exasperated, and helpless.

He strolled forward and she sank lower, knowing that there was little to hide her from him. Once again, she pulled her knees to her chest. He stood for a long moment and looked down at her. She knew he could do whatever he wanted to her, and no one would stop him. But he turned away and went to sit in a chair near the fire, where he could no longer see her body.

To her horror, she felt a tiny stirring of disappointment, and couldn't understand herself. To cover her confusion, she insisted, "I should have my own room, separate from you."

"And why is that? We've been bound together since your birth. We'll be married soon. In Scotland, all we need to do is profess it before witnesses and the deed is done."

"I am not professing anything, and it is not a marriage if not done by my own free will."

But he only continued to look at her with easy satisfaction. "Ye'll get cold if ye don't finish your bath," he said in a low voice. "These old walls hide the fact that 'tis summer."

"Then I suggest you leave." She sounded like a prim maidenly aunt.

He crossed one ankle over the other knee, obviously prepared to wait her out. But . . . he'd never tried to force her into anything intimate, had let her flee when he had her alone in bed. And though his word was law here, he seemed to be a man who believed in honor, in his own code, if not one she'd agree with. She was to be his wife, and he expected her to freely say her vows, and seemed patient enough to make it happen.

So . . . if he wanted to play these games with her, to tease and make her uncomfortable, she could do the same. He deserved to feel frustrated, because she certainly did. Knowing he was far enough away not to see beneath the water, she dipped her head back to soak her hair, then reached for the soap and began to lather it in.

And he watched her, his eyes going impassive rather than satisfied. She was glad to be able to affect him, even if only to make him shield his thoughts. She felt another surge of satisfaction when he glanced away.

"I'm here," he said, "because I want to know why ye didn't tell the entire clan that I forced ye to come here."

She worked her hands through her soapy hair

slowly, as if giving his question great thought. She surreptitiously watched him from beneath her eyelashes, not knowing what she was looking for, but he didn't seem to be having trouble with her brazen display of . . . cleanliness.

"You have me at a disadvantage," she finally said. "I know no one here—who would want to believe me or help me? And yet . . . I feel that you aren't all that comfortable here either, though it's your home. So if you want me not to name you a kidnapper, I'd like to know more about your youthful indiscretions before your mother took you away. I'd like to know how things got so bad with your father that you left, and how you ended up in London—I heard your men mention it."

"Ye're very curious for a woman alone in a precarious situation."

"Believe me, I know precarious—I felt it for nearly a fortnight, have I not? You frightened me and overwhelmed me and dragged me across the country and into the middle of a feud that has nothing to do with me. But I also have some power here now, and I want answers."

"A woman who professes herself willing to be my wife deserves those answers."

"Why would a woman *ever* agree to be your wife without those answers in the first place?"

"We seem to be at a stalemate."

He stood up again and advanced, this time coming right to the edge of the tub. Soap bubbles hid the sight of her from him, but they were no true protection. But she was sick of constantly showing her fear, so she stiffened her shoulders and tried to meet his cool glance with one of her own.

He lifted the bucket of clean water left to rinse her hair and raised it above her head.

"McCallum—"

"Tilt your head back—ye wouldn't want me to get soap in your eyes."

"McCallum—!"

But he wasn't stopping, so with a gasp, she put her head back and met his amused gaze with her furious one, even as the water began to run through her hair and down into the tub. Seeing that his gaze lowered, she had a terrible feeling that the water was not only removing soap from her hair, but driving it away from her body.

She covered her breasts with her hands. "Just finish!"

He did at last, and she bowed her head, knowing he'd gotten the best of her once again. Still feeling watched, she at last opened her eyes to see him crouched at her level. Water dripped down her face and she blinked rapidly.

"Ye may feel ye have power here," he said in a hoarse voice, "but 'tis only at my whim. Ye could make things as unpleasant as ye'd like, and I would survive it, for I am laird here, and all ken the terms of the betrothal and how important our marriage is. There's many a man who would cheer me on for taking matters into my own hands when your father tried to betray me."

She didn't bother to deny her uncle's relationship to her—McCallum wouldn't listen. And she found herself unable to speak, caught up in his intensity and nearness—and passion for his clan. She'd never met anyone who made her emotions waver so wildly from anger to despair to intrigue. She didn't want to feel this way, out of control, racing toward some desperate clash between them. He was right—they could be married by tonight, and really, could she deny him if he would have his way? Or would he simply take what he wanted?

She shivered, but it wasn't from the water's chill. It was from the frightening realization that there was something powerful between them, something that called to her, that made the risks he'd taken to have her for himself seem arousing, not just self-serving. There was a place inside her she'd never sensed before, surely a recklessness, a weakness.

"Ye're strangely quiet, lass," he murmured.

His gaze lazily moved over her face, dipping to her breasts, where the upper curves were displayed above the soapy water. Her skin felt . . . prickly, sensitive, even inflamed.

"I'm not done fighting you," she said at last, almost wincing at how breathless she sounded.

A slow grin curved his mouth, even as he reached his hand to cup her face and tilt it toward him. The shock of his warm palm settling so gently on her skin made her tense, but she didn't pull away, as if that would show that she'd given up, that she was afraid of what he could do to her . . . what he could make her feel.

He leaned over the tub and kissed her, his palm guiding her head. She wanted to show him he didn't move her, that this display meant nothing to her. But his lips were warm, and glided over hers with purpose, parted gently as if he wanted to taste her. She'd never been kissed . . . She felt her head swim at the sensation that seemed to travel down her body, to her breasts, to the pit of her stomach and between her thighs as if he'd touched her in her most secretive places.

When his tongue traced her lower lip, she jerked back in surprise. He didn't laugh, just studied her with those gray eyes that were considerably warmer. He kept his hand on her face, and his thumb caressed her cheek over and over.

"Our first kiss bodes well for the future," he said.

He glanced down to her breasts again, and she stiffened. With a faint smile, he let her go and stood up.

"Dry off," he said, back to ordering her around. "We have things we need to discuss."

Not the topics *she* wanted to discuss, apparently,

but she didn't argue. He turned his back and went to the window, while she hastily dried herself and pulled on a dressing gown Mrs. Wallace had laid out for her, trying to forget the feel of his mouth on hers, and how instead of being afraid or disgusted, she'd felt . . . aroused. Cat had told her one could feel overwhelmed when in intimate situations with a man, and Riona hadn't been able to understand what she meant. She did now, and felt a new kind of fear—fear of her own reaction and response to this compelling persuasion of his.

"Come sit by the fire and dry your hair," he said.

Gritting her teeth, she obeyed because it needed to be done. She had a comb this time, and worked slowly on the tangles, letting the heat dry and soothe.

"So ye did not name me a kidnapper of women because ye ken ye're a Duff amidst a sea of McCallums."

She harrumphed, but said nothing.

"I would prefer that my clan not learn that the earl meant to betray us and break the contract, so I will not speak of that."

"Am I supposed to thank you for not making my *uncle* out to be a villain?"

"If they knew your *father* had tried to renege, he would be more than a villain. There are some who would demand a justified retaliation, and I don't want the feud to resume. I want my marriage to be the beginning of a new peace."

Without thinking about it, she almost said *"our* marriage" just to annoy him, and then realized what it implied.

He continued, "So now that we agree that we'll keep silent about the real circumstances of our meeting—"

She laughed without mirth. "Meeting? As if we first saw each other across a ballroom?"

He ignored her outburst. "I think we should simply say we met when I came to bring ye to Scotland, exactly as I intended to do if your father hadn't—"

"I know, I know, fine, have it your way. We were introduced, and my whole family agreed to rid themselves of me by letting a veritable stranger take me away."

She looked up at him through the strands of her hair as she combed. To her surprise, he wasn't angry. He reached into the pocket of his coat and removed something that was wrapped in a delicate piece of tartan cloth in the same colors she'd seen his clan wear.

"This is the gift I had brought for ye," he said.

The gift he'd brought for Cat. She let the comb slowly settle in her lap as she stared at the item.

He held it out, and though she hesitated, she took

it from him. The tartan easily fell away to reveal a small, decorated wooden box that looked quite old. Inside nestled a necklace that glittered in the setting sun when she lifted it out.

"It has been in my family for many generations," he said gruffly. " 'Twas made here, of pearls from Scottish rivers and amethysts dug out of Scottish hills, set in gold captured in our rivers."

He was obviously proud of his heritage, the heritage her family had scorned and avoided. It was . . . jarring, strange. But the necklace was truly lovely, and it made her feel conflicted to be wearing something that represented his clan.

"I thought dower gifts were of cattle," she said at last, trying to sound scornful.

He answered as if he didn't take offense. "Our fathers decided to share land instead."

"Do not forget the money from my uncle that would have gone into this marriage."

He rose, then while heading for the door to the dressing room, he ordered, "Wear the necklace tonight."

He didn't look back, as if he didn't expect a refusal, then closed the door behind him.

For some time, she sat looking at the necklace, spreading it out in her lap, the pearls creamy, the amethysts pale purple crystal. It wasn't gaudy, but it definitely spoke of wealth the clan had had sometime in the past. The McCallums didn't seem terribly poor now, but if they'd been desperate for her—Cat's—enormous dowry, there was need. But they weren't going to receive Cat's dowry, and the contract would be broken. They were going to lose their special land, too, the one that produced their whisky. McCallum didn't want to believe the truth, and he would suffer for it in the end. She wasn't going to feel sorry for him. Civilized men did not respond to problems by kidnapping women.

She leaned back in her chair and tried to imagine Cat here, kidnapped in the dead of night and dragged across the country. If Cat had known about the marriage contract, she might have accepted it, while still feeling the pain of helplessness. Cat felt more a part of Scotland than Riona did, being the daughter of a Scottish earl. Cat had visited their estate a few times with her brother, Owen, the heir, and Cat always spoke about the beauty of wild Scotland. But both women had thought they'd marry Englishmen . . .

Her depressed thoughts were interrupted by a knock on the door that opened to the corridor. Pulling her dressing gown tighter, she walked to the door, then opened it to admit Mrs. Wallace, who pushed a stumbling young woman in front of her.

"Lady Catriona," Mrs. Wallace began, "I ken that fine-born ladies have maids of their very own, so I brought me niece, Mary, who's been wantin' to work in the castle. There's mostly men here, o' course, but I thought servin' you, she could be of help and learn a thing or two."

Surprised, Riona said, "Thank you, Mrs. Wallace. Hello, Mary."

The girl didn't raise her eyes, only nodded and whispered, "Good day, my lady."

Mary was dressed in a plain gown with an apron pinned to the front, and a little mob cap perched amid brown curls tamed into submission at the base of her neck. Though she was thin, her red chapped hands bore evidence of hard work and the strength necessary for it.

Mrs. Wallace clapped her hands together, and her niece jumped. "Then 'tis settled. I'll help for a day or two, and between us, Lady Catriona, we can train our Mary in what pleases ye." She opened the wardrobe doors and pulled out the first gown. "She's a good little seamstress, Mary is, and ye might be needin' that skill for a while."

They spent some time choosing an outfit for Riona to wear to her first dinner with the clan. It was a deep maroon that Mrs. Wallace thought highlighted her green eyes. The stomacher revealed by the lacing was cream with lovely flowered embroidery, which was echoed in the fancy petticoat on display beneath the open skirt. After two weeks without wearing stays, it was rather jarring for her rib cage to be laced so tightly. Jarring, yet also familiar, as if she was almost back to herself, instead of a prisoner.

Making "ooh" noises of appreciation at the sight of the McCallum necklace, Mrs. Wallace proudly put it around Riona's neck, where it sat like a weight of expectations Riona would never meet.

She sat at the dressing table looking into the mirror as Mrs. Wallace worked on arranging her hair into a chignon, leaving random curls to drape against her neck. She knew her old life was gone. Whether she married or not, she could never again be considered an innocent, virginal potential bride. No man would want her now, she thought, swallowing hard.

"Are you and Himself harkenin' back to the old ways for the start of yer marriage?" Mrs. Wallace asked as she worked.

Riona frowned. "Pardon me?"

"Ye're here, livin' in the chief's rooms. Will ye be handfastin' then?"

"Handfasting?" Riona echoed uncertainly.

"I ken there's a contract, o' course, but neither of ye knows the other. Perhaps ye'll handfast—live together—for a year, then make a decision. Make sure ye can have children together. All would understand."

Riona had to work hard to keep her mouth from sagging open. She could not reveal her feelings to Mrs. Wallace, regardless of how friendly she seemed. No one at Larig Castle would ever be Riona's true friend.

McCallum had installed her in his rooms, as if she was his wife. Had he planned this handfasting all along? Did he intend to come to her rooms this night to make her his, and the kiss had been a prelude of what was to come?

CHAPTER 7

As he bathed and dressed in his plaid, Hugh knew he was doing the right thing—Riona had to leave her childish ways behind and accept the duties of a woman. She couldn't change the agreement between their families, just as he hadn't been able to change things when he was nineteen and desperately wanted a different bride.

He would treat her well and make her see that they could have a good marriage. Love was not something to be expected in an arranged marriage, but they could find respect and understanding with each other.

He would make that happen.

Was kissing her against her will the best way to do that? He didn't know, but it had tested the limits of his control to be there when she was bathing—again. He should have realized what he'd be walking into as she prepared for the evening meal after

a long journey. But he'd been so focused on anticipating his clan's questions that he hadn't thought
of anything else. He'd burst in and found her once
again naked, wet, and alluring. She'd been full of
fire and insult, and he'd admired every bit of it, especially since she was all alone at Larig Castle, with
no one she knew to look out for her.

But that kiss . . .

She was obviously an innocent, but she'd caught
on quickly. Her lips had been so soft and moist, her
taste exotic to him. He'd almost shaken with restraint when he'd desperately wanted to deepen the
kiss, to explore her mouth, to discover and inflame
her passion.

Maybe he needed to douse himself in the tub
again, now that the water had turned cold.

Instead he fastened the brooch that held his plaid
over his shoulder and headed toward the dressing room, to escort Riona and face the people he'd
barely seen in ten years.

RIONA paced her bedroom, waiting for McCallum.
She wasn't about to come to him—he had to come
to her, to bring her to his people. He planned to
use her to strengthen his bond with the clan, but
she knew that would never happen. Somehow she
would make him see that—

A knock rattled the door that led to the dressing room. Part of her wanted to put a pillow over

her head and make Hugh go down alone, humiliate him as she'd felt humiliated when Mrs. Wallace had talked about handfasting. But that wouldn't incline him to eventually see her side of things, so she simply called for him to enter.

He stopped in the doorway and looked at her, as she looked at him. He wore the clan plaid pleated and belted around his waist. A long length of it crossed his chest and was pinned to his coat at the shoulder. He wore tartan stockings to his knees and leather shoes. There were some in England who thought the Highland dress ridiculous, but she was not one of them. His legs were fine and well made, and his pride in wearing his clan colors was evident. Instead of wearing a wig, he'd pulled his dark, unruly hair back in a queue, and she was no longer surprised that he forswore the custom. He was a man who did what he wanted—she of all people knew that.

He studied her, his expression full of pride, contentment—and yes, passion, passion for her. Feeling overwhelming and confused, she had to look away. He'd stolen her life—how dare he act as if it was so easily accepted, as if he felt something more for her when he was just using her.

An insidious voice whispered in her head, *But what kind of life did you have?*

That wasn't the point—she wanted to make her own decisions. She'd made no decision for herself, unless it was what book to read to Bronwyn, what song to play for her on the spinet. Her parents had always told her she could be involved in choosing her husband . . . someday. And every year, "someday" had become the next year, and then the year after that. She'd felt that the best years of her life had been spent in a sickroom, where she'd alternated between feeling loving pity for her sister, and sadness and frustration that her own life was just as confined. True, she'd been allowed to accompany Cat to the occasional dinner or musicale, but she'd never been free to enjoy the entire evening, because her parents had insisted Bronwyn needed her help to fall asleep.

But Bronwyn had been well enough to travel to the Continent, and that had given Riona hope that when they returned it would be Riona's turn for an elaborate Season in London. Her mother had promised it, confiding before she left that it was time for Riona to relax after all her years nursing Bronwyn. Riona had cynically suspected that her mother was growing jealous of the closeness between the sisters, and had deliberately denied Riona the chance to see Europe.

The kind of life her future self would have didn't matter right now. At some point, McCallum would finally realize and accept that he truly had the wrong bride, and everything he'd planned would be ruined.

"So you wear the plaid," she said.

He smirked. "Highland women don't like being denied the sight of their men's naked legs."

She rolled her eyes.

"Ye're a bonny lass, Riona."

He'd taken to leaving off the honorific of "lady" when they were alone, and the intimacy unnerved her. He would not be "Hugh" to her. That would be playing into his hands.

She didn't say anything as she set her hand on his forearm and allowed him to lead her into the corridor. He went first down the spiral stairs as if to catch her if she stumbled. He fancied himself a gentleman, did he?

As they descended, the noise from the great hall increased. Friendly discussion and laughter, the sound of pipes warming up, all of which made a cacophony of sound.

"Ye're trembling," he said as they reached the arched stone entrance on the first floor.

He covered her hand with his, and instead of soothing her, it made her feel powerless against his strength. She wanted to shake it off, but didn't. "I'm fine."

He eyed her narrowly, but nodded. When they stepped into the entrance, in full view of the people, Riona inhaled sharply. There had to be over one hundred people packed into the hall, which was lit by torches along the walls, their light reflecting off the silver platters displayed on several cupboards. A hush seemed to spread outward from them, and even the piper hit a sour note of surprise.

Every pair of eyes was focused on them, and the expressions ranged from curious to worried to skeptical to hopeful. A clan chief was the focus, and from him radiated prospects for the future. These people didn't know if they could trust Mc-Callum, absent so long from their lives, beginning when his mother hadn't trusted his father. Did the clan worry he would be just another drunkard? Or would he be weak because he'd been raised by one for the formative years of his life?

And then Dermot rose to his feet on the dais, and lifted a goblet of wine toward his cousin. "The Mc-Callum!"

A sudden roar of welcome made her start. Only when she felt the release of tension in McCallum's arm did she realize how tense he'd truly been. He did not grin, for he wasn't a man given to easy amusement, as she already knew. But his expression was proud and gratified, even as he led her to the dais and up the short staircase. She stood to his right and stared out at the curious crowd.

McCallum raised both hands and began to speak, and she realized she could understand none of it. Whatever he said to his people, they nodded or smiled or looked solemn. Many snuck glances at her, and she knew it must be easy to tell that she didn't understand a word. Some would look down on her now as a Duff who wanted so little to do with their homeland that she hadn't learned the language. Her father and uncle never spoke it in front of her, and her mother was English. It had never even been a consideration as she learned French and Latin. Now she felt guilty, as if she should have known, at eight years of age, to find a Scottish tutor.

And then she heard her name in the midst of the Gaelic words, and Hugh lifted her hand up as if presenting her. No one booed her as a Duff, but the applause was only scattered and dutiful. She looked speculatively at Dermot, but when her gaze met his, he glanced pointedly away. Hugh released her hand and went on speaking.

"Good evening, my lady," whispered a man to her right.

She turned quickly, only to find herself relaxing with relief. "Oh, Samuel, you startled me."

He bowed his head, even as she considered her reaction. He'd been complicit with his chief in capturing her, yet she almost felt him some kind of ally, which was ridiculous. He would never be the man she might beg to help her. She'd already tried that. He'd seen her terrified and afraid, and he'd done nothing to help her escape, simply hid her rebellion from McCallum after the highwaymen attacked. But at the moment, he was a sympathetic face, the only man who spoke to her in English.

Samuel held up a hand, as if he understood her confusion, and they both waited while McCallum finished speaking. When at last he sat down, voices rose again, the musicians started playing, and serving men and women appeared from a far corridor carrying wooden platters above their heads. A burly man came to stand behind Hugh, bristling with weapons, and giving everyone a menacing stare of warning that their chief would be well protected.

"Ye look well, Lady Catriona," Samuel said.

"Thank you. It is good to feel clean again."

He grinned. "Aye, I understand the feeling well."

"What did your chief just say?"

"The right thing, I believe," Samuel responded, looking out over the relaxed crowd. "How glad he was to have returned, and how he looked forward to proving himself as their chief."

"Proving himself?"

"Aye, he hasn't been inaugurated yet," Samuel said, wearing a small grin. "Not that I'm worried about such formalities."

She glanced at McCallum with interest, but he wasn't looking at her.

The platters were brought to the dais first, and McCallum and Riona were presented with the choicest lamb, chicken, and trout. She was surprised by her wooden trencher, but it was finely crafted and rimmed with silver. Using a drinking bowl that Samuel called a *cuach* with handles covered in silver, McCallum drank a large mouthful, gave an appreciative nod, and passed it along to Dermot.

"'Tis our famous whisky," Samuel told her, "the makings of which your family coveted for generations."

"Which led to the infamous betrothal," she said, keeping her expression neutral. "Are these people angry that your precious land has been shared with the Duffs these last twenty years?"

"Impatient, perhaps, for the day their generosity would pay off with the generosity of the earl and the tocher offered on your behalf."

There was nothing she wanted to say to that. That contract was the reason she'd been stolen away and most likely ruined in the eyes of Society. Hugh had probably ensured that his people would never have the tocher they expected.

She glowered at her food, but forced herself to eat. Someone began to speak as if to entertain, and she recognized the lilting tone of a poet or bard, which Samuel confirmed for her.

"He speaks of the ancient deeds of our people," McCallum added from her left.

She turned to face her captor. "Perhaps much of it in battle against my people?"

His faint smile contained real amusement and his silver gray eyes glittered. "Some, yes, but there's always a Campbell to be angry with in every generation."

He and Samuel looked at each other with understanding, and she barely resisted rolling her eyes. Men and their feuds and their battles. If women ruled the world, things would be different. Of course, Queen Anne had ruled Great Britain until just over ten years ago, and nothing much had changed. In fact, most in Scotland would deem her rule, during which Scotland had become united with England, as a detriment to them all.

To change the subject, she asked Samuel, "Do all of these people live within the castle?"

"Some of these men are chieftains with their own lands who owe fealty to the McCallum. They traveled to Larig upon hearing that Hugh was approaching."

She hadn't even known McCallum had sent word ahead, but of course, he'd often been apart from her in Stirling.

"Many of the young men live here," Samuel continued. "They're the chief's gentlemen, chosen from the finest youth from our best families. They're well trained in battle, but they're also tacksmen, who act as the administrators for all the land and people."

Riona eyed McCallum, who was listening to Samuel talk. She asked, "So Dermot chose all these men?"

"As did my father, of course," McCallum answered. "I am confident they chose well. I look forward to becoming reacquainted with them all again."

It sounded to her like divided loyalties were a problem waiting to happen, but that could only help her cause. If McCallum was distracted, he wouldn't notice her focus on Dermot. Hugh took another deep sip of the whisky being passed in the *cuach*. He'd mentioned his father's reliance on strong drink, and wondered if that made him careful about it for himself.

When the meal was over, McCallum came out from behind the dais and talked to many people. She simply watched him, glad he didn't ask her to join him since she wouldn't have a clue what they were discussing. No one came to talk to her except Samuel, and when he was drawn away, she stood alone beside her chair, feeling lost and alienated.

And then she saw Dermot momentarily alone as he turned to take another swig of the whisky being passed. Inhaling a fortifying breath, she approached him, wearing a forced smile.

If Dermot was surprised, he didn't show it.

"Lady Catriona, glad I am to finally meet ye," he said, bowing over her hand.

"Glad or relieved, sir?" she asked.

He smiled, and it was an easier thing on him than it was upon his cousin, although there was a resemblance in the strong bones of the forehead. "A chief is only happiest when he has a good wife at his side, my lady. With you, Hugh has found luck and favor."

Riona tilted her head. "High praise, sir, but you have yet to truly know me."

"We can all learn about each other."

"Then tell me of yourself. As the McCallum's cousin, were you raised within the castle?"

"Nay, I am the son of a chieftain from lands to the east of Loch Voil."

"How does one become the tanist?"

"I was selected at the great gathering that followed the old McCallum's death, just as Hugh was. Hugh could have attended, of course, but he felt it important to bring home his bride."

The disapproval was obvious in his voice, and she was surprised he didn't hide it from her. It gave her hope that focusing on getting to know him was the right course.

"Laird McCallum was selected as the tanist for his father?" she asked.

"When he reached adulthood, aye, the summer after Sheriffmuir. He was well admired for his bravery during the Rising."

There was an edge to his voice that intrigued her. "Were you there, too?"

"I brought him home after fighting at his side," Dermot said, his gaze now on McCallum as he talked with several young men. "I can attest to the bravery of all the men of our clan."

"Yourself included," she murmured.

His gaze sharpened on her, even as he gave a small smile. "Surely I cannot be expected to speak of *that*, my lady."

She chuckled, and it felt rusty, for she hadn't had a reason to laugh in a long time. But she was playing a part now, and it made it easier to hold back her fear.

"Do you have a wife to perform brave deeds for, Dermot?"

He shook his head, then spoke dryly. "Not yet. I've been busy these last months with the McCallum lands, including helping my father. There doesn't seem to be enough time to court a young woman."

If Riona decided to come to him for help, at least he wouldn't have a woman distracting him.

"Did you know Laird McCallum growing up?"

"Of course, Lady Riona. We often ran the hills together."

"I understand he was something of a scamp."

Dermot's dark eyebrows rose. "A scamp? Are not all little lads?"

"So he was like other boys?"

His expression clouded with the memories, and they didn't all seem to be good ones.

"As many lads are wont to do," he said, "Hugh played the occasional prank on the farmers, leading astray cattle so that it looked like we'd been raided. No true harm was done."

But she sensed the disapproval that even youthful Dermot had felt. She got the impression that he and McCallum had never gotten along well, and that could prove to her advantage. He might be eager to help her convince McCallum that he'd made a mistake kidnapping her.

"Often he'd disappear into the hills for a day or two, upsetting his mother, but not his—" Dermot broke off.

"But not his father?" she finished for him.

McCallum was suddenly beside them, a frown darkening his brow. "My father little cared what I did, Lady Catriona. Did Dermot mention that?" He eyed his cousin coldly.

"I was simply asking what you were like as a boy," Riona said, knowing she'd made a mistake being so curious where he could overhear.

Dermot crossed his arms over his chest and said nothing. The brooch pinning his plaid matched McCallum's, and she couldn't help wondering if clan loyalty was all they'd ever had in common. For although they seemed like two serious men now, she sensed their youths had been vastly different.

"If we're exposing past sins," McCallum continued, his voice practical but cool, "did ye tell Lady Catriona about our encounter with the redcoats?"

Dermot's eyes were now like ice as he stared at his cousin. "I did not."

McCallum's expression was pleasant, as if he

were about to relate an amusing story, but there was nothing amusing about the tension that crackled between the two men.

"We were bold that day, the three of us, weren't we, Dermot?"

When Dermot said nothing, Riona asked, "Who was the third?"

"My foster brother, Alasdair," McCallum said. "For a year or so we were raised in each other's houses, a tradition among our people. But when we were all twelve or thirteen, we spied a party of redcoats across the hills, and for a lark, we followed them." He glanced at his cousin. "Dermot was against it, of course, because being elder by a year, he'd decided it was his duty to look out for us."

"Someone had to," Dermot said impassively.

And now Dermot had been looking after the clan for McCallum, Riona thought, echoing a time in their lives when the boys had obviously been at odds.

"What happened next?" she asked, more intrigued than she wanted to admit.

"We followed them for a day," McCallum continued, "and when they made camp, we lured away their guard, slipped in, and stole their muskets."

Riona gasped. "You weren't caught?"

She glanced at Dermot, who spoke without emotion. "Nay, they were not. I remained as lookout, and did not go into the camp myself."

"Which helped him in the end. Being the son of the chief helped me," McCallum added, bitterness beginning to thread through his voice.

"I don't understand," she admitted.

"When my father found out what we'd done—"

Dermot interrupted, "Ye couldn't help bragging to the other boys."

"Aye, I didn't always think things through in those days. Word got back to my father. Many ghillies—"

"Ghillies?" she interrupted.

"Regular clansmen," McCallum clarified for her. "Well, they boasted to each other how mere boys had outwitted British soldiers, and of course, someone finally congratulated Himself on our daring. My father claimed—rightly so—that we could have led the redcoats right back to Larig Castle and caused major problems between the clan and Fort William to the north. He ordered a whipping to teach us a lesson."

She winced. "A harsh punishment."

"Not for Dermot or me. Dermot hadn't stolen the rifles and was excused. And I was the McCallum's heir."

She blinked in confusion. "Then who suffered—your friend Alasdair?"

"He had to take the whipping for all of us," McCallum said.

Though he kept his voice neutral, as if it was long

in the past, she recognized that it must have been terrible to have his foster brother punished in his place.

McCallum shook his head. "Though but thirteen, he was incredibly brave. Any blame he could have attached to me for my father's cruelty, he put aside."

"Which meant they continued to court trouble," Dermot said dryly.

Something passed between them, an escalation of tension, as if both were remembering other deeds from the past.

"More stories you'd like to share?" Riona asked.

"Nay, I think I've lowered your opinion of me enough for tonight, Lady Catriona," McCallum said.

"So ye haven't told her about Agnes?" Dermot asked silkily.

McCallum's eyes narrowed, and the gray roiled like storm clouds. " 'Tis unworthy of ye, cousin. The poor lass is long dead."

He took Riona's arm, his grip harder than he perhaps realized.

"Come, Lady Catriona, allow me to introduce ye to some of the wives of my chieftains."

Riona couldn't help glancing at Dermot as they left, but his expression revealed nothing.

CHAPTER 8

Riona was allowed to retreat to her room within the hour, claiming exhaustion. McCallum had shadows of his own beneath his eyes, but she knew he would stay with his clan as long as he felt necessary.

The little maid, Mary, was asleep in a chair by the fire, but she jumped to her feet when Riona entered, as if she thought herself derelict in her duties.

Riona smiled at her. "I did not mean to disturb you. I should have been more careful shutting the door."

"Nay, my lady, I should never have fallen asleep."

"Of course you could. It was a long evening. Think nothing of it."

Color flooded back into her thin face, and although she didn't smile, the worst of the tension seemed to leave her shoulders. "Thank ye, my lady. I've put your nightshift near the hearth to warm.

Though 'tis summer, this old castle feels like winter year round."

It was the most she'd yet spoken, and the tips of her ears went pink as if she thought she was babbling. Riona allowed the girl to help her out of her garments, and heaved a weary sigh when the stays were loosened and she could take a deep breath again. Mrs. Wallace had seemed to believe that if the garment was painful, it was doing its job.

The nightshift truly was warm. After Riona had wrapped herself in a dressing gown over it, she sent Mary to find her own bed, so that Riona could wait in peace. She knew that McCallum was coming. He'd put her in his own rooms for a reason, and now that she'd heard of this trial marriage arrangement, she wouldn't put it past him. Her nerves began a little dance of worry that made her pace.

She tried to think of anything but what might happen tonight. She thought of serious McCallum as a carefree boy who ignored the rules—well, the "rules" part was still true. He'd had no problem kidnapping her and dragging her home. But the conversation between Dermot and him had truly been enlightening. Who could Agnes be, that Dermot would sound almost triumphant bringing her up, and McCallum would look as if it were a sin to mention a woman long dead?

Though Riona regretted using such a memory to

drive a wedge between the two men, she'd do what she had to do to escape marriage to a stranger.

But there'd be no escape from McCallum tonight if he chose to confront her. Would she scream until help came? Hardly—what good would that do? She was at his mercy, because they all thought she was his betrothed, and of course, hadn't she seemed all too willing today?

So . . . would she try to talk McCallum out of seducing her? The way he'd studied her when he'd first seen her in the gown made her wonder if he wouldn't care about her protests. But she held tight to the memory of his promise not to force her to bed.

She didn't know what she was going to do if he changed his mind, so she simply paced back and forth for what seemed like hours. He never came. At last, she made herself crawl into the box-bed and pull the curtains tight—as if they were any defense against the chief. She kept her dressing gown over her nightshift, holding it closed at her throat, listening to the wind outside the castle walls. But she heard no footsteps. At last, she sank into a troubled sleep.

WHEN a servant brought a breakfast tray at dawn, Hugh thanked him, then took it to Riona's room, closing the door quietly behind him. He left the tray on a table and approached the box-bed. The curtains were drawn, but moved soundlessly when he slid them aside.

Riona, still wearing the dressing gown over her nightshift, lay on her side, her hands tucked beneath her chin. Her lashes feathered across her cheeks, and the golden strands of her braided hair almost glittered as the light from the window touched her.

He wanted to waken her with a kiss, but knew she might panic and give him a good bite. That would hardly start their day well. Instead, he leaned against the bed frame and remembered how she'd looked last night, her blond hair gleaming against the ruby red of her gown. He'd been proud to display her before the clan, and though she'd understood nothing of the language, she hadn't worn a bored expression. Bewildered, maybe, and he knew there would be some who'd look down upon her for her ignorance of Gaelic.

And then Dermot had decided to relive the past. Hugh grimaced. It wasn't as if Riona would never learn of his foolishness, and he certainly could have told her himself during their journey. But keeping a woman imprisoned, then talking idly about childhood memories, had just seemed wrong.

There was more he could tell her, but it could wait. Besides, only Dermot would be fool enough to bring up Agnes to his chief.

So . . . should he awaken Riona? He was debating

the thought when she stretched like a cat and rolled slowly onto her back, arms above her head, torso arched. He got another brief view of her unbound breasts beneath the garment as the bedclothes slid down, but then she opened her eyes and gasped at the sight of him.

He gestured toward the table. "Good morning. Breakfast is served."

She caught the counterpane to her chin again, and he found himself repressing a smile at her version of battle armor. He knew she wouldn't appreciate the humor. So he went and sat down, glad for the hot oatmeal porridge, warm bannocks, boiled eggs, and fried herring after days traveling.

"Will ye join me, lass?" he asked.

She pushed back the bedclothes and slid her dainty feet into mules before approaching almost cautiously to sit down opposite him.

He began to eat hungrily, while she just watched him. Finally, he asked, "What ails ye, Riona?"

"I thought . . . I was worried . . ." She took a deep breath and met his eyes solemnly. "I thought you would come to me last night and demand . . . a handfasting."

Surprised, he set down his knife. "I promised that I have yet to force myself on an unwilling woman, and I make no exception for my betrothed."

She let out a long breath and sagged back in the chair.

"I'll try not to take offense," he said dryly.

"I care not if you take offense," she retorted. "I am your prisoner and I never know what you might have planned for me."

"So ye remember what handfasting is, do ye?"

She said nothing, just picked at the cuff of her dressing gown.

"My people will believe what they want, of course," he continued.

"Well, I don't want them believing that!"

He broke off a piece of bannock and put it on her plate. "Eat something. Ye look as blanched as a clean sheep."

She coated the bread in butter and took a bite, then shuddered at the proffered ale. "I usually have chocolate to drink at breakfast."

"No chocolate here. But we can find ye some tea. And of course, there's buttermilk." He took a deep draught of his and smacked his lips.

They ate in silence for a few minutes until she raised her gaze to study him.

"So what *do* you have planned for me?" she asked. "What am I supposed to do with myself all day?"

"First, I'll be having your word that ye won't try to escape."

She stiffened. "I cannot give you that. I'm a prisoner! *You* would try to escape being held against your will."

"I've already told ye," he said with a long-suffering sigh, "that I long ago accepted my duty to my clan. Ye'll come to accept your duty, too. Until then, if ye cannot promise me to stay put, then ye're confined to the castle with a bodyguard."

"A bodyguard?" she repeated blankly.

"I'll not make it so obvious, for I don't want to embarrass ye."

"You mean you don't want to embarrass yourself by showing the clan that your bride is unwilling."

"Again, ye forget that everyone kens ye're a Duff. They might assume ye to be not so willing. Ye'll have free run of the castle grounds, but beyond that, ye cannot be going. Not without me."

As usual, her very expressive face revealed her emotions: dismay, frustration, stubbornness. When at last she seemed calm, he thought that now it would be time to worry.

She swallowed a bit of egg and eyed him with curiosity. "My conversation with Dermot was interesting."

He eyed her right back, boldly. "Dermot's memories aren't always to be trusted."

"So you're saying his mental acuity can't be trusted? Amazing that your clan elected him your tanist."

"Oh, he's a canny man, as ye can well see."

"But you don't trust him."

She was too eager for all his secrets. "He's my

cousin. A bond like that goes deeper than trust. He'll do what's right for the clan."

"Ah, but will that be what *you* think is right for the clan?"

He leaned toward her. "What I think is right is all that matters, lass."

She scowled at him and he resisted a chuckle. It wouldn't do for her to know how amusing he found her. She might think she was more special to him than just part of an arranged marriage.

"Who was Agnes?" she asked.

To his surprise, he had to swallow heavily at the onslaught of memories, but he met her gaze. "A village maid who died long ago."

"So I understood from you last night. But who was she?"

"She's in the past, and cannot be hurt anymore, can she."

Riona blinked at him, then opened her mouth as if to say more, but he interrupted first.

"I'll be out and about all day, and will plan to see ye at supper tonight."

"Perhaps I don't wish that," she said stubbornly.

"How else will ye get to know your bridegroom? We'll not have a good marriage otherwise. And I'm determined that we'll have a good marriage."

He left her stuttering and fuming. He needed a solid marriage and heirs, so he would have to come up with a better plan to woo her.

RIONA was still fuming after she dressed and sent Mary to find Mrs. Wallace. But there was nothing she could do about McCallum or his infuriating arrogance. All she could do was focus on her own plan to avoid this marriage. She might not be able to leave the castle, but it was important for her to know every inch of it, just in case.

Mrs. Wallace was thrilled and proud to show her Larig Castle. Everywhere they went, people broke off their Gaelic conversations and either bowed or curtsied to her. She wasn't used to being so noticed, so catered to. She could see the curiosity, and even the occasional skepticism—because she was a Duff, no doubt.

But as for the castle itself, away from the main public rooms, there was more of an air of neglect, sparse furnishings, shutters instead of glass casement windows that could swing open for fresh air. The landscapes that graced the chief's rooms were absent on plain stone walls. Even the wainscoting in other rooms held only the occasional dour portrait.

"Not much of a living to be made as a painter in Scotland," Mrs. Wallace said lightly.

When they came to a withdrawing room meant for the chief's family, Riona was surprised to find a spinet beneath the windows.

Mrs. Wallace chuckled at her look of surprise. "The chief's mother had it brought here. She needed something to do when Himself . . . well, I'll not be spreadin' stories."

"The McCallum has told me his father wasn't a good-tempered man."

"Nay, he was not, and poor wee Hugh and Maggie suffered for it."

"When did their mother die?"

Mrs. Wallace's eyes widened. "She's not dead, lass, but living in Edinburgh near her family. Did Himself not tell ye this?"

Riona flushed. "We've only . . . just met. We haven't had time to discuss much of anything, really."

"Ah, no wonder he plans to have supper at yer side every night. Ye have a lifetime of learnin' ahead of ye."

Not a lifetime—not if she could help it. "Do you have a library?" Riona asked to change the subject.

Mrs. Wallace's look was uncomprehending. "Any books are in the McCallum's solar. Who else would need to read them?"

"Other members of the household?" Riona ventured. "Ladies?"

"Sadly, ye'll not find many women here with much use for reading, except on the Sabbath."

"Oh." She was used to reading as much as she wished, and discussing the latest books with her partners at dinners. Did the McCallums care nothing for education?

They left the main towerhouse and explored the other buildings constructed into the curtain wall, many for the servants, like the brew house, the dairy, or the woman house, where village women spun and wove cloth. The kitchens were on the ground floor beneath the great hall, and next to them was a half-walled vegetable garden, and more gardens beyond the curtain walls themselves, Mrs. Wallace told her. Always they were watched by men patrolling the battlements along the curtain wall, as if they thought the British intended to attack at any moment.

Or the Duffs, she reminded herself. Or the Campbells, or any of the clans, for they were a warfaring people, or so her father always told her with disdain. And there had just been a series of battles with the English a little over ten years before. Of course all of the McCallums would be prepared.

They stood in the arched entrance to the lower courtyard, out of the way of the men who came and went. Except for the stone barracks, wooden buildings surrounded this courtyard, where the clansmen trained for war. There were large muck piles from dealing with animals, many of whom roamed freely in both courtyards, chickens, dogs, and even pigs. There were stables and shops for craftsmen, like the smithy and the carpenter.

She studied the clansmen as they battled each

other with swords, holding shields called targes to deflect blows from their opponent.

To her surprise, she saw McCallum in their midst, fighting against an opponent. And if this was simply training, their battle looked far too real, provoking an occasional wince out of her. A rare summer sun beat down on the training yard, and most of the men had shed their coats, and some even their shirts—like the McCallum. His plaid was still buckled around his waist, but the loose ends hung over the belt without being attached to his garments by brooch. Many of the men had gathered around to watch, and she couldn't blame them. He'd been elected their chief because he was the heir and a hero at Sheriffmuir, but they hadn't seen him for ten years.

His body gleamed with sweat, and she was able to see a scar or two slicing across firm muscle. His abdomen had actual ridges. Staring at him made her feel hot and uncomfortable, so very aware of him as a man, and not just as her captor. The memory of his kiss suddenly seared her, and she felt the heat of a blush. She didn't want to be drawn to him, had been fighting this betrayal of her body all along, but her resistance didn't seem to matter.

"Ye'll be noticin' the scars," Mrs. Wallace said, not bothering to hide her amusement.

"Oh . . . of course. Sheriffmuir?"

"Och, and as a lad. Broke a bone at least every

other year, it seemed. I'm still amazed he turned out whole." She sighed with contentment. "He is a fine lad, and the worryin' of some was for naught."

"He hasn't been here these last ten years, I know. What was he doing?"

"Another thing ye can ask him when ye don't ken what to say at supper."

How was she to discover anything if people didn't want to talk? "Who is that he's training with?"

"Ah, that's Alasdair Lennox."

"I've heard that name," she said, relieved to concentrate on something other than McCallum's superior physical condition. "He and the McCallum were friends as boys."

Mrs. Wallace nodded, eyes narrowed as she studied the two who'd grown into men. "Aye, foster brothers who took turns bein' raised in each other's households. Friends sometimes, opponents others, and I can see that might not have changed."

"It's been a long time since Alasdair took the whipping that McCallum deserved."

The housekeeper's gaze flashed to her in surprise. "Ye be knowin' about that already?"

"Dermot and Himself told me."

"I wouldn't have wanted to be a part of *that* conversation."

"It was certainly uncomfortable," Riona admitted. Mrs. Wallace eyed her, then looked past her at

McCallum and shook her head. "I'll be leavin' ye then to learn yer way about. Dinner will be at one by the mantel clock in the great hall. Until then!"

And the cheerful woman bustled away, leaving Riona alone. Truly alone, for as she stood in the archway, more than once she saw people who hadn't been in the great hall, and didn't know who she was, give her strange looks. She received the occasional nod or curtsy, but everyone seemed too intimidated to talk to her. She was used to feeling inconspicuous, and had often wished someone, anyone would notice her as she cared for the ill Bronwyn.

Now she had all the notice—the notoriety—as the McCallum's Duff bride brought to end the feud.

She stood for a while longer, watching the training, especially watching McCallum. She'd felt his strength when he'd tossed her over his shoulder and carried her off her balcony; she'd felt the smooth, warm firmness of his muscles when she'd pressed against him in her sleep. But seeing him half naked in front of so many people—it seemed sinful.

She leaned against the ancient stone, pretending she was out of the way, and tried to understand him. He spoke to his men with conviction, as if he'd been born to rule. He was forceful and aggressive in his mannerisms, then demonstrating a technique with patience, even when one of the men was slow to learn.

What did his people see when they looked at him? Where had he been for ten years, hiding away from his father?

Then the man who'd first been his opponent clapped McCallum on the shoulder and suddenly pointed at her. She stiffened when McCallum looked up at her, and though they were separated by half a courtyard, she felt the pull of him, the awareness of what he wanted of her, of how he wanted her to submit. It was as if he kissed her even now, and everyone could see.

The men shared a laugh, and though McCallum raised a hand to her, he did not leave his training. She turned away and had to force herself not to run back to the safety of her bedroom—but really, it was his, wasn't it? Everything she had, everything she did, was only because of him. She was as under his control as she'd been under parents' control, like trading one prison for another. But then, she hadn't exactly known it was a prison—she'd simply been a daughter without the means to set up her own household unless at her father's whim.

Now? Now McCallum wanted to make her his wife, to give her her own household—her own castle! But it was all against her will, against the very contract he thought he was upholding. It was a terrible mess. When these people who now looked at her with confusion or skepticism discovered the truth, and perhaps lost the precious land they counted on for the whisky they sold—their expression would turn to betrayal and disgust.

She shuddered and hurried back toward the laird's towerhouse.

CHAPTER 9

Hugh watched a moment too long after Riona ran away from the lower courtyard.

"Your bride doesn't seem in a hurry to be with ye," Alasdair taunted lightly.

Hugh eyed his foster brother. They hadn't seen each other for years after fighting side by side at Sheriffmuir and the disastrous summer after Hugh's recovery. Several years back, Alasdair had journeyed to Edinburgh for a family matter and contacted Hugh. They'd met at a coffee house, and it had been like they were lads again, away from the Highlands and the influence of their fathers.

But now that Hugh was back at Larig Castle, and been nominated as the chief? There was a change in Alasdair, too, almost a need to prove himself Hugh's equal—when that had never been in doubt.

Hugh told himself to be patient, that it was only

his first day testing the preparedness of his gentlemen.

But the two men once closest to him, Dermot and Alasdair, had not granted him the reunion he'd hoped for. And the rest of the men?

He eyed them as they traded partners and prepared to test each other's swords. In this time of uneasy peace, they were close enough to battle-ready for him not to complain. Since his father's death, and the illness of the old man who'd been his war chief, Clan McCallum had gone without one. That was one of the first things Hugh intended to fix. Was Alasdair ready for such a position? He'd fought at Sheriffmuir with the clan, had roamed these hills outwitting Duffs and Campbells and Maclarens for more years than Hugh had. Could he do justice to the position? Hugh would have to discuss it with Dermot, he thought, grimacing at the prospect.

THOUGH Riona had meant to rush right to her bedroom and hide, she ended up pausing at the woman room to watch the skill of the local women with spinning wheel and loom. Some spoke English, and they seemed awed and excited to meet a woman who'd spent her life among the Sassenach. Riona answered questions, and ended up with needlework supplies to keep herself occupied, and a promise to return again. It all felt wrong. She didn't belong here; she wasn't the bride McCallum was supposed to have, and these women would look at her with anger when they discovered the truth.

When she left them, she kept her head down and focused on following the corridor, wanting only to return to her room, when she almost ran right into Hugh's foster brother, Alasdair. He didn't see her as he remained poised in a doorway, as if looking at someone in the room beyond. Not wanting to disturb him—perhaps unwilling to face him—she retreated to where the corridor took a turn, trying to remember a different way back to her room.

"Dermot, ye don't plan to train with Himself?" Alasdair asked, his voice heavy with sarcasm.

Riona's head came up in surprise. Though she knew she should not eavesdrop, being kidnapped had made her willing to ignore propriety. Alasdair stepped within the room, and she was worried she'd no longer be able to hear any part of their conversation. After creeping back down the hall, she impulsively spilled the basket of skeins of thread and dropped to her knees to gather them. Alasdair chuckled, and she realized she'd missed Dermot's response.

Alasdair said, "Surely ye cannot avoid the training yard forever."

"I do not plan to," Dermot said, his voice heavy with exasperation. "I just did not anticipate how difficult it would be when he returned."

Riona held her breath.

"But he's been elected by the clan," Alasdair said, with some compassion in his voice. "Ye knew this day would come—we've known it our whole lives."

"Aye, but I thought I'd be more certain of my place at his side, and instead, I found myself questioning all he's done leading up to this moment, especially the time he's spent away."

"Dermot—"

"I know he represented us in Edinburgh and beyond," Dermot said furiously. "I know what kind of man his father was—but *we* were here dealing with the old chief, and Hugh was not. Just because he's been elected our laird doesn't prove to me that he deserves such an exalted position, that he'll know what to do with it."

"Dermot," Alasdair began quietly, "ye cannot let people hear ye talking against him."

"I'm not against him—I just need proof he's worthy to be our chief, that he's become a man we can trust, no longer the hotheaded lad who—" He broke off.

"'Tis not your place to control him," Alasdair said. "Ye couldn't then, and ye cannot try now."

Riona thought she heard footsteps heading back toward the corridor, and she quickly picked up the last skein of thread and fled.

Only when she had her back against the closed door of her bedroom did she feel like she could

breathe again and think about what she'd overheard and what it might mean for her. She wasn't
concerned with Hugh—he'd caused all his own
recent problems and he would have to accept the
consequences. Right now, it was all about her, and
somehow finding a way to freedom. She'd never
have her old life back—being kidnapped was more
than enough ruination for a lady—but she didn't
want that life anyway. There had to be something
more for her, and she wasn't going to find it at Larig
Castle in a forced marriage.

Was Dermot the key to unlocking this prison?
How could she use his dissatisfaction?

As the sun was setting that evening, Riona was
standing in her bedroom, looking out over the
courtyard, when the door opened behind her. She
turned to find Mrs. Wallace and Mary carrying
supper trays.

"'Tis so romantic that Himself wants to dine
alone with his bride," Mrs. Wallace was saying to
Mary, who blushed upon noticing Riona.

Riona gritted her teeth and forced a smile.

McCallum entered then, his hair drawn into an
untidy queue, his garments stained from a day in
the training yard. "Forgive me for not bathing before joining you. I lost track of the hour. We can eat
while my bath is prepared."

She should be repulsed by his earthiness, but it

seemed manly and invigorating to be reminded of the way he'd used his body under the sun, his muscles rippling with every thrust of the sword, every jump to miss a swinging blade.

She had to stop thinking about this or she wouldn't be able to meet Mrs. Wallace's kind eyes.

When they were at last alone, he dug into his food as if he hadn't eaten at dinner, when she knew he had, along with the men he'd been training.

"What did ye think of Larig Castle?" he finally asked, as he took a drink of whisky.

She eyed the strong drink. "In England, wine would be served with dinner, and the men retire for more potent libation away from the ladies."

"Ye might have noticed," he answered wryly, "but we aren't in England."

She nodded with a sigh and returned to his question. "The castle is impressive, of course, although I'm given to understand that the only books are within your private solar—locked away from the rest of the household."

"I'll see that ye're given access, of course, although I don't know if my father had the kind of books ye'd be interested in."

"How do you know what I'm interested in, when you know nothing about me?" she asked sweetly.

"Very true," he said, wearing a reluctant smile. "We could change that."

She ignored that and wondered why did he have

to catch her eye like this? He wasn't even that handsome. But she was learning that a man didn't need a classic profile to be masculine and appealing.

She hesitated, not wanting to give him the satisfaction of wifely conversation, but she needed to know everything she could. "The men you trained with today—they didn't seem to have a problem with you having been gone all this time."

He shrugged. "If they did, 'twas no matter to me. I don't need to be liked, only respected."

"Now that sounds like wishful thinking."

He paused while slicing a piece of mutton. "That I be respected?"

"No, that you don't care if you're liked. You've brought a bride home—the wrong one, I'll remind you—and you're supposedly fulfilling this contract that will help your clan. You want them to like you for it."

He sat back in his chair and wiped his lips with a napkin. "These things I do out of responsibility and duty, Riona. We all have such things in our lives. Did ye not have obligations at home?"

"Obligations you took me from?" she shot back.

"Obligations that every young woman leaves behind when she marries."

She sighed, knowing he spoke the truth. "I nursed my sister through illness much of the last ten years."

His dark eyebrows rose. "Ten years? You were but a child then."

"I believe you were stealing muskets from red-coats at that same age."

A smile quirked the corner of his mouth. "True. What illness does your sister suffer?"

"Consumption."

He frowned. "I'm sorry."

She felt a pang of old sorrow at the thought of her sister dying someday. "Bronwyn is younger than I, and when she was a child, I was the only one who could keep her resting abed with stories."

"Ah, the Scottish blood is yet strong in ye," he pointed out. "Ye ken how important our stories are. The bard sings of them enough to remind us all—especially me, who's supposed to live up to the bravery of McCallum ancestors."

"So the performance last night wasn't just for entertainment?" she asked, surprised.

"Aye, there was that. But also specifically for me to hear and remember."

"They expect a lot of you."

"Just as your parents expected much of ye, when ye should have been allowed to be a child. At least I was allowed that."

"What about after you'd recovered from your wounds at Sheriffmuir? Didn't they all expect much of you then? How were you permitted to leave?"

His face, once open and pleasant, seemed to shutter with impassivity. "I played my part in the welfare of our clan, and served them well from Edinburgh."

She remembered Dermot saying that as well. "And London? I heard that mentioned. How was that a part of serving your clan?"

"I was elected a Member of Parliament for our county."

Her mouth dropped open. "You sat in the Commons?"

"Where else could I sit, since the Crown went back on its promise to allow Scottish nobility an immediate seat in the Lords? Not that I'm a nobleman like your father."

She blinked at him. "It takes me a minute to remember you don't mean my true father when you say such things." He just looked at her, and she waved a hand, dismissing that topic. "I am still trying to picture you as an MP."

" 'Tis not an easy thing for a Scotsman to be. Ye saw what the journey is like, and most MPs do not have coaches. We come down by horse the whole length of Great Britain, a journey of weeks, only to be treated as if we're country simpletons with no understanding of our land. Contempt is too mild a word for how we are viewed."

"And you've done this for ten years, from January to August," she said slowly, seeing him in a new light, rather than simply an uneducated villain.

"Seven years."

So that left three more unaccounted years, but

she'd think about that later. "How could I never have met you?"

"And did ye meet many untitled Scots at your fine London dinner parties and musicales?" he asked sarcastically.

"Oh. No, I did not. Unless you count men like my father, the sons of noblemen."

"Not often invited, were we, the sons of chiefs? Some of us could not have afforded the necessary garments, of course. Living in London was an expense many had not anticipated, and few could tolerate for long."

"You did."

He nodded slowly, taking another bite of goose and chewing before continuing. "Aye, I wasn't going to turn tail and head for the Highlands at the first sign of trouble. I even served on a parliamentary committee long enough to be named the chairman."

"What committee?" she asked curiously.

"Gaols. Few wanted to discuss or implement prison reform. Perhaps my early lawbreaking against redcoats, that could have landed me in gaol, subconsciously guided me."

She still couldn't believe he'd been in London all those years and their paths had never crossed. "Did you wear your plaid?"

"Nay, that would have kept Scottish MPs permanently on the outside. Londoners could almost pretend we were English northerners when listening to us speak. But to wear colorful tartan? Nay, I chose to blend in with my breeches and coat."

Just as she'd first seen him. "Ye did not try to meet Cat?"

His face hardened. "I met your father once and he gave me strict orders to stay away from ye, said ye were having a difficult time accepting your duty to your family. And I believed him. When all the while, ye were simply kept ignorant of the whole situation."

She froze when he reached across the table and touched her hand.

"If I'd have seen ye on the street," he said huskily, "I would have followed ye anywhere."

His gray eyes were not so wintry when he looked upon her, and they strangely drew her in with a feeling of intimacy and focus she wasn't used to experiencing with men. She pulled away, uncomfortable.

He didn't protest, just went back to eating, and she did the same. For several long minutes, the silence seemed to stretch into a tension she'd only ever felt with him. He was watching her too closely, seeing things about her, intimate things, she hadn't known she could feel. She didn't want to feel anything but loathing for him after how he'd forced her from her family against her will.

But . . . none of that seemed to matter where her body was concerned. She could hear him breathing, knew that it quickened, which somehow made her own lungs labor. The weight of his stare was like a caress, and gooseflesh spread across her skin. She shivered.

"Are ye cold?" he asked quietly.

She shook her head, unable to meet his eyes. It was as if her lips remembered the feel of his upon them, and she could not forget the sight of his naked chest.

She forced herself to remember her plight. "I've thought of a way I could prove my identity to you."

He groaned and took a deep drink.

"Send a man to my uncle's castle. Discover that Cat is in England, that she is my cousin."

"What would that prove? I already knew ye were in England. And I won't be risking the life of my man by sniffing around Duff lands."

"But you said this marriage was a bridge between clans. Surely he'd be safe—"

"Nay, I'll not do it, Riona. Stop trying to change what cannot be changed."

She jumped to her feet. "I—I should like to retire," she said furiously.

"I shall bathe while ye prepare for bed."

He bowed and retreated to his own chamber before she could speak. She frowned at the closed door. What did he mean by *that*?

For just a moment, she contemplated surprising him at his bath, so he could see how it felt. And then she realized he would love nothing better. She would stay far away from his chambers.

Just when she was about to climb into her cozy box-bed, Mrs. Wallace knocked and entered, looking . . . uncomfortable.

Riona frowned. "Mrs. Wallace? Is something wrong?"

"Nay, my lady, at least . . . I don't think so. Himself asked me to wait here for him."

When the housekeeper kept her eyes downcast, Riona became truly concerned. They didn't have long to wait. McCallum entered from the dressing room, wearing a shirt and breeches, and carrying a length of rope.

Riona's lips parted with distress. "What is *that* for?" she demanded.

"Since ye've heard of handfasting, I thought I'd introduce ye to another Highland tradition. Bundling."

She blinked at him. "But—but—"

"Ye've not heard of it? 'Twas even common in parts of England. During courtship, the woman's legs are tied together, and the two lovers lie talking in bed getting to know each other."

"I've heard of bundling!" she finally cried. "But I never thought I'd be part of it. It is such a—a country custom."

"Ye want to know me better, and I want to know *you*. I thought ye'd be most comfortable with this." His voice deepened as he came closer. "Climb into bed, lass, and I'll tie ye up."

Short of running screaming into the hall, what could she do? Fuming, she sat down on the edge of the bed and watched McCallum kneel before her and remove her mules.

Mrs. Wallace took a deep breath, and as if to distract Riona, said, "Now, this is a proper courtship, my lady, the one ye couldn't have because of that silly contract. Himself has the best intentions."

Riona clenched her jaw and said nothing, because she wasn't sure McCallum's motives were all that pure, at least not tonight. After this, Mrs. Wallace surely couldn't see him as her little lad, come home to settle down and do his duty.

Oh, she was just trying to distract herself from feeling McCallum's hands on her bare ankles. His skin was rough with calluses, something she already knew and which . . . didn't bother her. He had a man's hands—and she saw that those hands now had abrasions and cuts from the afternoon's training. And, of course, he had no problem touching her with conviction because he always believed he was right.

At last he straightened and glanced at the housekeeper. "Thank ye for being a witness, Mrs. Wallace, should there be a question about this someday."

"O' course, Laird McCallum. A good night to ye both."

And without meeting Riona's beseeching eyes, she left, shutting the door behind her.

McCallum went around the room and, one by one, blew out the candles until just the faint glow of the peat fire left the corners of the room in shadows. Then he approached and leaned past her to draw down the bedclothes.

They were alone for the night. She stubbornly remained seated, arms crossed over her chest, trying to give every evidence of fury.

While her insides melted. They'd been alone countless times on their journey—why did this seem so different? Why did her limbs tremble, her mouth seem dry, her heart tumble about in her chest? He loomed over her, and with a gasp she fell back onto her elbows.

He braced a hand on the bed frame and frowned. "Are ye still afraid of me, lass?"

How could she say that she was afraid of herself? Afraid that she'd reveal this unnatural desire for him, the man who'd kidnapped her? There must be something wrong with her, to have such feelings. But she couldn't say any of that.

"Yes, I'm afraid," she whispered. "I know you've promised not to—to take me to bed before I give my consent, but I have heard whispers that a man in the throes of passion is not always . . . rational."

"Is that what virginal lasses discuss when we're not around?"

She said nothing, then gave another gasp when he picked her up against his chest, then laid her out closest to the wall. He stretched out beside her on his side, head braced on his hand. She felt trapped between his big body and the wall, the width of his chest practically all she could see. His shirt was unbuttoned at the throat, dark hair scattered there, and she could smell soap from his bath.

She closed her eyes and slowed down her breathing.

His chuckle was deep and raspy. "So ye think 'twill be so easy to forget I'm here?"

"I certainly did so at the inn, until you rudely pulled me to you." She didn't open her eyes.

His breath was soft on her face as he spoke. "I seem to remember us cuddling together quite mutually."

"You have a habit of believing what you want to believe. I'm trying to picture your real bride tolerating these strange advances. Cat would never stand for it." She tried to move her legs, but he'd expertly tied her without hurting her.

He put a hand on her knee. "Hush, there's no reason to struggle."

Even through the fabric of nightshift and dressing gown, she could feel the heat of him. With a low groan, she turned her head to the wall.

"So I have a sister, and you have a sister," he said.

For a long minute she said nothing, then spoke between gritted teeth. "Unhand me, and we can talk."

He did so. "That's better. Don't ye want to know about my sister?"

"Fine, go ahead and speak of her."

"Maggie is younger than me by four years. She draws attention to herself, and not just because she's pretty—her eyes are two different colors. One's blue, and the other's green."

That made her turn her head to give him a skeptical stare.

He raised his free hand. "I swear. There are other things about her that are unusual, but since ye'll meet her eventually, I'll let her choose what to tell ye."

"I know Scots are a superstitious people—"

"Ye make that sound like ye're not one of us," he teased.

She ignored that. "So did the clan treat her differently?"

His amused look faded. "Some do. She's not yet married, and I worry that she's holding back out of fear a man won't understand her . . . differences."

"So you're not forcing her to marry?" she asked dryly.

In a solemn voice, he said, "Do to her what was done to us? Ye forget, lass, that perhaps there was someone else *I* wished to marry."

She looked up at him in surprise, then took an educated guess. "Agnes?"

He studied her too long before looking away. "It doesn't matter, does it? Did ye have someone else?"

She wanted to lie to him, hoping to hurt him as he'd hurt her. But she felt too wounded, too raw, to be convincing. "No."

"Perhaps your family kept ye away from suitable men because of the contract?"

"And not tell me? I mean, tell Cat? That makes no sense. No, I was more important to them for Bronwyn's sake."

He touched the braid that had tumbled over her shoulder and gave it a wiggle. "How old is she?"

"Twenty. She is a true innocent, so naïve about the pitfalls of life."

"And ye're so very worldly?"

She sensed laughter beneath his calm surface, but he didn't release it, and she reluctantly appreciated that. "I didn't say that. But if you'd have done to her what you did to me, she'd have stayed in a perpetual swoon."

"Instead of fighting back and trying to escape? Maybe I'd prefer that."

But there was admiration for her in his tone, and it made Riona uncomfortable. She was always uncomfortable, forced to be on alert, to be wary. She didn't remember what it was like to feel content and happy.

Perhaps because she'd never truly known such a state.

"Ye look sad," he whispered.

He dropped his head and pressed a gentle kiss to her temple. And just like that, her sadness was drowned in a sea of conflicting emotions, passion and need and desperation.

His face was just above hers and he only breathed the words, "I want ye to be happy."

He pressed another kiss, this time to her forehead, to her cheek, to her chin. Her hands might as well have been tied, for how little she could move them. And if she did move them, it would only be to put her hands in his dark hair, pull the leather tie free and let his wavy hair fall about his face.

He stopped when his lips were just over hers, their panting breaths mingled. The moment extended on and on, exquisite torture that she made worse by lifting her head and kissing him. With a groan, he slanted his open mouth against hers, forcing her lips apart, and then his tongue began a delicious exploration she'd never imagined. She was pressed back into the pillows by his body half over hers. He cupped her face in his hands and kissed her deeply, wildly, drawing a moan from her that he answered with his own. He tasted faintly of whisky, as if he'd needed something to bolster himself before confronting her. She knew that probably wasn't true, but it gave her a wild thrill regardless, as did the hard pressure of him against her hip. Riona might be an innocent, but Cat had whispered details of lovemaking that she'd gleaned from friends.

Riona's hands crept up to his powerful shoulders and then into his hair. She arched into his chest, feeling the pressure against her aching breasts. She wanted him to touch them—

And she realized that could push him past restraint. He'd tied the ropes—he could untie them, and who would ever know?

She twisted her head to the side, her voice a rasp as she said, "We must stop."

He didn't answer, just buried his face against her neck, kissing and licking as he made his way down to the edge of her dressing gown. When his hand slid up her rib cage, she caught it with her own.

"Please, Hugh, stop."

Hearing his Christian name seemed to bring him back to awareness. He lifted his head slowly and looked at her with heavy-lidded eyes. His mouth was still moist with their kiss, and she had an irrational desire to lick him there. She was trembling at the restraint, yet she continued to hold his hand tightly until he pulled away.

He lifted his body off hers, rolled onto his back at her side, then flung his forearm over his eyes, his chest rising and falling like the bellows in a smithy. They said nothing for long minutes in the shadowy darkness. The bed wasn't big enough to keep them apart, and his arm still touched the length of hers. To escape, she'd have to crowd into the wall. With a sigh, she knew she wasn't going to do that.

She debated what to say, how to tell him that this should never happen again, how to make him believe that he wasn't always right.

And then he snored.

It was her turn to throw an arm over her eyes and groan. But she couldn't sleep, not with thoughts dancing in her head. She had to get away from here before things went any farther. She wondered if her uncle had even bothered to inform her parents that she was gone. What had he told *Cat* about Riona's absence? Besides her sister, her cousin was the only one who truly loved her, who didn't want anything from her. She must be frantic and terrified. Perhaps the earl had created an elaborate lie about how Riona had left of her own free will . . .

Oh, she had to stop this wild imagining. She had a plan in place, and now she knew that Dermot was the one to approach with her secrets. But how? He might not trust Hugh, but he certainly wouldn't trust a Duff. If she went to him now, he'd feel no compulsion to help her. She would try to become friendly with him, so that he'd relax around her and believe her when she finally spoke of her need for his help. If they approached Hugh together, perhaps Hugh would at last be convinced that she was telling him the truth.

Hugh rolled over and slung an arm around her waist, his face pressed into her hair. She couldn't escape, not with her legs tied, and she wasn't about to wake him up and risk another seduction . . .

A seduction to which she was growing more and more susceptible.

CHAPTER 10

Hugh could have lain within Riona's arms forever. One of her soft, warm arms was beneath his neck as she curled against him. It wasn't dawn yet, but his body was awakening—in more ways than one.

He was filled with satisfaction and confidence in the future. Riona wasn't immune to him; it would just take a little time to make her see that their marriage could be happy. They might not trust each other, but that didn't really matter. Trust was something that could get a person killed. Attraction was more important to him than some mystical feeling like love that could hurt her in the end.

She gave a little sigh, and he could feel the exhalation through her chest, which was pressed along his arm. This was a good way to wake up.

Until she went all stiff and affronted; she opened her green eyes wide and gazed into his.

"I can't get up," he said with amused apology in his voice. "Someone is holding on tight."

With a sigh, she rolled onto her back. "I cannot control what I do in my sleep. Please sit up and free my arm now."

"Ye mean ye can't hold back your desires when ye're asleep."

"Just untie me, please."

He chuckled and stood up, then squatted as she put her legs over the edge within his reach. He untied her a little slower than necessary, making sure his fingers had to repeatedly touch her soft skin.

When she gave several exaggerated sighs, he glanced up at her. "Ye just like having me at your feet."

"Only if I can kick you," she grumbled.

He slid the rope free. "See, not a permanent mark on ye."

She bent her knee and put her heel on the bed, the better to look at her shin. There were faint impression marks there.

"Shall I kiss them better?" he asked softly, leaning forward.

She swung her legs away with the speed of a swordsman and tucked them beneath her. "No, thank you. You can leave now, go about your day, whatever you'd like to do."

He stood up. "I hope the day passes swiftly, so that we're soon together again."

She looked aghast at the notion, and with a shaky finger pointed at the door. "Please leave! If you thought tying me up would help your cause, you've miscalculated. I'm more offended than ever by your uncivilized behavior."

Leaning against the bed frame, he eyed her rumpled garments with interest. "I think ye're lying to yourself. You enjoy kissing as much as I do. Ye'll enjoy what follows even more."

She came up on her knees and screeched, "Out!"

He laughed, and wearing a victorious smirk, he left.

RIONA ate breakfast in the great hall without Hugh, and at first she thought that was better than staring at him across an intimate table in his suite. But she was eating in the company of a household of mostly men, and though they obviously tried not to stare at her, they all took turns sending her surreptitious glances. She'd never felt so on display before, regarded with such curiosity and speculation. She was their enemy—many must think it. Some might also consider her their clan's very salvation. It was an awkward, scary place to be. She'd spent much of her childhood and young womanhood praying someone would notice her; she'd gotten her wish and the irony was keen.

She was grateful Samuel made time to see how she was doing, but other than that, conversations continued in Gaelic all around her, and she felt very alone, an outsider in every sense. But to bolster her spirits, she reminded herself that she would leave someday—she *had* to leave, she thought firmly, considering all that had happened between her and Hugh last night.

She explored the castle for much of the morning, opening random doors, speaking to servants, reluctantly introducing herself to Hugh's young gentlemen who helped him run the business of the clan estates. She didn't see Dermot. Everyone was polite but distant, sometimes even wary, and she felt very much like the enemy, a Duff in the midst of McCallums. But she'd be a Duff who knew Larig Castle if an opportunity to escape presented itself—not that she was counting on that.

As the day went on, memories of her night tied in bed with Hugh began to overtake her, and anticipation built stronger and stronger. Though she told herself she'd use the opportunity to learn more about him, learn his weaknesses, deep inside she imagined how he might touch her, and how it would feel, and what would come next.

Why was she having these kinds of thoughts about her cousin's betrothed? Much as Cat didn't even know about him, their families had this marriage long planned. Riona should respect it, even as she tried to escape it for herself. Instead she was discovering a wicked part of her she'd never imagined.

To distract herself, she went to the kitchens and watched the cook and servants prepare tarts they'd be serving with the main course for dinner. Mrs. Wallace was there as well, chatting cheerfully as if she hadn't seen Riona tied up by the McCallum. Riona couldn't stop blushing, but perhaps they'd think the cause was merely the heat in the kitchen. Then a ragged man entered, and Mrs. Wallace called him a gaberlunzie, a beggar granted a license to beg. Apparently he was a regular gossip with the servants, and brought news in exchange for a meal. Mrs. Wallace asked hesitantly if Riona wished to have a say in whether he was still welcome, but she demurred. She wasn't going to be the mistress of the castle and didn't want to give that impression.

But . . . it had been rare to be asked her opinion, and she'd been grateful that Mrs. Wallace had given her the chance. To turn down having her own say had been bittersweet.

After the midday meal, she wore a hooded cloak and boots outside into the cloudy, misty—muddy—day. She was used to occasionally walking alone in London's public parks or shopping on Regent Street, so it was strange that someone would be assigned to watch over her. She didn't know who it was, and there were so many people in the courtyard that his identity was well hidden. But she couldn't let that stop her from exploring, because she'd go crazy with nothing to do. She briefly considered just walking through the gatehouse and into the forbidden world, but what was the point? She could get nowhere on her own, didn't even know where the nearest village was. And it wasn't like there was a road with a sign pointing the way. The trails that crisscrossed the mountains as they'd approached could have been from cattle roaming and might lead nowhere. She wasn't about to risk death in so foolish a manner. But she did spend a while studying the guards' focus on people entering the castle, and realized they were far more indifferent when people left.

She wandered through the castle buildings, probably making the servants nervous as she watched them brew beer or soak the castle laundry. In the lower courtyard, she stared fascinated as the smithy worked glowing metal into a horseshoe.

But it was all an excuse to watch Hugh with his men. Sometimes he seemed like different people to her—the merciless kidnapper, the clan chief wanting respect and authority, the potential bridegroom who kissed her with barely restrained passion. But he wasn't her betrothed, and he was never going to be her husband.

But one thing she'd never expected was how taken he was by a shaggy little terrier hanging around the yard, mud caked on the lower half of his tan body as if he'd been running through a bog. On top of his head was a burst of fur like a hat. His tongue hung out with doggy happiness as if he'd found his perfect master, his gaze never leaving Hugh. Riona leaned against the wall and watched the entertainment until the training session broke up. The terrier followed Hugh as he headed toward the upper courtyard. Hugh stopped to talk to the smithy, gesturing back toward the dog, but only got a shrug out of the man.

Then Hugh headed back across the yard and the dog followed obediently, little legs trotting to keep up. Riona stepped into the shadow of the wall near the smithy, glad for the cloak that hid her. She wasn't ready for Hugh's gray eyes to focus on her, to roam her body, to make her feel . . . wicked.

A young groom, who couldn't be more than ten years old, was leading a horse from the smithy to the stables, but came to a stop when he saw Hugh, as if the McCallum awed him.

Hugh pointed to the dog and spoke in Gaelic. The boy led the horse into the stables and came back with a length of rope, which he slipped around the dog's neck. Dog and boy watched Hugh walk away, the dog full of yearning, the boy much more wary.

And then she really looked at the boy, and something strange moved through her. He had dark shaggy hair and a prominent forehead. His body looked healthy, even big next to some of the boys she'd seen, as if he'd be a tall man someday. She shivered. What color were his eyes?

With a glance to check that Hugh had reached the upper courtyard, she strode toward the stables, where the boy was talking to the dog in Gaelic. The terrier just continued to look at him with expectation.

"Hello," Riona said.

The boy glanced at her, and his gray eyes shocked her. He resembled Hugh.

She was speechless for a moment at the implication, and then told herself that the McCallums were mostly related, where similarity in looks would be common. Hugh wasn't going to be her husband, so this wasn't her problem.

The boy bowed his head. "Mistress."

To her relief, he spoke English. "What is your name, young man?" she asked.

"Brendan. What's yours?" he asked boldly.

She briefly pressed her lips together to hide a smile at her own assumption that *everyone* would know who she was. "My name is Catriona."

Those gray eyes went wide. "*Lady* Catriona? The McCallum's wife?"

"I'm not his wife yet," she said with a smile. "That's a nice dog."

"Himself asked me to take care of it." There was both pride and wariness in his tone.

The wariness could have been about her, of course. She couldn't help wondering about him or his family. Did he notice the resemblance to his chief?

She looked around. "I see other dogs roaming the courtyard. Is this one special?"

He shrugged thin shoulders beneath his shirt. For a boy who worked in the stables, he seemed remarkably clean.

"The McCallum said this one was young and wouldn't leave him alone. Might make a good stable dog. Terriers hunt badgers, Himself said. Maybe I can train it to hunt rats."

"Do you live here in the castle?"

He gave her a look like she was crazy. "Nay, I live in the village with my granny. My mum's passed on."

He didn't mention his father, and she decided not to ask. Instead, she bent and rubbed the furry head of the dog.

"Do you have a name for him yet?"

"I'll be thinking about it. Unless ye'd like to do it," he said hastily.

"No, of course not. You're in charge of him."

He relaxed, then looked over his shoulder. "Got work to do. Begging yer pardon, my lady." And he led the dog into the stables.

Riona watched him go, trying to tamp down her curiosity.

At dinner that afternoon, Hugh strolled between the tables, talking to his gentlemen and meeting the occasional wife. Training that morning had been a little more difficult than yesterday, as the awe of his arrival was wearing off, and the distance of ten years' absence was settling in. They'd all been afraid of his father and his drink-filled rages, but they didn't know what to expect of him.

It wasn't as if a chief normally trained the men, but he'd yet to name a war chief and wasn't sure if he should until after the ceremony. He was frankly surprised the clan had elected him their chief at all, considering his childhood rebellion and the scandal of Agnes. But his work on behalf of Scotland in Parliament seemed to weigh in his favor, as well as being the direct descendant over many generations. And then there was Riona's dowry . . .

He spotted Brendan McCallum eating at the rear of the hall with several other boys. Hugh had questioned his factor about the boy after seeing him at the stables and wondering why he wasn't at home helping his grandmother. The factor was as clueless as Hugh was. They had a good house in the village, which Hugh had seen to, and money enough for a comfortable life.

Yet Brendan was at Larig Castle, working in the stables, and it didn't make sense. Hugh would have to talk to the boy's grandmother.

The terrier had been the perfect excuse to talk to Brendan, and it had been as easy a conversation as possible between a chief and a nervous groom. If Brendan had thought it strange that Hugh gave him charge of the dog, he didn't show it. All it had taken was Hugh expressing concern that such a little dog would be dominated by the rest of the pack, and Brendan had responded.

And it had given him a chance to look the boy over, and be glad of what he'd seen. But sad memories were hard to escape . . .

LOOKING out her casement windows, Riona could just see Loch Voil glimmering in the setting sun. It was a beautiful sight after a day of rainy mist, but she still felt melancholy. She'd just come up from supper in the great hall, determined to be alone as little as possible with Hugh, but of course she'd felt him watching her all during the meal. As if he'd understood why she was seeking out the company of his gentlemen, he'd merely given a small smile and waved for the harpist to play for her.

But as one by one everyone had retired for the night, she'd had no choice but to do the same. Hugh had followed close behind her, but it had been almost an hour, and he hadn't emerged from his room for a second night of bundling.

Then without knocking, he strode into her chamber, his hair wet from a bath, wearing just a shirt and breeches again.

As if she'd been given a signal, Mrs. Wallace knocked and entered from the corridor. She smiled at Riona. "Well, I hope ye two had a good long conversation last night."

"We did, Mrs. Wallace," Hugh said, all innocence.

The housekeeper looked at Riona, who could only nod.

Hugh rubbed his hands together. "Shall the bundling commence? Where is the rope?"

She was tempted to say she'd lost it, but knew he'd just find more. She went to the chest. "I hid it from the maid so that gossip would not result."

"Clever."

He waited by her box-bed as she brought him the rope, feeling like she was playing a part for Mrs. Wallace. His eyes gleamed with candlelight mirrored in their depths. He took the rope in his big hands, and to her surprise, she shivered, and not with fear. The thought of being at his mercy would once have terrified her, but now she recognized that being bound meant none of it was her fault, that she could accept what happened—accept and secretly enjoy it.

She looked away, mortified, then closed her eyes when he lightly ran the rope along her cheek.

She jerked her head back and shot a glance toward Mrs. Wallace, who pointedly fiddled with the keys hung at her waist.

"Sit down," he said in a low voice.

Riona did so, keeping her gaze averted when he knelt at her feet. There was something far too meaningful about looking into his eyes. She saw passion and desire, and it appealed mightily to her to be wanted by someone—by him.

"I've never tied a woman up before," he said for her ears alone. "It seems to be rather . . . stimulating."

She wished she could kick him, but the rope was already wound about her ankles. She settled for an aggravated sigh that made him chuckle. When he was finished, she used her hands to slide backward into bed before he could touch her.

"Good night, Laird McCallum, Lady Riona," Mrs. Wallace called as she closed the door behind her.

Riona rolled her eyes at the warm humor lacing the woman's words. She stared at the ceiling of the box-bed while he blew out the candles and joined her. She lay there stiffly, determined not to play along with this farce, to discourage conversation. But the silence lengthened and filled with undercurrents of awareness and tension. His big body sagged the mattress, subtly encouraging her to move closer, and she had to fight to stay on her own side. He gave off heat, too, and within the cold stone walls of the castle, it was alluring. And he smelled of soap. At last, she had to distract him—or to be honest, distract herself.

"When will you officially be declared the chief?" she asked, risking a glance at him.

When he folded his arms behind his head and stared up as she had, she breathed a little sigh of relief.

"At a ceremony in a week or two. 'Tis a foregone conclusion, unless ye wonder if ye're to marry a different chief. After all, your dowry is a powerful incentive, and the clan wants it for their own."

She grimaced, knowing the clan was not going to get Cat's dowry any time soon. "No, I wasn't thinking that. I was just thinking about the duties of a chief, and since my uncle did not live in Scotland, he did not train the Duff clansmen as you do."

"Usually we rely on the war chief for that, but as ye probably realize, I need them all to become familiar with me again."

"But ye have no war chief?"

"I'll name one. Probably Alasdair."

"That man who seemed to take such delight in fighting you?"

Hugh harrumphed. "Aye, him. He's younger than a chief usually appoints, but his father was war chief many years ago, and Alasdair knows these mountains as well as anyone."

"And warfare? Does he know that?"

"He was with Dermot and myself at Sheriffmuir. We all know the folly of bad choices. I can never forget our retreat from Perth, when some of the soldiers, under orders from the bumbling Earl of Mar, burned three of our own villages to slow the advance of the Duke of Argyll. Homes and livelihoods wasted because Mar was ineffectual and lost the initiative."

The sadness in his voice made her look at him at last. His brows were lowered in a frown, muscles in his jaw working as if he clenched his teeth.

"Alasdair may have the background you require," she said hesitantly, "but does he have the temperament? He seemed like he rather enjoyed taunting you in front of your own men."

He glanced down at her, the storm clouds leaving his eyes. "Are ye upset on my behalf, like a true wife?"

"Of course not," she said hastily. "You can certainly take care of yourself." Changing back to a safer subject, she said, "Wasn't there another Jacobite battle after the Rising? Was he there with you as well?"

"We didn't send men because Scotland and its problems were only being used by Spain to harass the British government. Spain promised a fleet of soldiers would land in southern England, and a small fleet would meet with the Jacobites in Scotland. But just like the last Spanish armada of the sixteenth century, storms caused this fleet to founder and turn back. Only two Spanish ships came to the Outer Hebrides, and their force and the small contingent of Jacobites were no match for the redcoats and the royal ships that sailed into Loch Alsh. They fought briefly at Glen Shiel and then went into full retreat, without any Scottish deaths. A farce, the whole thing."

She nodded, knowing this was the history of her people as well—and her mother's people on the opposite side. Who was she to be loyal to? Or could she just stay separate and hope the conflicts never touched her? That seemed cowardly, and she shied away from the thoughts.

"As for Alasdair," Hugh went on when she remained silent, "he was a friend to me when I didn't have many."

Unable to stop herself, she said, "You were the son of the chief—how could you not have friends?"

"Remember who my father was. An unpredictable drunkard with the power of life and death over his clan. They all feared him, and feared provoking him. 'Twas easier to keep their children away from me and my sister—and Maggie didn't make it easy for anyone to approach her."

This Maggie was more and more intriguing, but she didn't ask questions.

"But Alasdair's father asked if he could foster me, like the other boys were able to do. Even my own father was shocked at the suggestion, but he willingly got me out of the castle. It was the best year of my life. Alasdair was a true brother to me, and when I found out about the contract at thirteen and did what I could to rebel, 'twas Alasdair who tempered my wild plans. I would have done more than steal muskets from redcoats were it not for him."

"And then he was whipped in your place," she said sympathetically.

She glanced at his profile again, and rather than ferocious, his expression was pensive.

"We were never quite the same after that," Hugh admitted. "And then my mother sent us away. And though she meant to protect us, it alienated us. Going to battle with my clan cemented some of the bond but then . . ."

Agnes. She thought the word, but didn't speak it. She didn't want to know how Agnes died or if Brendan was the son she bore Hugh. But if it was true, what kind of man let his son become a stable groom to survive?

She stopped those thoughts, reminding herself that Brendan could be another cousin. There seemed to be hundreds and hundreds of them.

And then she had a terrible thought: Was Agnes the girl Hugh wanted to marry but couldn't because of the contract?

She felt a slash of guilt she had no business feeling. She wasn't the coveted bride, this wasn't her life, and she was determined to leave it. She'd warned Hugh that he was making a mistake and he'd chosen not to believe her, had forced his will upon her. The consequences would be his to accept.

And his clan's. If Hugh couldn't make it right for them . . . She thought about the hidden land in the mountains, where they seemed to believe mystical faeries made the best water, grew the best peat and barley, as if their whisky was some kind of talisman for the clan. Hugh had already made himself untrustworthy in their eyes, with his youthful immaturity and whatever had happened to Agnes. And perhaps they all even knew the truth about the boy.

But if they lost the land, they might never forgive Hugh.

CHAPTER 11

Lying wide awake beside Riona, Hugh found his thoughts lingering on Alasdair, and how the bond they'd shared had frayed and weakened. The only way to make it better was to show his foster brother that he was there to stay, that the clan meant everything to him.

He didn't actually like talking about it, but knew women appreciated that sort of thing. If Riona was ever to accept her life, to trust him, she wanted to know about him. All he wanted to do was move forward, to prove himself.

He had to prove himself to Riona, too. She wasn't like other women, content to accept that men made the rules. He'd been exasperated by her need to fight her fate, but he was learning that such spirit made her interesting and appealing. He would find a way to make her understand that submitting could be pleasurable, that being his wife would make her happy.

He rolled onto his side, braced his head on his hand, and looked down at her. He couldn't miss how she tensed, how beneath her nightshift and dressing gown, her legs tightened futilely against the restraints.

He put a hand on her thigh, and she startled. "Settle down, lass. Fighting the ropes will only chafe your delicate skin. And then I'll be forced to nurse ye, to rub salve into your flesh . . ."

She so completely stilled that he had to chuckle. He leaned down and spoke into her ear. "That's better."

He waited for her to tell him to move his hand, but it didn't happen. She was trembling, her eyes downcast, but he knew this wasn't fear, not after the incredible kiss they'd shared the previous night. Or maybe it was a kind of fear, but of herself and what would happen if she gave in.

He took his hand from her thigh, then plucked the tie from her braid and used his fingers to comb out the locks. He spread her blond hair across the pillow like a halo. She wasn't an angel, but he didn't want her to be perfect or lofty or pure.

"Beautiful," he murmured, lowering his face to inhale the floral scent of her hair.

He picked up a curl and used it like a paintbrush

across her cheek. She twitched, bit her lip, and kept her gaze firmly on the ceiling. He traced a path down the slope of her nose and over her lips, lingering to tease her chin.

"Hugh," she began with exasperation.

"Shh."

He used her hair for feathering touches down her neck to the edge of her dressing gown. The lock of her hair did his touching for him, traveling down between her breasts even as he imagined what it would be like if it were her bare skin.

Her breathing was swift and unsteady, and ceased altogether when he circled her breasts at a slow pace, first one and then the other. He traced the little false paintbrush very near the peaks, but always backed off. He was waiting for her groan of disappointment and need, but she withheld it with some sort of herculean effort. Her tightly closed eyes and need to moisten her dry lips was not only a balm to his pride, but made him long to show her more.

At last he could resist no longer, and he twirled the end of her hair across her nipple. She gasped and shuddered, pulling her hair free of his hand.

"Stop! Hugh—you shouldn't—I mustn't—"

"Mustn't feel pleasure? Our bodies were designed for it, lass. Every part of your skin will crave my touch before long. And I not only want to touch"—he let his lips brush her ear as he spoke—"I want to taste."

She made a strangled sound and turned her flushed face away from him. His blood was afire with need, his mind trying to stop him, knowing he would not have release this night, or perhaps not any night soon.

This was a seduction that would last a lifetime. He'd spent his adulthood learning patience, and now he could put it to the test. She was worth it.

"Sleep, lass. But I'm not leaving your bed."

He rolled onto his back because he didn't trust himself not to touch her again. He listened to the gradual quieting of her breathing, felt the trembling slowly fade away. Turning his head, he saw her eyes closed, her expression relaxed as she slipped into sleep.

How long would she fight him? And would her resistance outlast his ability to control his passion for her?

RIONA awoke when Hugh left the bed at dawn, though she kept her eyes closed as he tucked the counterpane around her. Through the faint gray out the windows, she watched him put another brick of peat on the coals of the fire, as if he cared about her comfort.

He cared about making her want him, wanting her to stay, she thought with resignation.

She might be an innocent, but she knew enough about the world to know he could simply force her to accept him in front of his people, force her to accept the marriage because of the contract, but he wasn't doing that. And she had to reluctantly admire him for that—even if she thought he was a stubborn fool for not believing that she told him the truth.

But if he believed her, then their wedding would be a lie, and he wasn't ready to accept defeat.

But she wasn't ready to hang around just waiting and hoping for it, she thought, watching his body as he walked toward the doorway to the dressing room. His shoulders were so incredibly broad and masculine, full of muscle from wielding a sword, and she couldn't help her fascination. His hips were narrow, as if built to lie between her thighs. That forbidden thought brought on a physical ache of need that scared her. Last night, when he'd teased her with her own hair, she'd been shocked how desperate she'd been for him to caress her breasts, how disappointed when he'd only teased the peaks for endless minutes. And then when he'd actually touched them, the shock had gone through her body and to that most secret place between her thighs. She was aware that touching herself felt good, but when *he'd* touched her . . . She'd had no idea a man could do that to her, even though she was so unwilling to be seduced—even though he was her cousin's betrothed.

She covered her faced with a pillow and groaned

into it. She had to bring about an end to this farce before it was too late.

At breakfast in the great hall, she discovered he'd already left for the day, off to see nearby rigs of land. Samuel had told her Hugh had been studying new agricultural methods and wanted to try them. Dermot had gone with him, and she was relieved Hugh hadn't insisted she attend.

She returned to her room for her cloak. It was another gray, rainy day, which fit in perfectly with an idea she'd just had. She was testing the castle's defenses—and Hugh's promise of a secret body-guard watching her every move.

She left the castle as she did each day, and began a slow walk around the courtyards. People were used to seeing her now, and some even nodded, but no one gave her more attention than that. Maybe there was no bodyguard at all, and Hugh had lied to keep her in line.

She decided to leave through the main gatehouse, where far more people came and went, hoping she'd remain inconspicuous. Packhorses with sup-plies and travelers on foot entered each day. Guards stopped everyone arriving, but those leaving seemed free to do so. Just in case the guards had been told to watch for her, she timed her departure for when sev-eral packhorses were leaving together, and walked on the far side of them. She kept her hood up, her head down, while her heart pounded. Guards spoke to new arrivals in Gaelic, horses neighed, chickens squawked, but she just kept moving.

The packhorses distanced themselves from her as she followed the winding trail down the hillside toward Loch Voil. Her hopes began to rise with every footfall—there was no bodyguard! How could she use this new knowledge?

"Lady Riona, allow me to accompany ye on your walk today."

She winced and stumbled to a halt, recognizing the voice. Turning, she found Samuel ambling toward her, wearing a pleased smile as if he was glad for her company.

"So ye'd like to stroll by our loch," he said as he came abreast of her. " 'Tis a rainy day, but the beauty of our mountains framing the water cannot be denied. Shall we go?"

Silent in defeat, she trudged at his side, going ever downward toward the water. She looked wistfully to the east, wondering if she would ever leave this place again.

"Samuel, are you the mysterious bodyguard Hugh told me about?" she asked, when they reached level ground near the water's edge.

There was a log on its side, perfectly placed as if for sitting and admiring the view. Samuel gestured, and she sat down, grabbed a stone, and heaved it into the calm water. The splash and the widening circles didn't make her feel better.

"The guards knew to contact me if ye left," he said, not exactly answering her question. "Hugh made sure they believed he was only worried for your safety in our wild, dangerous land, that ye needed an escort into the village. But ye weren't going to the village."

"Of course I was."

With a faint smile, he shook his head. "Nay, Lady Riona, that will not work with me. What did ye think ye'd accomplish like this?"

"I knew I would not have freedom," she whispered, lowering her head to her folded arms and trying desperately not to cry.

Samuel said nothing for several long minutes as she got herself under control. She heard birds, and the faint plop of something landing in the water, but whether it was a fish jumping or not, she didn't care.

"Will it be so bad to be the McCallum's wife?"

"I'm not his wife," she said fiercely, raising her head to glare at him. "I'm his prisoner. And I wasn't foolish enough to risk being alone in this savage country, but I had to know if I was constantly under watch."

Samuel's expression remained mild. "I understand that among the nobility, arranged marriages are common."

"I'm not the child of a nobleman," she insisted. "My father was the child of an earl, but I am not. This isn't a fairy tale I've invented, but the truth. Why do you not send word to the earl's castle and confirm that there are two cousins named Catriona?"

"As if we speak often to each other, ye mean?" he teased.

"Well, shouldn't you all be civil, with a marriage erasing a feud?"

"'Tis not that simple, my lady," Samuel said, his smile fading. "There are hundreds of years of warfare, with cattle reiving by Duffs that risked our very survival through terrible winters."

"And McCallums sat innocent on their lands and didn't respond or initiate any of these raids? Surely there are two sides to this feud."

"My clansmen haven't forgotten that one hundred and thirty-two years ago, a McCallum chief was a guest of a Duff, and he and his wife were found murdered in the bed provided by their host."

Riona sighed. "That is a terrible story, and I'm sorry for it. But that was one hundred and thirty-two years ago, Samuel. Shouldn't it be left in the past?"

"And hence, to make that happen, a marriage between a McCallum and a Duff, and the sharing of ancient land."

"And the obtaining of Duff money," she said skeptically.

Samuel shrugged. "A dowry is typical for weddings, Lady Riona. In the contract, ye'll be given ample dower land and money should ye someday be widowed."

She shrugged. "What care I? I will never marry Hugh."

"He aims to change your mind, my lady. Is it so difficult to imagine that he can do so?"

She felt herself blush and wondered if Hugh had spoken of their private business. How many men knew that Hugh tied her up to keep her in bed? But she couldn't ask that. She stood up. "I'm ready to go back."

Samuel rose as well and gestured for her to start up the narrow path ahead of him. "If it helps, my lady, Hugh has already sent an escort to his mother and sister in Edinburgh to tell them that ye've arrived. They'll come soon, and then ye'll not feel so lonely."

Riona gritted her teeth and said nothing. The news didn't make her feel any better. There'd be two more women in the castle on Hugh's side, women who wouldn't understand why she didn't want to marry their precious Hugh.

Hugh and his small party returned to Larig Castle before dinner the next day, and he was in a foul mood. Dermot had infuriated him, the tenants had been obstinate and—he'd missed Riona, which annoyed the hell out of him.

As he'd lain wrapped in his plaid on the hillside, the horses hobbled nearby, he'd thought of her lounging in her cozy box-bed, alone and gleeful at his absence. Every time he'd almost fallen asleep, he'd imagined that she'd shed her dressing gown, and her thin nightshift would be translucent in the firelight. While he'd shivered in the damp chill, she'd been warm beneath the bedclothes, relaxed in sleep.

And just the thought had given him a cock-stand and further ruined his night.

At the castle, Dermot took leave of him without a word of farewell or conciliation. When Hugh arrived in the great hall, Riona took one look at him and her eyes went wide. She said nothing, only gestured to the servant, who pulled out his chair. A washbasin was brought forward, and when he was clean, he dug into stewed venison with a ferocious appetite.

He wanted Riona to ask how his trip was, like a loving wife. But she didn't want to be that wife, didn't want his caresses, didn't care that he could make her feel such pleasure she'd never want to leave the bed.

In fact, she looked suspiciously nervous and chastened, and he didn't know why. He took a deep sip of whisky, felt it burn his throat and warm his gut, but that only helped a little. He poured another.

"Dermot is a fool," he finally said in a low voice that only Riona could hear.

She eyed him as she daintily broke a piece of bread and buttered it.

She didn't ask him why, and he went on.

"I've spent years learning the newest agricultural methods that have had such success in England, field rotation, marsh drainage, cattle enclosures to keep the crops from being ruined."

"You don't have hedges or walls?"

"On our hillsides? Nay, the cattle roam free on our lands, but that only ruins crops and good land not meant for pasture. But does Dermot—or the tenants—care? Nay, they only wish to do as we've always done, as our fathers before us have done. If only they could see how much more successful farming is in England, but they don't believe in change."

"Then as chief, I imagine you just order them to do as you want," she said mildly.

He saw her studying the second whisky in his hand, which only made him frown harder. "And ye're proof that trying to force a person against her will is a successful strategy?"

Her eyes widened, and for a moment, he thought he might see her smile, but she controlled herself.

"But the clan lands are yours to oversee," she countered. "Do as you wish."

He grumbled and sawed at a piece of venison with his knife.

"There could be another reason Dermot is being so obstinate," she mused.

He eyed her.

"He's not against agricultural improvements—he's simply against *you*."

And then he did receive her rare, satisfied smile, not quite what he'd hoped for. He rolled his eyes and went back to his food. Riona turned away and began to speak to Samuel on her other side. Hugh knew Samuel often translated for her, and he hoped that she felt like she had a friend here. If she let herself, he suspected she had the sweetness and generosity to make plenty more . . .

He considered Samuel for a moment. When Hugh had first arrived home and been greeted by him, Hugh could have sworn Samuel had meant to tell him something, hesitated, then changed his mind. Hugh shrugged. Samuel would speak when he was ready.

Alasdair took a seat in the empty chair to Hugh's left, the one that would have been Dermot's if the man hadn't stiffly excused himself.

"Alasdair," Hugh said warily.

Alasdair nodded. "Hugh." He looked past Hugh at Riona and Samuel talking together, then said in a low voice, "There's something ye should know."

CHAPTER 12

Riona knew that something had happened between him and Alasdair by the thundercloud that was Hugh's lowered brows. The bard sang as if to distract him, but it didn't work. Hugh glowered at her and drank too much, and she began to feel uneasy. Tonight she could be trapped with—or tied to!—a drunken Highlander in a terrible temper. What was he capable of?

They retired to their separate rooms soon after, and she found herself pacing. She'd ordered a bath to be brought to him, and she hoped the heat was soaking away the alcohol.

She paused, straining to listen when she thought she heard something from his room. Her curiosity began to get the best of her, and she wanted to be prepared, so she gently opened the door and crept into the dressing room, lit only with a candle. They hadn't used this room much yet, for they hadn't entertained family or friends. She had no ladies to sew with—although Hugh's family was supposedly arriving soon, and that would change, she thought glumly. At least now, her days were her own.

At the door to Hugh's room, she leaned to put an ear next to it. Misjudging in the dark, she gently banged her head against it instead. Wincing, she began to retreat.

"Lingering at my door, Riona?" he called.

His words didn't sound slurred, and she tried to take that as a good sign. But she said nothing, hoping he'd think it only a castle cat.

"Open the blasted door and get in here!" he shouted.

She let out her breath on a shaky exhale and did as he commanded. Running away would only make him chase her, and might end up worse for her.

She froze in the doorway upon finding Hugh still in his bath before the fire. His wet shoulders gleamed above the rim, his dark hair was damp and hung in waves to those broad shoulders. There was a goblet on a stool beside him, and he reached for it and took a drink, head turned to eye her.

"Close the door; there's a draft," he said coldly.

She did so, then leaned back against it.

"You were so curious about my bath. Come closer."

She wanted to refuse, but found herself taking several steps. She wasn't curious—she was afraid, she reminded herself sternly. He was like a god here, and she was his prisoner.

Luckily, the room was lit only by a few candles, and it was rather murky and soapy beneath the surface of the water. She shouldn't be looking.

She concentrated on his face and spoke matter-of-factly. "Why are you in such a foul temper? There has to be more than your problem with your tenants and Dermot. Or do you let such a little setback bother you?"

He leaned his head back and stared at her with narrowed eyes. She should focus on that, but the hair on his chest was damp, and seemed to point downward . . .

"Alasdair had news for me tonight, but ye didn't hear him tell me."

She frowned. "No, I didn't. Was it bad?"

"Seems there was some talk about ye being alone with Samuel by the loch, as if ye were meeting in secret."

She stiffened, opened her mouth to retort, then closed it. Wasn't this farce better than him knowing what she'd actually done? Because apparently Samuel hadn't told him she'd tested the truth of a bodyguard.

But he was scowling at her, and she realized he thought his friend Samuel was either leading her astray or being led. She shouldn't care if there was a rift between them, but . . . Samuel had tried to help her in his misguided way; she didn't want to see him suffer.

She crossed her arms over her chest and said heatedly, "Samuel was not trying to get me alone, and believe me, I wanted no company."

He took another swig of whisky, and when he set it down hard, some sloshed onto the stool and dripped to the floor. "Then explain, because this doesn't make sense. Alasdair—my foster brother!— looked devilish and satisfied with himself. I couldn't decide if he thought he was helping and taunting me at the same time, or trying to hurt me." He lowered his frowning gaze.

She couldn't believe he was speaking to her so intimately about his feelings, and not just about passion. He was obviously affected by drink. "You can't be hurt by anything *I* do," she insisted, trying to ignore the pangs of sympathy that stirred in the corner of her soul.

"Tell me what happened, woman!"

He put both hands on the rim of the tub, as if he meant to heave himself out. That was all she'd need, a naked Hugh advancing on her. Instead of running, she might fling herself on him, and then what would he think? And what would she think of herself?

"All right, all right!" she said, holding up both hands. "The only reason we were alone was because I went for a stroll, and didn't know the grounds around the castle are off limits to me. There are gardens there," she added quickly, seeing him focus on her face with eyes as cold as mirrors. "Women work in gardens!"

"Ye tried to escape," he said slowly. "Ye waited until I was gone, and ye tried to escape."

"I'm not that stupid," she said wearily. "I had to see if you truly have someone spying on me. And apparently you do."

"The guards told Samuel ye'd left?"

She hesitated, then gave one quick nod.

He relaxed back in the tub and raked her with a baffled stare. "Where did ye think ye'd go, you a woman all alone?"

"I told you I didn't try to escape. But if I had, where do you *think* I'd go?" she countered with sarcasm.

"To your father's castle."

"To my *uncle's* castle."

"Are ye not tired of lying, lass?"

She wanted to yell to the rooftops, but kept her voice calm. "I am not lying."

"I ken ye're afraid to be married, but—"

She advanced on him and pointed a finger at his face. "I am not afraid of you, nor would I be afraid of a husband I chose. But I did not choose you!"

"Your father did, lass, and surely ye're an *obedient* daughter."

Was he *taunting* her now? His gaze was certainly sly enough.

With a frustrated groan, she grabbed the pot of soap off the stool and tossed it into the tub. It hit the water with a satisfying smack, splashing Hugh in the face. She turned to run toward the door, but he caught her skirts in his fist and pulled. She toppled right into the tub, landing bottom-first across his lap. Water sloshed out and splashed onto the rug all around them.

"Hugh!" she cried, flailing, trying to find a way to leverage herself out of the tub and away from his slippery, warm skin. But her lower legs dangled over the edge and water soaked her through the hips and up her torso.

With an arm across her body, he held her still. "No more squirming," he said against her ear, his voice rumbling, "or I won't be responsible for what happens next."

She froze as she realized that right beneath her backside, she could feel the hard length of his erection. She couldn't look at him, fully aware of a surge of pleasure and longing and an unbearable need to . . . squirm. A long, tense moment passed, with only the sound of water dripping, and both of them breathing shallow and fast.

She glanced at him from beneath her lashes. His gaze was hard, a tic jumped in his jaw, and he was looking down at her chest. Following his line of sight, she realized her dressing gown had parted when he'd yanked on her garments. The only thing obscuring her nudity was a soaked nightshift that clung to her skin and starkly showed her nipples.

Before she could hide herself, he lifted her and covered her breast with his mouth, sucking on her right through her clothing. She cried out, but it wasn't in fear or denial. A hot wash of passion overcame her, heating her face, her body, her blood. He took turns suckling and then nibbling her, holding her tightly against him, until she was a shuddering mass of need. Somehow her arms were around his head, holding her to him, making it far too obvious what she wanted.

And then he lifted his head and she dropped hers to kiss him, boldly slanting her mouth over his, as he'd taught her. For endless minutes they practically fed from each other, exploring with eagerness. She suckled his tongue; she tasted the whisky and didn't even mind, for it was all a part of him. When she felt his hand cup her breast, she moaned into his mouth. He rolled her nipple between his fingers, plucked at it, then soothed it with a caress, leaving her trembling and gasping.

He broke away and kissed down her neck and found her breast again. She dropped her head back over the edge of the tub, which shamelessly thrust her chest higher.

He put his hand on her leg and slid it beneath her hem. "Come to bed with me, lass."

Those words brought home the reality of what

she was doing—what she was encouraging. She came upright so fast that more water surged onto the floor.

"No," she said, her voice hoarse. She had to clear her throat to be louder. "No! Hugh, let me go. We aren't married and we never will be. This is wrong."

He kept his arms around her for too long, and she almost started struggling, but at last he released her. With a hand on her backside, he heaved her out. She stood bereft and lost on the rug, water dripping down her body, her wet clothes sodden. She shivered uncontrollably, too shocked to cry.

"Go get warm," he said between clenched teeth. "I'll not be joining ye tonight."

She fled to the door, then paused and said over her shoulder, "I hope . . . I hope you are not jealous over Samuel. I would never use him against you."

"Ye think I would punish an innocent man?"

"I don't know. I just want you to know the truth, that he is protecting you."

"Ye didn't want to tell me the full truth a moment ago."

She shivered. "I couldn't let your loyal man be harmed. I lied to protect myself," she said without thinking.

"Ye're very good at that, are ye not?"

Why was it such a personal affront that this particular man thought her a liar? She opened the door, then slammed both it and the next door that separated them. In her own room, she stripped off her garments and toweled herself dry. Unbidden, images of him doing the same bombarded her. It was a long time before she fell asleep, and though it was summer, she felt cold without him beside her in bed.

RIONA couldn't remain inside the castle, where Mrs. Wallace was beginning to seek out her opinion on the running of the household, as if breaking the new wife in slowly. She wasn't going to be in charge here and didn't want to mislead the well-meaning housekeeper. And it was far too much of a lure, that her opinion counted, that she could make decisions.

The rain had stopped, and so she wandered from shop to shop in the lower yard, watching the craftsmen work, receiving the occasional confused or apprehensive stare in return. The clan didn't know what she was doing—neither did she. Though she reminded herself she did have an idea to ask Dermot to go with her to convince Hugh, her plan seemed to be moving so slowly. She could never find time alone with him to build any sort of connection. So she floated through the day as if she were only waiting for what happened next, whether it was Hugh's family arriving, word from the earl that sealed Hugh's fate with his clan, or Hugh losing patience and taking her to wife. She hated the waiting, without the ability to make her own choices. She'd spent too much of her life doing that.

And then she heard Hugh's voice, and it was as if she was suddenly back in his room again, in his bath, his mouth so intimately giving her pleasure. He might as well have been touching her at that moment, so overwhelming was her body's reaction.

But he wasn't touching her. In fact, his voice was raised in anger. It made her shiver, and she saw more than one man glancing over his shoulder as if he didn't want to be next in line. Her instinct was to run away, but that infuriated her, so she followed the sound of his voice to the stables and stood just outside the large double doors. She realized that Brendan was doing the same thing on the other side of the doors. She ducked back before he saw her.

"These stalls need to be raked out on a regular schedule," Hugh ordered, "and I'll not see ye feeding oats that have spoiled. I don't know what ye thought ye could get away with under my father's rule, but I demand a higher standard to benefit the beasts that serve us."

He went on for far too long, until Riona began to think he was being unreasonable. She heard him stomp out of the stables and decided to stay hidden.

"Good day, Laird McCallum," Brendan said in a small, defensive voice.

Riona figured Hugh must have caught him

eavesdropping. She admired the little boy for not running away from all that dominant-male wrath.

The change in Hugh's voice was surprising. It went from fury to controlled neutrality. "A good day to ye, too, Brendan."

She found herself peering around the corner, but all she could see was Hugh's impassive profile. Brendan was holding a rake in both hands—as if he'd been charged with mucking out stalls. She held her breath, waiting for the yelling to commence— or would he favor the boy? Which would be worse for Brendan?

Hugh glanced at the rake. "There will be new orders to follow for the care of our horses."

Brendan nodded, his head lowered. There was a sudden high-pitched bark, and Riona saw that the little terrier had been tied up near where Brendan now stood.

Hugh looked down with a frown. "Is the animal behaving?"

"Aye, sir," Brendan said.

"Have ye named it?"

It was almost painful yet sweet the way Hugh was trying to connect to the boy through the animal.

"Hamish, sir."

To her surprise, she could read the amusement that Hugh held back but for the raising of one eyebrow. " 'Tis a big name for a little dog."

"He thinks he's big, sir."

Riona realized she was not the only one watching this little scene. Next door, the carpenter had put out his head and frowned. Several of the gentlemen on the training yard were standing together whispering, watching Hugh and Brendan.

Men made bastards all the time, she told herself. She wasn't even certain this boy was one, yet . . . it made her nervous on Hugh's behalf, seeing the reaction of his clansmen.

Little Hamish started barking, and she realized it was in her direction. Both Hugh and Brendan turned their heads in an almost identical manner.

Riona gave a little wave. "I didn't want to interrupt. Forgive me."

"Lady Riona," Hugh said, a note of curiosity in his voice.

Hamish kept barking furiously at her.

She had to raise her voice. "I was simply learning my way about, seeing what your people do each day."

Even Hamish seemed suspicious of that, and just kept barking.

"Wheesht," Brendan commanded, dropping to one knee and putting an arm around the dog's shoulders.

Hamish subsided into low growls.

Hugh was no longer trying to hold back his amusement. "I believe Hamish has decided ye're the lowest member of this pack, and a threat to him." He gave Brendan a nod. "See to your duties, lad." He turned to her. "Lady Riona, please meet me in the great hall in one hour's time."

He didn't wait for her response, and she studied his retreating back with curiosity. The pleats of his belted plaid swayed with his walk, and she could see his calves move beneath the tight stockings. So perhaps Scottish ladies had a reason to like seeing their men's bare legs.

Riona had never been afraid of dogs in her life, especially not one of this diminutive size, so she walked to Hamish and bent to offer her hand. He gave several sniffs, and then a low growl, but not quite so menacing.

"I'll win you over yet, little Hamish," Riona said, smiling.

"I've got to work, my lady," Brendan said, coming to his feet and reaching for his rake.

"Then I'll leave you to it."

She watched the boy disappear inside the gloomy stables, and so did Hamish, who sank down on his haunches and rested his snout on his paws.

Glancing up, she saw Dermot leave one of the workshops and stride with purpose toward the upper courtyard. She hurried to catch up with him.

Hugh resisted the need to turn around and watch Riona. He'd certainly seen more of her last night, and he was trying not to let the memory intrude on the day's work, but it was difficult. Their argument had been stimulating in more ways than one, and now he could barely remember what they'd been arguing about, since images of her drenched in his bath, her clothing translucent, her nipples hard, would override every other thought in his head—if he allowed it. And he must not. He had to pretend to be a new bridegroom, putting aside the nights with his wife until they'd retired. Every night of their journey to marriage, he learned more about her, grew a little closer, touched a little more. Soon, she wouldn't be able to resist him.

Hugh found Samuel in the armory, inspecting the castle's supply of weapons. An increase in arms was one of the things Hugh had planned when he received the dowry. He'd been waiting to hear from the earl, but nothing had come yet of his first move to negotiate. He was confident that word would come eventually. The earl wouldn't want it known he'd backed out on a signed marriage contract.

Samuel finished talking to the armorer and stepped out into the sun. "Ye needed me, Hugh?"

"Walk with me." When he was certain no one overheard them, he said coolly, "Why did ye not tell me the lass left the castle yesterday?"

Samuel continued to walk with his hands behind his back, his expression rueful but not terribly concerned. Hugh didn't know whether to be irritated or amused.

"So the lass confessed?" Samuel asked.

"Nay, not at first. But ye put yourself in a bad light, Samuel. Ye've been with me all these years, and people here don't know ye. When ye were seen talking to my lady by the loch, rumors spread and Alasdair heard them."

"So ye confronted her, did ye?"

"Of course I did. And she admitted the truth readily rather than see ye suffer for her mistakes. I'm not sure how ye've befriended her when ye helped me kidnap her."

Samuel shrugged. "'Tis easy for her to absolve me—I'm only one of your men, following your orders. And she and I did nothing improper down by the loch. We talked for but a few minutes, then I returned her to the castle. Of course people are talking about her—she's not yet your wife, though it looks like 'tis a trial marriage ye're after, since she's installed in your rooms."

"Are ye commenting on my private business, Samuel?" Hugh asked, wearing a frown.

"Course not. Ye have my loyalty—ye ken ye always have. But I've been a part of this private business from the moment I drove your coach beneath her balcony and helped ye steal her away. Ye had your reasons, and I'm not arguing with ye. But I sympathize with the lass's fear and frustration, and so I thought 'twas no harm done to keep secret that she'd made a mistake. Now she understands that she's being watched all the time. She had to test that—wouldn't ye in her place?"

"Whatever I might do matters naught. I need your word ye'll tell me what she's up to from now on. I'm protecting her, too, can ye not see that?"

"Aye," Samuel said slowly. "I do—now," he added.

Hugh rolled his eyes. "Ye'll accompany me to the village in an hour's time. See to three horses and provisions for an afternoon ride."

"Aye, sir," Samuel said, before walking away.

Damn the man for the smile he barely bothered to hide.

As Hugh entered the upper courtyard, he was surprised to see Riona talking alone with Dermot, but he didn't interrupt them. She was already upset enough with having guards watch over her—she didn't need to think he was following her.

But he was curious. Perhaps she was finally attempting to get to know people, to become a part of life at Larig Castle.

A quarter hour later, when Riona entered the great hall, Hugh called her over to the hearth. "I've sent Mary up to your chambers to find your cloak and sturdier boots."

"It's not raining," she said with confusion.

"But it might, and we'll be gone for the day."

That perked up her interest. "Where are we going?"

"Into the village—if ye can promise to be good."

"Oh, I can be good. I'd enjoy getting out of here for a day."

"Without having to sneak off?"

She only lifted her chin rather than respond.

"Sula is the nearest village of the many that are part of Clan McCallum," he continued.

"Will I get to see more?"

"Someday, perhaps. If ye're good."

"Do not treat me like a child, McCallum."

"Do not try to run away from your responsibilities."

He saw the fierce defensiveness come over her, and then the way she corralled it and remained silent. He knew that was difficult for her—just as he knew she was desperate to escape the castle, even if it had to be with him.

CHAPTER 13

On the sloping path to the village for the two-hour journey, Riona rode between Hugh and Samuel, and said little to either of them. She was still annoyed that Samuel made her feel conflicted, both upset he'd been part of her kidnapping and chagrined that he treated her gently. She didn't want to like him, but he seemed a good man, loyal to his chief.

As for Hugh, she was still having difficulty meeting his eyes. It would have been easier if he was his impassive self, but the more intimate time they spent together, the more it showed in his eyes when he looked at her. And she was succumbing to the lure of his desire for her. She was already a fallen woman, having been taken away by a man and having spent weeks in his company, and now nights within his rooms. It didn't matter that she hadn't gone with him willingly. But she had to focus on remaining true to herself, to make the best of her life. She couldn't marry him and she wouldn't become his mistress. All she had was her promise to herself to leave this place someday. Finding out about the surrounding countryside would help when she finally made her way out of here. Because when Hugh and the clan found out the truth . . .

Not that she knew when that might happen. Her conversation with Dermot had been disappointing, although she wasn't sure what she'd expected. He was a man, the tanist to his chief. She was simply a woman the chief meant to marry. They hadn't spoken long, and Dermot had made it very clear that her attempts to engage him in conversation were keeping him from *real* work. Trying to get to know him had only made her feel like a silly decoration hung about the castle. Women certainly had much to contribute to the running of such an immense and complicated household, but apparently he didn't see it that way. She was offended on behalf of Mrs. Wallace and Cat, the woman who should be mistress at Larig someday.

Not that she was giving up using him to reach Hugh. Dermot had just made it clear it would be harder than she'd thought.

Upon reaching the path that ran along Loch Voil, they turned east and walked their horses along the water. In the glen at the end of the lake, she now could see the small village, with its tiny church and graveyard with a half wall all around it. Several dozen stone cottages surrounded it, topped by thatched roofs above and surrounded by small gardens and fields of long green stalks of oats beyond. In the center was a triangular village green, where several cows now roamed free.

There were men lounging outside their cottages, sharpening weapons as they talked to each other. Women worked in their gardens or stirred huge boiling cauldrons of laundry over fire pits outside. Children ran and shouted, tossing hoops back and forth.

But everyone stopped what they were doing when they saw Hugh, Samuel, and Riona arrive. Their expressions ranged from wariness to outright skepticism as Hugh approached, but most changed those into impassive or pleasant nods. It had been ten years since Hugh had caused a scandal with Agnes, the girl who was long dead. It didn't seem as if people had forgotten, but then this had been Agnes's village, and Brendan came home here every night.

"There don't seem to be any merchants in a village this size," Riona said as they reached the green.

"Did ye expect a milliner?" Hugh asked lightly. "Even Edinburgh only has one."

She inhaled on a faint gasp. "In truth?"

Hugh and Samuel exchanged an amused glance. "In truth," Hugh replied. "Tailors and cobblers wander from village to village for a week here and there until the work is done, and then they move on."

"But we do manage to have an alehouse for the occasional traveler," Samuel said with satisfaction.

"Or hardworking clansman," Hugh said.

He slid from his horse and came to her side. To her surprise, he lifted her knee from the pommel of the sidesaddle, put his hands to her waist, and set her on the ground. She told herself he was putting on a show.

The alehouse had obviously been someone's two-room cottage at one time, but now the front room had a bar, tables with benches, as well as a wooden settle before the fireplace for the occasional private conversations. Behind the bar was another room, probably for storage. Hugh dwarfed the small room. His head almost touched the rafters, and he'd had to duck several hanging cheeses.

A man dressed in shirtsleeves, waistcoat, and breeches emerged from the back room, an apron at his waist. He was thin, not much more than thirty, with a neat beard and mustache. "How can I help ye fine folks?"

And then he stopped, truly seeing Hugh for the first time.

"Hugh McCallum." The man breathed the name as if in shock. "I'd heard ye were back, of course, but—God, ye look good."

"Donald Ross," Hugh said, a rare grin splitting his face.

The two men hugged hard, clapping each other's backs. Riona watched in amazement, for no one had given Hugh this kind of welcome yet. Several men at another table watched the reunion, and she wondered if they would spread word that their chief was not a man to be wary of.

"Sit down, sit down," Donald said, gesturing to a clean table where a lantern dispelled the gloom. "Let me bring ale for ye strapping men, and for the lady?"

" 'Tis my betrothed, Lady Catriona Duff," Hugh said. "She'll take a goblet of your best wine."

The pride in his voice was like a knife prick to her heart. He was proud, perhaps of her looks—which wasn't truly her, deep down—but definitely most proud of the money she was supposed to bring to the clan. The money Cat was supposed to bring, she reminded herself. Her own dowry was much smaller and would disappoint many.

The ale keeper lifted her hand with the gesture of a courtier and kissed the back of it. "Lady Catriona, a pleasure to meet ye. I know your betrothed from when we took a degree in master of arts at university together in Edinburgh."

Riona barely kept her mouth from sagging open. The ale keeper had studied at university—as had Hugh? She should no longer be surprised by anything she heard about Hugh's past, but he just kept surprising her. And Donald—for a literate man, he seemed reduced to hard circumstances in this out-of-the-way village.

"We spent several years there after the Rising," Hugh was saying, grinning at his friend.

"And the times we had," Donald added, shaking his head. "The women—" He flushed and glanced at her, donning an apologetic expression. "Forgive me, my lady. Those might have been exciting years, but then your betrothed decided he could serve his county better in Parliament. And I went off to improve my fortune, and ended up losing it."

Hugh's smile faded. "Donald . . ."

"Nay, none of that. I invested unwisely. Your family gave me another chance here, Hugh, and I won't forget it." He clapped his hands together and looked from Hugh to Riona and Samuel. "My wife has a delicious soup heating in the back. I'll bring ye some."

He went to refill drinks at another table before going behind the bar. Riona kept staring at Hugh. Donald brought tankards of ale for Hugh and Samuel and set a surprisingly delicate glass goblet before her, brimming with rich red wine. He bowed again to her and disappeared into the back room.

"Ye look surprised, lass," Hugh said in a low voice, forearms folded on the table. "Ye have questions?"

"So many, but . . . it must be difficult for your

friend to have been so wealthy that he went to university, and now . . ." She looked around at the plain stone walls and thatched roof.

"Here in Scotland, no one thinks less of people in reduced circumstances," Hugh said matter-of-factly, then added dryly, "Not so in England."

"You are right about that. So much for Scotland being uncivilized."

Hugh nudged Samuel. "Did ye hear that? We'll bring her around yet."

Ignoring their teasing, she sipped the wine. "This is very good."

He slammed the tin tankard into Samuel's as if in toast to each other. " 'Tis glad I am that Donald was able to make a life here. Many young men fell on hard times after the Rising and had to leave, never to return. The American colonies are the recipients of too many of our good young clansmen." He eyed her with amusement. "I'll be able to help many people with your tocher, lass. Don't be thinking I'll spend it on myself."

The wine suddenly tasted bitter in her mouth. She couldn't let herself think of how these poor people might be waiting in anticipation for the tocher they'd never get, so she let barbed words distract her. "Your people don't exactly seem to trust you. Will they trust you to spend such a sum wisely?"

"They have nominated me as their chief," he said, full of confidence, "so that means they trust me."

"Or they want the money," she said in an overly sweet voice, "which is tied to *you*, not a random chief."

Hugh's smile didn't lessen as he let her words bounce right off him. Donald returned then, along with a young woman, carrying bowls of soup and platters of fresh bread. He introduced her as his wife, Rachel, and she shyly retreated to the kitchen without saying a word.

"Are your parents still here in the village?" Hugh asked, when Donald sat down on the bench next to Samuel.

Donald's smile faded. "My da died a few years back, and my mum is in frail health. Consumption."

Riona looked up in surprise, and felt a surge of sympathy for the family.

"Sorry I am to hear that," Hugh said.

She hesitated, then found herself saying, "My sister has consumption. I've nursed her for many years."

"Ye're a Duff, aren't ye?" Donald asked, but with curiosity, not dismissal.

"I am, but I've spent my life in England, much of it in London. My sister saw many physicians there."

Donald leaned toward her. "Maybe ye would visit my mother? See what ye think?"

"I—I'm not a healer myself," she demurred, uneasy, though she didn't know why.

"But ye know more about modern treatment than

we do. In Stirling, all they wanted to do was bleed her, and that seemed to make her much worse."

"Yes, it is the same with my sister," Riona said. "Of course I will see your mother."

Hugh had the glint of pride in his eyes again, and she deliberately looked away. She couldn't cure the woman—there was no cure. But some people lived longer than others, and their lives could be extended with knowledgeable care.

She was rather surprised by her own eagerness to be of help. She'd spent much of her youth closeted in a sickroom with only Bronwyn's gratitude, while her parents had acted as if anyone would give up their daily activities to nurse. *They* hadn't, she remembered. And she also remembered Bronwyn's guilt that Riona had been forced to spend so many hours with her. No one was forcing Riona now. She might not be able to help herself escape Hugh's plans, but perhaps she could do something for another woman's suffering rather than dwell on her own plight. It felt good to be able to make her own decision for once, because seldom in her life had she had such a chance.

For the next hour, they ate soup and oat bread, and she listened to stories Donald told about Hugh at university. She placed these stories in a timeline in her mind, occurring after he wanted to marry Agnes. It seemed to have taken Donald a long time to coerce Hugh into doing anything more than studying, but after a while, they'd enjoyed parties and drinking and probably women, as all young men did.

When Riona had eaten her fill, Rachel took her to the simple cottage just behind the alehouse, where an elderly woman sat within, watching over a little boy and girl rolling a ball to each other. Riona wasn't surprised to see a handkerchief clutched in her hand for the occasional cough, and wondered if there would be blood upon it. The room itself, though clean and with a wooden floor, was closed in, the shutters drawn though it was summer, the heat almost unbearable. The first thing Riona did was throw back the shutters and talk about the healing qualities of fresh air and walking out-of-doors for exercise, along with wholesome food to help strengthen the body. She mentioned an infusion made of chamomile flowers to aid digestion.

The elder Mrs. Ross looked upon Riona as if she were a ministering angel, which made her uncomfortable at first, but she well understood how an illness could make one dependent on the goodwill of another. She stayed for an hour, chatting with the women about news from the south, and life here in the village, and took her leave after promising to return again soon.

For a long moment, she stood outside the cottage, alone but for the distant sound of villagers near a neighboring cottage speaking in Gaelic, and the lowing of cows on the hillside. The mountains rose up on either side of the glen, bare of trees at the crown, and she could see the glimmer of Loch Voil down the center to the west of them. She didn't think about trying to run—what would be the point?

With a sigh, she returned to the alehouse. She felt warm from Donald's ensuing praise and gratitude, the way Samuel smiled at her—and the pleasure and pride in Hugh's eyes when he looked at her.

That evening in her bedroom, she awaited Hugh's entrance, hoping he was too tired from the long day outdoors to bother her. Of course he was a fine physical specimen, and it was she who was tired, not him. But to her surprise, after he arrived, he sat in front of the fire and pulled her onto his lap. She stiffened warily, but except for absently play-ing with her fingers within his big, rough hand, he spent an hour telling her more about Donald and his family, and others like him, the people he'd wanted to help as an MP in London. The sound of his voice was soothing, and soon she found herself resting her head on his shoulder. She must have fallen asleep, because she awoke in the middle of the night, alone in her cold bed. She was mostly re-lieved, but part of her was . . . disappointed.

HUGH came up to change after a morning spent on the training yard. He was meeting with his factor to discuss leases that had just been vacated, a dry topic, but necessary. He had his agricultural books, the ones he'd sent home over the years and no one had studied, at the ready to show his factor—and Dermot. These vacant leases were perfect to begin an experiment in improving the crop yield in their harsh growing climate.

To his surprise, he heard voices from within the dressing room, and opened the door to see Mrs. Wallace and Riona with lengths of fine cambric stretched out over a long table.

Though both women looked up at him, only Mrs. Wallace smiled. Riona just nodded and went back to her work. He tried to imagine Riona smiling with pleasure when he entered a room, but it was difficult. He'd realized that a kidnapping ensured a lengthy, slow courtship, but he was still surprised it was taking this long.

"Ye need some new shirts, Laird McCallum," Mrs. Wallace said. "Yer future wife has asked to sew and embroider them for ye. Did ye know ye were wedding such a talented woman?"

"Aye, I knew," he said.

Riona's cheeks reddened, but she didn't meet his eyes.

"She could be sewin' her weddin' clothes, but she insisted that the chief's shirts were more important."

"Did she now?" Or was she still playing at the

fallacy that she didn't need wedding clothes because she wouldn't be here long?

He'd thought after their visit to the village yesterday, and her interest in helping the Rosses, that she might have mellowed, but apparently not. She wasn't going to sew gowns for a future she didn't want to have. He was still willing to be patient, but he'd been with her almost three weeks now, and she showed no signs of admitting to the truth. She was definitely a stubborn woman.

Lingering in the doorway, he unpinned his plaid at the shoulder and let the loose ends dangle from his belt. He thought of the hour by the fire last night, when he'd gradually felt her defenses come down the closer she got to sleep. She'd let him hold her, had even allowed him to touch her hand. To his surprise, once she'd fallen asleep he hadn't felt the overwhelming urge to awaken her senses to pleasure. She'd looked so . . . innocent in his arms, shadows beneath her eyes as if it had been a long day. He'd watched her sleep some time before gently placing her in bed. He still wanted her, but . . . there was time.

When he did nothing but watch them work, the two women eyed him, then went back to discussing measurements and embroidery.

"Mrs. Wallace," he said suddenly, "I forgot to ask if ye had any trouble preparing for the council of gentlemen tomorrow. If ye need me to contact someone on your behalf . . ."

He trailed off because he saw Riona's surprised expression before she ducked her head back to her sewing. Mrs. Wallace eyed Riona with her own surprise, then sent a frown Hugh's way.

"Ye did not tell yer own betrothed about a feast in the great hall?" Mrs. Wallace asked, speaking as freely as a mother would.

He brazened it out. "I spoke to ye directly, Mrs. Wallace. I did not think it fair to bother my betrothed when she's not yet the mistress of the household." That sounded as if he'd given it some thought.

Riona snuck an amused glance at him that said she wasn't believing a word out of his mouth.

Mrs. Wallace harrumphed. "Very well, I see that, Laird McCallum. But such an undertaking . . ." She mumbled the last part under her breath.

"I know you have everything well in hand, Mrs. Wallace," Riona said, a hint of smugness in her voice that Hugh knew was directed at him.

"Ladies," he said with a nod, and retreated.

But once he'd arrived in his study and seen the skepticism of his factor and the unyielding face of Dermot when he lectured on how agriculture was changing, he almost wished he was back with the women.

The men might be resistant, but in the end, his

word was law, and it was time to try some new experiments on McCallum lands.

AFTER a morning spent with Mrs. Wallace, Riona was beginning to think Hugh had tried to save her by not informing her in advance of the council. Instead she was forced to follow Mrs. Wallace throughout the household so the housekeeper could show her how they prepared for all the guests and how the kitchens seemed to explode with extra servants, dozens upon dozens of plucked fowl, and enough pastry dough to line a path back to Stirling. When Riona was granted some relief, she hurried outdoors.

She slowed her pace upon receiving several curious stares. If this had been her household, she would have willingly done even more to prepare. But it seemed . . . cruel to have the staff, and especially Mrs. Wallace, become used to looking to her for guidance, only to learn the truth. They'd hate her soon enough for being the embodiment of monetary salvation, only to take it all away from them again.

But . . . she'd felt wanted, needed, and hadn't been able to resist answering when asked her opinion. She had so little control over her own life that it felt good to make decisions, even small ones.

When she saw little Hamish tied up next to the stables, tongue lolling out beneath the flop of hair on top of his head, she felt her heart lighten just a bit. He barked when he saw her, but she simply sat down on an overturned pail beside him and gave him a frown.

"You aren't in charge, little Hamish," she said sternly. "I won't let you chase me away."

The barking stopped, and he tilted his head as if listening.

"Now if we're going to be friends, you have to learn not to bark when you see me."

She put out her hand again, and he did the same wary sniffing. When he looked away as if disinterested, she briefly ruffled the fur on his head.

She thought of the little dog's owner, and how she'd been questioning Mrs. Wallace about him. It was good that Hugh hadn't overheard *that* part of their conversation. Not that the old woman had been forthcoming. She didn't have much to say except that Brendan's grandmother was her particular friend, and that they had a much nicer cottage on a larger piece of land just past the village. This made Riona feel better, that even if Hugh didn't acknowledge the boy, at least Brendan was being taken care of. But . . . was this how it should be handled, especially when all the residents of the castle watched disapprovingly every meeting between Brendan and Hugh?

Brendan stuck his head out of the wide stable doors, but the tension left his face when he saw her. "Afternoon, my lady."

She smiled. "Hello, Brendan. I think Hamish is starting to like me." She attempted to pet the dog again, but he ducked away. Ruefully, she added, "It looks like I have to take things slow."

Wearing a crooked grin, Brendan wiped his forearm across his sweaty brow.

"Working hard?" she asked.

He nodded and spoke softly. "The marshal took the words of Himself seriously. Never have the stables been so clean." He looked around as if making sure no one overheard them. "I'm little, but even I knew it was bein' done wrong, but what could I say?"

"Of course," she said solemnly, trying not to smile at how seriously he took his work.

"There's another groom being trained," Brendan said, his face reddening. "He's younger than me, so when he didn't do things the new way, our master got real mad at the thought of Himself seeing it. Well . . . I couldn't let that happen. So I said it was *my* fault, thinking Himself might go easier on me than someone else."

Riona's eyes widened at those words. The boy was young and innocent, but . . . did he suspect the truth? He couldn't be ignorant of how people looked at Hugh and him.

Brendan slowly grinned. "Seems I was wrong, and got punished just the same. I was fine with that."

Did being treated like everyone else make him think his suspicions were wrong, and he wasn't Hugh's son? As she started to pet Hamish, who seemed to accept reluctantly, she realized that she could no longer live with this feeling of suspicion. She was going to have to discover the truth, and that was a decision that could have unpredictable results.

CHAPTER 14

Riona thought she had a plan for how to handle Hugh that night, but then he was there in her room, large as life, this time wearing only a black and red plaid belted loosely around his waist and nothing else. Plans faded right out of her mind. A new brick of peat had just caught fire, and it seemed to flicker across his damp skin. He'd obviously bathed again—she'd never met a man so focused on cleanliness, she thought, flustered, as she remembered how good he'd smelled when she'd been curled upon his lap. His black hair had been drawn back in a queue then, but now it swung freely to his shoulders, slightly curled with wetness.

What was wrong with her, that it had been so easy to relax into his arms last night, to listen to his voice, to forget that she didn't belong here, that he'd stolen her away against her will? She was starting to forget her old life of calling upon ladies with

Cat, spending hours every day with Bronwyn, or being the less appealing cousin during dinners and soirees in the evening. She had not been able to compete with Cat's dowry. Of course, Cat's dowry had already been promised to the McCallums the whole time . . . what had the earl been thinking by keeping silent about it?

And then she couldn't distract herself anymore because Hugh was standing right before her, the rope in his hand. She arched her neck to look up at him. He didn't say anything, just stared at her with those gray eyes that sometimes showed the anger of winter ice, and other times glittered silver with passion. They were silver now as if metal touched by fire.

She had to distract him, and hopefully herself. It felt like an urgent need, like she was drowning in a rising tide of desire that she was afraid she could no longer resist.

"I—I talked to Brendan today," she said breathlessly.

He arched one dark brow, and his gaze began a slow path down her body.

"I have questions about him." She sounded anything but determined.

"Ye've told me repeatedly that ye don't want to be involved in my household, with my people. Until ye change your mind about that, he's none of your concern."

His searing gaze lingered at her mouth, her breasts, her thighs, until she felt the heat of a brand on those very places. She was sinking into a smoldering sensation, her body inflamed for his. Gooseflesh rippled across her arms, and her heart was beating erratically. But she couldn't give up so easily. She shook her head, trying to clear it of languor.

"You—you have so many scars." She focused on a ragged one along his ribs. "Tell me how they happened."

He wore a faint smile, just the twist of one corner of his lips—she shouldn't even be looking there. And then he took her hand and touched her finger to the scar on his side. She was startled at the sensation.

"Sheriffmuir," he murmured.

He gently traced her finger back and forth along the rough ridges of the scar, and she shivered at the heat of his skin.

"A redcoat tried to gut me with a bayonet. 'Twas almost a month before my fever abated and I could leave my bed."

She licked her dry lips. "Your recovery surely took many months. What did the physician have you do?"

He ignored her. Still holding her hand, he dragged her finger across the hills of his chest and up to the scar like a cleft in his chin. "A dirk in practice with the men." Next was his upper arm. "Musket ball grazed me when I was fourteen. We were stealing back cattle that belonged to us, and though I'd been ordered not to go, I went anyway."

She had to come up with something to say, even as her gaze was fixed on the hard muscles of his arm. "So . . . who stole your cattle?"

Ignoring her question, he traced her finger down his body, and she gasped when he slid it just inside the folds of his plaid, tugging downward until his hipbone was revealed. She was trembling now, and knew he felt it—just as he had to know it wasn't fear, not anymore, not after how she'd responded to his kisses and caresses these last few nights.

"A thief in Edinburgh tried to slice open my pocket and was too enthusiastic."

And then he was moving her finger again, but on the outside of his plaid, over his hip and lower, to his thigh. He was bending low to manipulate her, leaning so close to her that his hair slid against her head.

When he made her feel the bare skin of his thigh, then began to move her hand higher against his hairy flesh, she gasped, "Hugh!"

He grinned. "Ye don't want to know where the sword cut me?"

She couldn't find words. He held her hand hard to his thigh, and then began to kiss his way down her neck. With a sigh of surrender she closed her eyes and just let herself feel the gentle moistness of his mouth. He parted her dressing gown to reach her collarbone and trace his tongue along it. Her head fell back and she found herself clutching his bare shoulder with one hand to keep from swooning at his feet. She suddenly realized he no longer held her hand in place beneath his plaid, but she hadn't removed it. It was she who lingered there, enjoying his warm skin. She pulled back, and he laughed.

"Sit down, lass. I need to tie ye up before I try to talk ye out of it."

She sank back on the bed, feeling dizzy and almost disappointed. Apparently, he could have talked her out of the rope quite easily but she bit her lip to keep from saying so. He tossed her skirts up to her knees to reveal her ankles, and when he was done, his head came up slowly, on the same level as her trembling knees.

"If ye part your thighs just a bit, I can see heaven," he said softly.

As she pressed them quickly together, he gave another hoarse chuckle.

He didn't rise up above her, but stayed crouched low, kissing his way from her ankles, along her calves, and to her knees. She quivered beneath such simple ministrations, having no idea her skin could burn with his every touch. He didn't try to move her nightshift, but rubbed his cheek along her thigh above it, then lingered on the outside of her hip, before rising up above her and climbing on to the bed over her on all fours. This once would have frightened her, but now she relished feeling feminine and delicate and desired. Through her garment he pressed kisses on her hip and stomach, her rib cage and the very tip of one breast, where he lingered to torment her with light kisses until he gently bit her and she cried out.

She caught his head between her hands. "Hugh . . . please." A mindless need had taken hold of her, made her uncaring about something so unimportant as propriety. She now existed somewhere beyond herself. If he would have untied her and sunk between her thighs, she would have let him, anything to stop this desperate ache.

But he didn't untie her, just slid to one side and began to caress her. He took her mouth with a fierce possession she thrilled in, as she met his tongue with her own and explored his mouth just as greedily. His hands began to work magic on her body, fingers trailing across her breasts, teasing, plucking, caressing until she shuddered. Then he took those light touches farther down, and she willed him not to stop, although she couldn't quite use the words. The tips of his fingers brushed between her thighs, and with a moan she parted them as much as the rope and her nightshift allowed her. Every stroke of his hand was a sharp pleasure-pain that only made her want more. She writhed and gasped, and when his mouth left hers to suckle her breast, her body hovered on the edge of oblivion. He'd awakened her to passion, and she felt she'd never be the same. She plummeted over that edge at last, shuddering as the pleasure consumed her.

Dazed, she opened her eyes. He was seated beside her, leaning over, one arm braced across her body as he watched her. She thought she wouldn't be able to meet his gaze out of embarrassment, but that wasn't so. They studied each other as if something had shifted between them, but really, it hadn't; it couldn't. And she felt a terrible sorrow well up inside her. She covered her face with both hands, forcing back tears as much as hiding them. Hugh said nothing, and she couldn't explain this to him. Let him think she was just a stubborn girl who wanted to pick her own husband, who could continue these supposed lies out of spite. He didn't know her, even if he knew what to do with her body.

He slid down to lie beside her, maneuvering her like a doll until he could spoon behind her and still hold her close. She felt his erection against her backside, but he didn't do anything about it. He fell asleep before she did, and she could only watch the dying fire and wonder what she could do to stop herself from falling in love with her kidnapper, her cousin's betrothed.

HUGH was distracted all the next day, when he should have been focusing on what needed to be prepared for the council of gentlemen. He had reports to read from his factor, treasurer, and quartermaster, but every time he tried to concentrate, his mind returned to Riona.

Riona, who'd gloried in a woman's pleasure until it had moved her to tears. He'd known they weren't happy tears, much as he'd wished it so. She was still struggling against her future, against him, and he was running out of ideas to make her accept what must happen. He wanted to call her stubborn, willful, even blinded by her need to decide her own destiny for perhaps the first time in her life.

She couldn't change her future. Couldn't she see that, although he was chief, this household would be hers to run? What more could a woman ask for?

And once she accepted her life, he could answer her questions about Brendan. That made his thoughts veer to the young groom, who'd bravely taken the mild punishment meant for another. Hugh had admired him even as he'd been exasperated. The boy's grandmother had done an impressive job raising him.

But did Brendan know the truth about their relationship? And how was Hugh supposed to tell him?

Throughout the day, peddlers set up booths in the courtyard for the gentlemen and their wives visiting from other villages and estates. They displayed wine and fine fabrics, embroidery silks and jewelry. The atmosphere was as festive as a country

fair, but after dinner at midday, the men settled into
the great hall for the real work. Hugh heard reports
from his tacksmen on the leases and sub-tenants
of his properties, the taxes collected over the last
few years, reports on recent harvests. And then
he presented detailed explanations of the English
farming methods he wanted to adopt, and just like
in the nearby farms, there was a great outcry over
leaving behind the old ways.

Riona stood at the back of the great hall and listened long after many of the other women had gone
back to the peddlers, or gathered in the withdrawing room to sew and gossip. Most of the women's
conversation was in Gaelic, although they'd been
kind enough to speak English in her presence. Their
curiosity was great, and they asked many questions
about growing up among Sassenachs, not realizing
that her mother was English. And what could she
tell them—the truth? No, that would garner suspicion. She was a Duff, and though they were kind,
there was also a wariness and a skepticism over everything she said.

Donald was in the hall, since he was the tacks-
man of a small parcel of land with subleases beneath him. Riona made certain to ask about his
mother, and was glad to hear her spirits had improved.

During the council, Riona listened to Hugh talk,
understanding only the rare word here and there. It

frustrated her to know Latin and French, but nothing of her own father's language—how had she not seen that?

When Samuel walked past her, she called his name, asking, "Is there any news I should know? Are they as against Hugh's ideas as they seem?"

Samuel stopped beside her and looked over the hall, where men talked fiercely in corners whenever Hugh paused. "'Tis going as expected. Nothing can change overnight, and he knows that. He's begun a plan to work on several abandoned rigs of land, so that by this time next year, the gentlemen will see how much better the yield is."

"Oh, well, that was smart of him," she said reluctantly.

Samuel eyed her and shook his head. "Is that approval I hear?"

She stiffened. "I can approve of trying to better a harvest so people don't starve, can I not? It does not mean I have to approve of *Hugh*."

Hugh, the man who controlled her body and sometimes her soul, the man who could make her forget herself with just a touch. If she hadn't had her legs tied together, she might even now be worried she was with child.

Samuel studied her with curiosity, and she looked away, unable to meet his gaze.

"There is another announcement he's made," Samuel said. "He's going on a journey to all of his lands and villages sometime soon. The gentlemen will open their homes to welcome him, and prepare the lands for his inspection."

Riona tried to contain her excitement. "How long will he be gone?"

"Considering he plans to take you with him, does it matter?"

She exhaled loudly, then was distracted by the sudden applause and cheering. "They're happy we're imposing on their households?"

" 'Tis a great honor to house the chief, of course, although first the gentlemen will return for the ceremony officially naming Hugh the chief of the Mc-Callums."

She waved a hand. "A mere formality."

"But an important, sacred ritual that's been in our clan over five hundred—"

"Is that why they're cheering?"

"Nay," he said with a sigh. "Alasdair has been named war chief."

Riona stood on tiptoes, glad most of the men were still seated on benches facing the dais. She was able to see Hugh with a hand on his foster brother's shoulder, Alasdair looking surprised and proud, and on the other side of Hugh, Dermot with an expression of stone.

"I hope Dermot doesn't represent too many disappointed people," Riona said quietly.

"Do ye care?" Samuel asked.

She widened her eyes. "Well, I don't want warfare. That could spill over to my own clan, could it not?"

"I'm glad ye're so concerned about the Duffs," Samuel said, amusement laced through his voice.

She felt like elbowing him, but restrained herself. She saw Dermot lean over and speak to a man on his other side, and together they both watched Hugh impassively.

"Dermot could make a lot of trouble if he wanted," Riona murmured.

Samuel gave her another surprised look. She *did* care; she didn't want to, but she couldn't help it. Yet she had to put those feelings aside and remind herself that Dermot's discontent might be her chance to escape. Putting the truth of her kidnapping in the man's hands would certainly change Hugh's command of his clan, but she tried not to think about that. It was beginning to make her feel like a traitor to Hugh—which was ridiculous, because she'd been *kidnapped*!

Samuel explained Hugh's final announcement about organizing a large hunt to benefit the clan. There was much cheering and whisky drinking that lasted through supper and into the night, as musicians entertained the crowd. Hugh persuaded Riona to try a sip of their precious whisky, and all the men roared at the expression on her face as she downed the vile stuff. It did warm the belly, but that was the only good thing she could say.

Riona retired well before the gentlemen in the great hall, and she could hear their drunken singing long into the night. She didn't sleep easily herself, wondering how she'd handle a drunken Hugh wielding a rope, but he never came to her bedroom.

Many of their guests stayed an extra couple nights, distracting Hugh until late each evening. Just when Riona was growing tired of being on her best behavior, sewing with the ladies, feeling excluded by the language, they all went home. She thought she'd have some breathing room but then more visitors were announced.

Hugh's mother and sister were spotted near Loch Voil, and were winding their way up the path to Larig Castle. Riona was with Hugh at dinner when this was announced. They glanced at each other, her full of uncertainty. To her surprise, he didn't quite hide his own wariness. That made her actually look forward to meeting the woman who'd taken him away from his drunken father, yet still inspired such antipathy.

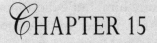HAPTER 15

Hugh stood in the courtyard waiting for his family's arrival, Riona at his side, little bothering to hide her curiosity. He could usually hide his own emotions from everyone, but with Riona, she seemed to see through the mask he'd learned to don long ago. Would she comprehend his wariness? Not about Maggie, of course, but his mother, that was another story . . .

Only a half-dozen riders finally came through the gatehouse, which annoyed him no end. He'd told Maggie over and over again that the several-day journey from Edinburgh could be full of dangerous men who thought nothing of kidnapping wealthy women—

And then he heard the voice in his head: *He* was a kidnapper of women. And money was even involved. But it was his by right, he reminded himself forcefully.

Riona had said nothing to anyone about the way she'd come to Larig Castle, and he wondered if that would change, now that his family was there to help pressure him. Little did Riona know, there was nothing his mother could do to impact him, not ever again. But Maggie . . . he had a soft spot for his younger sister, and been her guardian against the worst of their father's drunken outbursts. While Hugh had spent much of each of the last seven years in London, she'd been the one he'd written to, whom he'd missed the most.

"When did you last see your family?" Riona asked, as the guards dismounted and went to assist the women.

"Earlier this summer after my father died."

Her expression sobered. "Of course. Forgive me."

He frowned at her. "You have nothing to ask forgiveness for."

"But I thought your arrival with me was the first time you'd been here in years."

"It was. I was not here for the burial but I saw my sister and mother in Edinburgh later."

Hugh seldom stayed in the same room with his mother for long. At least she had not put on a show of mourning, but had been solemn with respect for Hugh himself, as the heir.

And then he smiled, for Maggie was running toward him. He scooped her up in a hug that made her groan.

"You're crushing my ribs, brother!" she said in Gaelic. When he put her down, she smiled at Riona. "Lady Catriona, how wonderful to meet you at last!"

At Riona's bewildered expression, Maggie repeated it in English, then impulsively hugged her. It was good to see Maggie looking happy. Hugh thought it had been a few years since she'd been the carefree girl he remembered, but then she had had to deal with problems few could imagine.

Maggie had dark, wavy hair like his, and she wore it pulled back to the nape of her neck under a jaunty straw hat tied beneath her chin with ribbons. She wore a plaid shawl to combat the breeze of a Highland summer over a dark green riding habit.

"Lady Catriona, may I present my sister, Maggie McCallum. Maggie, my betrothed."

"Please call me Riona," said Riona, smiling politely.

The two young women took each other's hands, and Hugh found himself hoping that at last Riona would find a friend, someone who could help her see that life as the wife of a Highland chief wouldn't be so bad.

But he hoped Riona wouldn't confide quite everything to his sister . . .

And then his mother approached sedately. She wore a frilly cap over her gray hair, and her gown was dull in color, as if still in mourning for the man who'd destroyed their family.

Riona curtsied to her as Hugh made the introductions. "Mother, this is Lady Catriona Duff. Riona, my mother, Lady McCallum."

"Lady Riona," his mother said in a formal voice, even though her eyes drank in the sight of Riona as if she were a lifeline back to Hugh.

Nothing could be that for Hugh, not after all the secrets and lies.

"So you met your betrothed at last," Maggie said, eyeing Riona from head to toe. "He has waited a long time, my lady."

Riona blushed, then glanced at Hugh with a worry that hopefully only he could see.

"So how did your first meeting go?" Maggie continued. "It must have been tense."

Hugh was tempted to jump in and answer, used to being in control, but he just gave Riona a smile.

"It was *very* tense," Riona said at last. "I—I had heard nothing about the marriage contract at all."

Maggie's smile faded. "Oh, how dreadful that your family didn't prepare ye." Then she glanced at her brother. "But ye're here with us at Larig Castle, so I'm hoping that means ye see ye've been blessed."

Riona could feel herself going pale, the blood draining away. Blessed? To feel so conflicted all the time? To not even be able to hate one's captor? And here she had the perfect opportunity to embarrass him before his family, and she couldn't even do it.

What did that say about her deepening feelings for him?

She told herself that it would be unwise to make enemies of them, because of course they would take his side. But she could still use this time to understand Hugh, to figure out the mystery of Brendan and help him if possible. Hugh's family must know the truth.

Hugh gestured her to precede him up the stairs to the entrance of the great hall. He took the arms of his mother and sister and followed behind. Riona glanced over her shoulder, to see him talking to Maggie, while his mother remained silent and pale. This was the woman who'd tried to save him from his father's drunken behavior. Wouldn't that inspire some sort of closeness or at least loyalty? Apparently not, for she'd never seen Hugh behave so coolly to one of his own clan, let alone his mother.

In the great hall, new platters of hot food were being brought out to serve the chief's family. They all sat down on the dais to eat, on display for those gentlemen and servants who watched closely. Maggie was seated to Hugh's left, and Lady McCallum was seated on Riona's right. Hugh spent much of the meal chatting with his sister about friends they both knew in Edinburgh. He spoke in English and kept drawing Riona in, which she appreciated, but then there was his mother, silent and withdrawn on her right. Riona couldn't ignore the woman.

"Lady McCallum," Riona said, "I am sorry for your mourning."

Lady McCallum blinked weary gray eyes, dull and tired next to her son's vivid coloring. "Mourning? My dear, in my opinion, the McCallum did not die soon enough."

Riona inhaled with surprise, as both Hugh and Maggie stared with almost the same impassive expressions at their mother. Riona noticed Maggie's eyes again, two different colors as Hugh had warned her, one blue, one green. The effect was . . . disconcerting, intriguing.

Then the siblings returned to their conversation.

"Oh," Riona said uneasily. "Hugh has told me some of his difficulty with his father, and that you took Maggie and him away to protect them. That was very brave of you."

Lady McCallum's eyes really focused on her then. "Thank ye," she murmured, then bent her head and took another tiny bite.

She was already thin, and if she didn't start eating more than that . . . And this wasn't mourning? Or was she mourning the loss of something else? Riona wondered, glancing at Hugh with speculation. He met her gaze impassively, giving nothing away.

While their chambers were being prepared after

the departure of so many guests—Riona realized she now occupied the room Lady McCallum had once called her own—Hugh brought his mother and sister to the privacy of the chief's dressing room. He relaxed away from the great hall, and Riona was able to see a playful, even tender side to him that showed how much he loved his sister.

And through it all, their mother sat alone and looked out the window.

Riona didn't want to care, but she'd always been too curious for her own good. She offered Lady McCallum an embroidery frame, but the woman declined.

"The trip simply exhausted me," she said in a quiet voice. "But thank ye."

"I'm certain Mrs. Wallace will have your room ready for you to rest as soon as possible," Riona said.

Riona worked on the simple embroidery for one of Hugh's shirts and thought of her own family. Perhaps they'd come across just as troubled as the McCallums. Like Hugh and Maggie, she felt close to her own sister, but her parents . . . they were another matter.

"How was the journey north, Riona?" Maggie asked.

"Long, although your brother was thoughtful enough to use a coach for most of it." She deliberately avoided Hugh's gaze.

"But a coach on some of these roads?" Maggie shuddered. "I prefer riding a horse."

Hugh said, "Ye wouldn't have said the same were ye caught in a few rainstorms."

"True." Maggie turned again to Riona. "I do believe you and I must have met as children, because I well remember your brother."

There was an edge to her voice now, and Riona couldn't help wondering about the McCallums and secrets. Maggie's unusual eyes seemed to be trying to see deep inside her, and it gave her an unsettled feeling.

"I was seldom in Scotland," Riona said. "Owen, being the heir, was here more often with the earl." Not her brother, not her father. She was feeling on edge herself, realizing she had her own secrets. She wanted to blurt them out, but caution stopped her. She was the enemy here. When they all found out Hugh had captured the wrong bride . . . "I'm curious how you and Owen knew each other, considering our clans have not always been on the best of terms."

Maggie and Hugh exchanged an unreadable glance.

"I tried to forge a friendship with the countess," Lady McCallum said, "for the sake of both our clans. 'Tis the reason your marriage contract even came about." She shot a concerned glance at Hugh, as if she expected him to retort.

Of course there'd been a time in his life when he'd wanted to choose his own bride regardless of the contract, Riona remembered. Had that been the reason he and his mother didn't get along?

"Whose idea was it to stipulate that the whisky land be shared?" Riona asked.

"There would have been no contract otherwise," Hugh said coolly. "Your father would not grant ye and your tocher to a McCallum without a great offer in return. Sharing the land for all these years has put a strain our own ability to profit from the whisky. But you Duffs were able to create your own recipe and succeed beyond what ye'd done before."

"And marriage is all about an exchange of goods, isn't it?" she said, bitterness creeping into her voice.

Maggie and Lady McCallum looked at her far too closely.

"It hasn't been easy for Riona," Hugh said to his family. "She's a Duff, who was taught to disavow the country of her birth, who doesn't speak our language. Imagine yourselves alone with another clan, knowing no one, never having heard that your family offered ye to settle an old feud. She's been taken away from everything she knew, everything she thought her future would be."

Riona blinked quickly, feeling the sting of tears she refused to shed. But she couldn't look away from Hugh.

"Well, it seems ye both have forged a beginning,"

Maggie said hesitantly. "Ye're not spitting hatred at each other."

Riona gave a hesitant smile, then bent her head over her embroidery. No, she didn't hate Hugh, though she once had. She was worried she felt too much for the man in this very impossible situation . . .

"Have ye made plans for a wedding?" Lady McCallum asked.

"Not yet," Hugh said briskly.

"But Lady Riona is housed in your rooms," his mother continued, confusion wrinkling her brow. "Is it a trial marriage of sorts?"

"No," Riona said firmly.

"Oh." Lady McCallum continued to frown at her son, who ignored her.

A naughty voice inside Riona wondered what they'd say if they knew she and Hugh were bundling . . .

Soon Mrs. Wallace came to escort their guests away, leaving Hugh and Riona alone. She studied his broad back where he stood at the window, hands linked behind as he stared out. She imagined he might not be seeing anything.

"Your kindness to my mother is appreciated, but not truly necessary," he said brusquely.

She stared at him. "I am not blind. I see that you and your mother have problems, but they aren't *my* problems. I was not raised to be disrespectful for no reason. Of course, if you *want* to give me a reason . . ."

"So ye're saying ye'll be my bride?" he countered.

And they were back to their stalemate again.

AFTER supper that night, the clan bard sang a long song celebrating the McCallum past. Thankfully Hugh's mother had retired, and he was able to sit with his sister and enjoy her eagerness to hear the old song. Occasionally he glanced to where Riona and Dermot sat together. Dermot was obviously translating for her, but that didn't make Hugh feel any better.

Maggie glanced past him at the couple, then back at Hugh. "Are ye troubled about something?"

"Nay, 'tis nothing."

"Considering Dermot is your longtime companion and now tanist, 'twould seem you would smile rather than frown when ye look at him. Or are ye frowning at Riona?"

"What do you think of her?" he asked, ignoring her question for one of his own.

Maggie cocked her head. "I've only spoken with her as an adult, and I have no memory of her as a child, although I think I should, if what Mother says is true."

"But she claims she was seldom ever in Scotland."

"Claims? Ye don't believe her?"

"A poor choice of words on my part. I knew before I went to England to find her that she'd rarely been here. I wanted to know what I was facing with the Earl of Aberfoyle."

"Seems wise to be prepared," she mused, though she still studied him closely.

Hugh looked at Riona again, then asked his sister, "Do ye . . . *see* anything about her?"

Maggie's open, amused expression was suddenly shuttered as if a lamp was turned off. "I don't do that anymore, Hugh. I've told ye that."

"Ye've said that, but . . . has your gut agreed?"

"My gut?" she echoed stiffly, her smile obviously forced. "A man has a gut, a woman has . . . intuition."

"So now ye've the same intuition as every other woman?"

She lowered her voice. "Hugh, don't do this. Ye ken I want no part of the strange gift I've been given."

"Ye used to call it a God-given gift."

"But it hurt me one too many times. It became a curse. I found a way to ignore it, to push the dreams away from me. I'm seldom troubled anymore by feelings and emotions that are baffling and in the end, useless."

"Not always useless. Remember the little boy that everyone feared had fallen in the loch and drowned? *You* knew he had not; *you* led the search party that found him huddled beneath a rocky cliff."

Her cheeks pinkened even as she exhaled slowly. "They would have continued the search without me. His parents were desperate and weren't about to assume he was dead."

" 'Twas winter, and if he'd have been out there all night . . ." Hugh let his words trail off. But his sister didn't look any happier.

" 'Twas a rare case. Mostly 'twas just my dreams giving me a fright. What good is that? Most of the time I felt like I helped no one, and all I received were wary looks and people warding me away like I had the evil eye."

"Ye often got us away from our father before the worst of his drinking."

She shrugged. "Not difficult to notice when *that* was about to happen. Subtle, he was not."

"Och, I don't like to see ye disregarding your gifts."

"I'm not. I'm just trying to forget about a time when I thought I was better than everyone else, when I was so arrogant I thought God had gifted me alone."

"Ye can say we all have our gifts, and maybe we do, but yours—"

"I'm finished with it, Hugh. I won't be a seer people look at with a sense of doom."

"So ye sensed nothing when ye met Riona."

Hugh was watching closely, and he saw the curious glance at his betrothed that Maggie couldn't quite hide.

"Nothing," she insisted. "And I never did 'sense' things. I saw them in dreams."

He let it go—for now.

"So . . . ye've put her in Mother's former bedroom?" Maggie asked, her curiosity returning.

"Riona's my betrothed, deserving of the best chamber in the castle."

"And she can be close at hand."

That conclusion was obvious, and certainly not the result of second sight.

"So ye have to work that hard to win her?" Maggie prodded. "She didn't swoon at the sight of your fine face?"

Hugh took a deep sip of whisky and grimaced. "She's a stubborn woman. Ye well ken how I took it when I found out I had no choice in my betrothed."

"Almost got yourself killed, several times over."

"She has that to work through, she does."

"So she's not doing herself harm trying to get away from ye?"

Hugh arched a brow at her sister.

She chuckled. "I did not think all was perfectly well, and ye need no second sight for that."

"I came up with a plan that seems to be working."

"And what's that? I might want to use it myself some day."

"Nay." He spoke in his firm chief's voice, forgetting whom he was talking to.

"Are ye saying nay to *me*? And what are ye doing that I should not?"

"We're bundling."

Maggie coughed on the wine she'd just sipped, drawing the attention of those at the dais.

"Shall I send for something different to drink, Mistress Maggie?" Riona called.

"Please, I'm just Maggie, and nay, I simply swallowed wrong, I did."

Hugh noticed that Maggie couldn't even meet Riona's gaze. "Your face is red. If ye start laughing—"

"I won't, I won't. Just . . . just give me a moment." She took another sip of her wine, a smaller one this time, then wiped the tears from her eyes. "Och, Hugh, ye always make me laugh."

" 'Tis a serious thing, Maggie. Riona and I don't know each other, and I spend my days learning to be chief since Father kept tight hold of the reins."

"Aye, and ye weren't here either, don't forget. Not by our own say at first, of course. That was all Mother."

They both briefly sobered, and again, he caught his sister's curious glance.

"Riona and I have no time alone together, and I thought . . . bundling is an old custom. Why should I not try it when nothing else seemed to work?"

She leaned toward him and asked eagerly, "And has it worked?"

He cleared his throat uncomfortably.

"And the rope—that helps ye talk rather than kiss?"

"Well, the point is, ye can kiss. Ye just cannot . . . This is far too uncomfortable to discuss with my own sister."

"But 'tis something I should allow if I were to decide to marry?"

"That's not necessary—"

She arched a brow with interest. "Truly? Ye're saying 'tis fine for you, but not for me?"

"I shouldn't be discussing it—'tis a private matter."

Maggie smothered her giggles behind her hand, and Riona glanced at them with interest. He nodded to his betrothed and didn't mind so much when she returned to her conversation with Dermot.

Hugh had hoped his sister would use her gift to confirm he was doing the right thing wooing Riona; instead, he only had his own judgment to go by, and if that was true—

The bundling wasn't about to stop. He thought about it all day, imagined what he was going to do to her, and how she was going to respond. He felt like a youth pursuing his first love.

But Riona wasn't the first girl he'd tried to marry; he refused to allow a relationship to end that badly ever again.

CHAPTER 16

When Hugh came to her room that night, Riona told herself she would be ready. She had a half-dozen questions to ask—even though she knew coming up with them was partly a distraction just for herself. She'd spent the evening in the great hall watching Hugh with his sister, and had been far too fascinated. She'd never seen him so talkative and cheerful and expressive. Before tonight, he'd seemed a man very restrained in his emotions from long practice. And that might still be true, but beneath, he was a man who'd once known how to laugh, who'd been an excellent brother, who knew how to treat his mother with some respect, even though something had clearly happened to alter things between them.

Thinking about this helped her forget the last time he tied her up, but nothing could distract her for long. Her body craved that experience again;

she'd lain awake each night when the gentlemen had monopolized Hugh and regretted that he would not be coming to her. She was wanton, she was wicked, she was losing the battle with her conscience. This would only bring her misery—she could never be Hugh's bride.

But when he arrived, all those thoughts fled, and the hot yearning seemed to pool in the depths of her belly and make her tremble. He stared at her like he was starving and she was his only food. As if in a dream, he came across the room toward her, pulling off his shirt and dropping it. The expanse of his chest made her breath catch. He'd replaced the plaid he'd worn earlier with breeches, so he'd taken some care against the risks. She had to do the same.

"So—I like your sister," she said brightly, breathlessly.

He came to a stop a foot away from the bed, and his focused stare faded. "What?"

He sounded as dazed as she felt, which she tried to take strength from. She had to keep control, because he was under no such constraint. He wanted her to lose herself in him, to deny him the need for the ropes, to make her his wife even with a trial marriage.

"You and Maggie seem like you've always been close," she continued.

"Aye. Ye have a sister; ye understand. I'd do anything for her."

"Did you help each other avoid your father when he was drunk?"

He frowned, and the dazed look began to fade, only to be replaced by consternation. "Of course. 'Twas my duty to protect her. Father didn't try to beat her, but . . ."

"You worried he might, since he beat you."

Hugh didn't answer.

"She was only your duty?"

His dark brows came together swiftly. "Of course not. I love her."

"Then you know how important love is, how difficult it must be when people don't have that within a marriage."

Rolling his eyes, he ran a hand through his long hair. "Riona, we haven't had enough time together to know—"

"And we cannot, Hugh. I cannot marry you, and I won't be your mistress, and that's the only way this"—she gestured between the two of them—"is heading."

He just stared at her, his expression blank, as if he was going to keep concealing anything he wanted from her.

"Your sister's eyes are fascinating. Do superstitious people stare at her?"

He opened his mouth, then closed it and turned away from her, slamming the door behind him.

Riona slumped back on the bed and covered

her face with both hands. Disappointment surged through her, and she almost—almost—went to him. But if she did that, her resistance would be over. He could get her with child, and when proof of the truth came out, she'd be as alone as Agnes had been.

There'd be no husband for her, no children. This solitary grief for the life she could never have was for the best. So why did tears continue to stream down her face?

HUGH departed with the men at midmorning on the promised hunt, though it was obvious he regretted leaving his sister just after she'd arrived. Riona stood beside Maggie and watched the mounted group ride slowly across the courtyard. Dermot and Samuel remained behind with some of the older men—none of whom were happy about it. But Alasdair was going with Hugh, and Riona hoped they could return to the friendship they'd once had.

Hugh saluted Riona and Maggie, but he didn't smile. He gave Riona a piercing look that warned her not to attempt to escape. She only lifted her chin and gave him a cool look back.

Riona found herself quite monopolized the rest of the day by Hugh's sister, who seemed delighted that her brother would be marrying at last. There wasn't a moment for Riona to corner Dermot and try again to win his regard, partly because she was worried how it would look to Maggie. Riona knew she shouldn't care, that the truth coming out was more important, that Maggie was going to be hurt regardless, but . . . she felt like a coward.

Lady McCallum spent the whole day in her room, and at breakfast the next morning, Riona questioned Maggie about it.

"Is your mother resting after the journey?" Riona asked.

"I believe so," Maggie said. "But she's not the most social of women anymore. She's behaving as subdued as if in mourning, though she lived apart from my father for many years before his death."

"Perhaps there are better memories she is mourning?"

"If so, I never heard them. He had control of himself when we were very young, although my earliest memories are still of him drinking heartily at every meal, becoming more and more vocal because of it. But in battle people feared him. In some ways Hugh resembles him, with his height and strength."

"Sometimes I think Hugh drinks a bit too much, like his father," Riona said hesitantly, then added, "But I've never seen him out of control, and he doesn't yell."

Maggie's lips parted as if Riona had given her the greatest shock. "I cannot believe that Hugh gets drunk often. Everyone here drinks the whisky."

"That's true. I don't mean to impugn his character." She felt a little sick inside, knowing her worry was making Hugh look bad in his sister's eyes.

Maggie nodded, through her frown still lingered. "I ken these last ten years have been difficult for Hugh, forced to be away from the clan by attending university, and then being an MP. Did the clan . . . accept him upon his return?"

"Yes, of course, but there was—is—a wariness. I imagine he needs to prove himself and this hunt will probably help. He trains with the men on the training yard, which certainly shows his skill, but it's not the same as what you do in the spur of the moment."

"True. He never stopped training. His skill with the sword was legendary in London."

"He does not speak much of his time there, and says Scottish MPs were not treated well."

Maggie nodded. "'Twas a scandal that the British government—of which Scotland is supposed to be an equal part—would allow some of its politicians to be degraded by others. But Hugh did his duty and bided his time until our father's death. Now 'tis *his* time, his turn to prove himself. With you at his side, I don't see how he can go wrong," she added, smiling.

Riona's own smile was tight, and she broke apart a loaf of bread in her hands. When they all found out that Hugh had left behind the correct bride, that he'd jeopardized the contract, the dowry—but especially the land—she didn't know what would happen.

But she had something to accomplish before this revelation, a decision she'd made that could have consequences for everyone involved. She wasn't backing down.

"Do you think your mother would like to walk outside with us?" Riona asked. "It might do her good to have fresh air. And there's a bit of sun between the clouds."

"A wonderful idea. I'll ask her."

Riona half expected Lady McCallum to decline, but within a half hour, she came downstairs with Maggie, her lace cap as wilted as her spirits.

Riona kept their pace through the courtyard slow, and she encouraged Lady McCallum with questions about how things had been done in the past. An occasional servant greeted them, with good cheer for Maggie, and with more reserve for the chief's widow. Riona kept them moving steadily, through the archway that led to the lower courtyard. There were a few gentlemen left in residence, and none on the training yard, but she could see watchmen on the battlements and grooms moving about within the stables. Most of the horses would be gone, and she'd heard Hugh give explicit instructions for a thorough cleaning.

There was Hamish the terrier, tied up outside,

and Riona took a deep breath in relief and expectation.

Maggie practically squealed and dropped to her knees. "How adorable ye are, wee little doggie."

"His name's Hamish, and he's not always friendly—"

But Hamish put his little paws on Maggie's thighs and would have licked her face if he could have reached.

"I guess I'm the only one he doesn't like," Riona said dryly.

Hamish glanced at her but refrained from growling.

"Why is the creature tied?" Lady McCallum asked, her voice already filled with fatigue though the day had barely begun. "I see other dogs running loose."

"Only the elderly, who couldn't go on the hunt," Maggie said.

"Hugh has given him to one of the grooms to care for," Riona explained. "The boy's name is—"

But she got no farther, for Brendan came out of the shadow of the stables and eyed them all with interest. His thin body, bony with the promise of future strength, already looked as if his shirtsleeves were too short.

"Afternoon, Lady Riona," he said warily.

Lady McCallum gasped, and her pale face drained of any remaining color. Riona tensed in case she had to support her during a swoon. But except for laying a hand on her daughter's arm, she seemed to right herself.

"Good day, Brendan," Riona said pleasantly. "This is the chief's mother, Lady McCallum, and his sister, Mistress Maggie."

Brendan seemed to stiffen, but he eyed the two women boldly.

"You are Brendan McCallum, grandson of Claire?" Lady McCallum asked, her voice slow and measured.

Brendan nodded, even as Hamish jumped and put his front paws on Brendan's leg. "Aye, my lady. Ye know my granny?"

"I do," Lady McCallum answered, "or I used to, before ye were born."

Riona studied Lady McCallum—was she this boy's granny, too?

Maggie regarded Brendan with bright-eyed interest. "Are ye not young to be working at the castle, Brendan?"

The boy shrugged and scratched the floppy fur on Hamish's head. "I like it. Granny doesn't need me so much anymore. She's hired a cotter to help with the grain and our cows."

Who was paying for that? Riona wondered. But she thought she knew, and it made her feel a little better.

"How nice that ye bring your dog," Maggie added.

"Himself gave it to me." And now Brendan seemed to be watching them.

Lady McCallum frowned, and Maggie glanced at her uncertainly.

Riona thought that their behavior was the best proof of Brendan's paternity that she'd seen so far. Brendan excused himself to go back to work, and Lady McCallum turned and headed for the upper courtyard alone. Riona and Maggie followed behind.

Riona took a deep breath. "Were you here during Hugh's recovery after the battle at Sheriffmuir?"

Maggie's smile faded. "I was. 'Twas a terrible time in Scotland. Defeat is a bitter thing, and many of the redcoats were cruel in their victory." She glanced hastily at Riona. "Forgive me. Ye have English relatives, I ken—"

"But I'm not a redcoat," Riona said wryly.

"Are people here treating ye differently because of your English relations?"

"I've heard the word Sassenach a time or two, but not out of cruelty. Being . . . with Hugh makes people respectful, of course. They're respectful to both of us, since he *is* the new chief, but I think trust is harder to earn."

Maggie nodded.

And I can't trust you, Riona thought. "Hugh has implied to me that his time here during his recovery was when the final break with his father happened. Would you tell me about it?"

"He has not?" Maggie asked, a frown growing.

"He's told me there was someone he wished to marry, but couldn't because of the contract. I also know there was a woman named Agnes who died. Were they the same person?"

After a long moment, Maggie spoke apologetically. "I think ye should talk to Hugh about this."

Riona sighed. "Of course. Forgive my curiosity."

"I understand. Ye're about to marry a man ye didn't know a few weeks ago. But . . . 'tis Hugh's story to tell."

Maggie glanced over her shoulder back the way they'd come, and Riona wondered if she was looking for Brendan. Riona silently berated herself— she should have waited to initiate this discussion. Maggie didn't know her at all. Or maybe she didn't want to show her brother in such a poor light.

As Lady McCallum ascended the stairs to the entrance to the great hall, Maggie caught Riona's arm. "Wait a moment, could ye? Let's go sit in the kitchen garden and talk."

Riona tried not to get her hopes up—Maggie had already ended the discussion about Hugh's past. But once they were seated side by side on a little bench overlooking the greenery of carrots and turnips, she watched Hugh's sister expectantly.

"I know this is a strange request," Maggie began slowly, "but how is Owen?"

She didn't use his honorary title as the heir, Viscount Duncraggan, which implied a familiarity that surprised Riona. Maggie thought Owen was Riona's brother, of course, rather than her cousin, but still . . . "He is well, last I knew, cutting a dashing figure in London while still attending his favorite science lectures."

Maggie nodded, but didn't smile. "That makes sense," she murmured.

"You know him? I did not think our families had intermingled much once the contract was agreed upon."

Maggie gave her a piercing stare, and Riona wondered if she'd made a mistake.

"Well, there's a little history to that," Maggie explained. "When Hugh discovered at thirteen that his future was decided, he . . . had trouble with it."

"I know. He told me about his reckless behavior, and the incident with the redcoats."

Maggie's tense shoulders relaxed. "Oh, good. Our mother was desperate to help him, and she decided to renew contact with Lady Aberfoyle, the better for our families to know each other. Though your mother never returned from England, as ye know, Owen and your father occasionally did. We had several dinners together. Very uneventful."

Uneventful? Riona thought, her curiosity aroused. If it was so uneventful, she wondered why Maggie would be asking about Owen after all these years.

Maggie cleared her throat. "I just . . . wondered how he was doing. So he's not married?"

The latter was said with such false brightness that Riona had to withhold a smile. "No, he's still unspoken for."

Maggie nodded and rose suddenly. "I hope he finds happiness soon."

"Are *you* still unspoken for? Hugh hasn't mentioned a betrothal for you."

"I am yet quite the independent young lady of Edinburgh," Maggie said with determination. "I possess a tocher and another small inheritance from my mother. I have time to decide my future."

"I'm glad."

But as they headed into the castle, Riona continued to wonder if there was more to the story about Maggie and Owen. Apparently the Duffs and the McCallums were connected in more ways than one . . .

"Let me teach ye Gaelic," Maggie suddenly said.

Startled, Riona eyed her.

"I saw how difficult it was for ye last night," Maggie continued. "Ye have Hugh or Samuel to translate, of course, but wouldn't ye like to be able to understand some of it on your own?"

"I would," Riona said slowly, her certainty growing. "It is a kind offer I gladly accept."

Maggie clapped her hands together. "Good. I know not how long we'll be here, but I'll help as much as I can." She twined her arm through Riona's. "This will be fun. I've always wanted a sister!"

Riona's "fun" drained away with those words.

THAT afternoon, a tailor arrived from Stirling to make Riona several gowns. All of it had been arranged for by Hugh, and both Lady McCallum and Maggie loved reminding Riona of his thoughtfulness. And it *was* thoughtful, she knew. Over the next two days, Riona posed for fittings and learned Gaelic words for basic items around the household. Maggie discovered Riona could play the spinet, begged her to play for Lady McCallum, only to make the older woman cry. Maggie privately confessed that her mother's melancholy was growing worse with every year, but her mother wouldn't speak of the reason for it. Riona privately thought it was something more than her estrangement with Hugh—although maybe it was related.

On the third day since Hugh's departure, Riona decided to ride to the village with Maggie and Samuel and call upon the Rosses. Samuel had acquiesced easily, and Maggie was excited to meet up with all the villagers she hadn't seen in a while.

As they rode past the alehouse, Riona was happy to see the elder Mrs. Ross sitting outside, watching her grandchildren play. She smiled upon seeing Riona and rose to her feet unassisted.

"Lady Riona," the old woman cried, waving. "Look at me, outside with the wee bairns."

Riona and Maggie dismounted and came to sit with her, while Samuel disappeared into the ale-house on the pretext of looking for Donald.

Before long, Maggie was telling Mrs. Ross about the musical gifts Riona had honed entertaining her sister, and a blushing Riona was asked to sing for the children. Three songs later, a little crowd of women and children and the elderly, those who hadn't gone on the hunt, had formed around her, seated on rocks and tufts of grass. Mrs. Ross was beaming as if she'd taught Riona herself.

It felt . . . strange and rather wonderful to have so many fresh, upturned faces look upon her with happiness. The usual wary suspicion of her as a Duff or a Sassenach seemed gone, even if only for a little while. Or perhaps they were coming to accept her as their chief's future wife. But that was a stab of pain she put aside. This life was not hers but Cat's, and though that seemed more and more bittersweet, Riona had never been one to live in a fantasy. But she tried to enjoy the moment, and take comfort in being admired for a skill she'd worked hard to perfect.

And then there was a shout from the hillside above the village, and a young man came stumbling over the crest, falling to his knees and lurching back to his feet. He shouted something in

Gaelic, and the crowd surged apart as if lightning had struck directly in the center.

Though Riona knew only a few words of Gaelic now, Maggie had taught her these: cattle thieves. Maggie translated the gasping boy's account of six men stealing away dozens of cattle. Then she and Maggie practically flew to their horses, where Samuel met them.

"Do you know where Hugh and the gentlemen are?" Riona demanded.

"Aye, they send missives every day, along with all the carcasses of the beasts they've killed."

"Then take word to him about the raid. He'll need to know."

Solemn, Samuel nodded, mounted his horse, and headed uphill, away from the village, away from the castle.

Riona watched him go, then accompanied Maggie back to Larig to await Hugh.

CHAPTER 17

Hugh returned by mid afternoon to find preparations already being made to leave at dawn to take back their cattle. Riona awaited him in the great hall, looking concerned. Then her expression altered with determination when she saw the men following him, wearing haphazard bandages.

"Mrs. Wallace," she called, "I need your help!"

Hugh watched in surprise as Riona, Maggie, and Mrs. Wallace tended to the mild injuries sustained by his men—a gash from a dirk through a man's hand, a sprained ankle, and a musket ball through an arm when another man had wandered in the way of a hunter's shot.

Riona worked with a kind efficiency that surprised him. He was so used to her reluctance and wariness that he sometimes forgot she hadn't always needed to be that way. She knew people's names now, and he could have sworn he heard her use a word or two of hesitant Gaelic. She seemed like the mistress of the household—like his wife.

It was some time before he realized his mother wasn't with the other women, and then only as an afterthought. It had been ten years since she'd betrayed him, ten years of her condemning silence. He'd grown used to putting her out of his mind, and it was still very easy to do.

Dermot came to let him and Alasdair know what had happened, that the Buchanans had used the absence of the hunting men for their raid. Dermot's tone grew cooler as he said, "I could have handled this, of course, for there were enough men for a chase, but Lady Riona alerted ye without consulting me."

"She was simply concerned for our property and people," Hugh said mildly. " 'Tis better if we give them a show of force since I'm the new chief. I'll lead the party myself."

Now it was Alasdair who frowned. "As your war chief—"

"I ken, ye'd normally go on my behalf. But as I said, I'm the new McCallum, and I need to project strength. Ye'll accompany me, of course."

"As will I," Dermot said.

Hugh debated keeping his tanist at home, but the odds of death were not great. "Very well. And when we return, Alasdair, give me details on the state of our security. But for now, let us assemble the men in an hour at the training yard and see to preparations."

Both Alasdair and Dermot turned away stiffly, silently, and Hugh held back a sigh. But then Riona came to him, drying her hands upon a cloth, lifting the gloom that had surrounded him. Dermot didn't bother to hide the frown he bestowed on her as he left.

Riona looked over her shoulder at Dermot, then turned to Hugh. "He's upset with me."

"Ye played the part of my wife too well," Hugh said lightly. "Ye ruffled Dermot's feathers by sending for me without consulting him."

He glimpsed a flicker of worry in her green eyes. "You know I did not mean to overstep my bounds."

"Ye cared about McCallum cattle—that's not overstepping your bounds."

But she continued to stare with concern at the door through which Dermot had disappeared.

To distract her, he asked, "Everyone will live?"

She gave a small smile. "They will, even the ones I cared for myself." Her smile faded again. "I heard Dermot and Alasdair talking with you. You're not very popular right now, either, are you?"

He snorted.

"Come, eat some food before you must rush outside."

She cut meat from the platters of mutton and

hares herself, dished him cabbage and kale, nettles and garlic, and as she was pouring him a goblet of wine, noticed that he was staring at her.

"Is something wrong?" she asked, turning around as if to look behind her.

"Nay, nothing. Ye're simply so . . . agreeable."

Maggie overheard them, and he saw Riona blush.

"Agreeable?" Maggie echoed. "Ye should have seen her in the village this morn. Mrs. Ross is feeling much better after Riona's advice and care—"

"Maggie," Riona said with exasperation.

Like they were already close friends, Hugh thought in wonderment and a growing feeling of hope.

"And then she started singing for the children," Maggie continued. "Singing! I knew she played the spinet beautifully, but her voice—"

"Ye play the spinet?" Hugh asked Riona.

She shrugged. "Remember how my parents liked me to entertain."

He studied her as if he couldn't get enough. And for these three nights away, it had seemed like it. During the days he'd been busy, but at night under the stars he'd thought of nothing but Riona, her smile, her kisses, the hope that she'd at last want to marry him and have children together.

Alasdair came bounding in the wide open double doors. "Hugh! We're waiting. Ye said ye needed to be out here with the men."

Hugh rose to his feet. "I'm coming." To his sister and Riona, he said, "Thank ye both for your help and for thinking to alert me when the raid happened." His eyes lingered on Riona even as he said, "Until the evening then."

And Riona blushed as if he'd said he'd meet her in bed.

RIONA paced in her room that night, knowing Hugh would not remain in the great hall for long, since they were leaving before dawn to take back their cattle.

She wasn't used to thinking of men she knew in this sort of danger. Oh, there were always footpads in London, or a hunter's mistake at a country estate, but this . . . Not that "this" was open battle, but it could be. Hugh had fought British soldiers not that long ago and barely survived.

And she thought of what she'd overheard, that Dermot was unhappy she'd notified Hugh about the raid without consulting him. She realized she'd made that decision without dwelling on it, letting her instincts take over. More and more she was trusting herself, taking for granted that her decisions would be accepted. She couldn't control much about her situation, but she was learning to appreciate what control she had. And when her decisions were met with acceptance and respect? It was a heady feeling.

But the decision to bypass Dermot might have

cost her her chance to have him listen to her story objectively. Why would he want to go to Hugh at her side, privately, when he could embarrass both of them by revealing the truth to the entire clan?

When the door opened and Hugh walked in, freshly washed and shaved after days in the mountains with his men, even seeing the scar on his chin gave her a soft feeling of tenderness. God, keeping herself distant was going badly.

And then he smiled at her, crooked and endearing, and her reaction was a deep pleasure that was also a pain, right in her heart. Talking, she had to keep talking, or she would run to him to be swept up into his arms. She would forget the future and the risks. How could she have fallen for the man who'd kidnapped her? The man who could never be her husband?

He cocked his head. "Ye're giving me a strange look."

"Am I?" she asked, forcing a lightness to her voice as she went to pour him a goblet of wine. But of course that meant approaching him, but she did so, full of trepidation and yearning. When he took the wine and saluted her with it before taking a sip, she asked, "I know the hunt was successful as far as the meat was concerned, but did it go well in . . . other ways?"

"Other ways?"

"You and your clansmen, you and Alasdair . . ."

"Are ye asking if we were good little laddies and started no fights?" he asked with faint sarcasm.

She sighed. Why *was* she asking about this? Or was she simply delaying? "I'm being silly, I know. We women think more about everyone having no conflict."

"Ye're not silly," he said softly.

He cupped her face with one palm, and a shiver moved through her. It had been a long time since it was a shiver of fear. She stepped away, forcing a smile, and poured herself some of the wine.

Hugh stared for a moment into the fire as he sipped his wine, before saying, "Alasdair and I will return to our old ways someday. He is still having difficulty with me 'usurping his role,' or whatever he believes I've done. As if I shouldn't lead our men in their search for justice. But he's been here all these years and knows the men—as he points out to me. And I agree. I've promised to take that into consideration more."

"It's a start."

"Now tell me how things went while I was gone. Did I hear you speaking Gaelic?"

He sat down in the cushioned chair before the fire, which eased her trepidation. She took the chair opposite him.

" 'Speaking' is not how I'd term my use of Gaelic," she answered wryly. "Maggie is helping me learn a few words."

"We'll have ye feeling more like a Highlander in no time."

She nodded, knowing it would be far too easy. "My parents denied me a part of my heritage, and it does feel good to learn what it's like to be Scottish. I like the stories the old men tell at night, and the superstitions Mrs. Wallace swears by. I was a little put off by how distant all the shops I take for granted are now—it seemed like my way of life was gone. But it was very thoughtful of you to send a tailor." She spread her skirts wide. "My new gowns are lovely." The only way she'd been able to tolerate their making was knowing someone else would have use of them someday.

His eyes shone as they studied her. "Ye look bonny. That deep green matches your eyes. I'd told him to look for that."

"You did not."

"I did," he said, hand over his heart.

"I appreciate you thinking about my comfort. Next you'll be telling me you're a poet."

Good Lord, she was teasing and flirting now. It was so easy with him. The pain of it was sharp, bringing on a grief she hadn't anticipated. She could fall truly in love with him, and was sliding down the slope toward it.

He smiled. "I'm not a poet. I simply appreciate fine eyes."

She could get lost in his. To stop herself, she

asked, "What do you know about Maggie and Owen?"

He frowned. "My sister and the heir to Aberfoyle? Why do ye even link their names together?"

"Because she asked me about him, if he'd married."

His frown intensified. "I ken little except that my mother and Maggie used to attempt an acquaintanceship with your family. It was awkward and eventually abandoned."

"What about when you were at university? Maggie was maturing into a young woman then. I get the feeling that something else happened."

"She didn't tell me. If he tried to harm her—"

"You mean kidnap or seduce her?" Riona interrupted, irony lacing her words. "What should a brother do when that happens?"

Hugh sat back in his chair, the goblet dangling from his hand as he studied her. "Ye still think to make me embarrassed by what I've done—and I'm not. A contract was entered into in good faith."

She waved a hand. "I know I can't change your mind, and I didn't mean to start in on it, not when you're leaving tomorrow."

"Ye don't want to send me away with an argument?" he teased.

"No, but . . . maybe you'll still want to argue when I tell you what else happened while you were gone." She watched him intently.

"Go ahead," he said, taking a fortifying swig of the wine.

"I was walking with your mother and Maggie when we met up with Brendan."

She paused, studying his face. Instead of displaying anger, his expression smoothed out into something neutral and impassive.

"I imagine my mother was not impressed with meeting a groom," he said.

"I don't know about impressed, but she practically swooned."

He rose to pour himself another goblet of wine, silently offering her one. She shook her head.

"You've got nothing to say, Hugh?" she asked softly.

"I've told ye my conditions for free and open talk between us, lass. Have you accepted that ye'll be my bride?"

She bit her lip and turned to look at the smoldering fire. "I've already told you I can't."

He came to stand before her, tall, imposing, but not menacing. He could never be that for her again. Then he took her by the arms and raised her to her feet.

"How can ye keep denying this?" he demanded, then pulled her hard against him and kissed her.

She didn't try to fight him—she was incapable of it, she knew that now. She could even admit to herself that she missed him, that she put her arms around his neck to hold him to her, as if she could cling to him and push away the future where he'd suffer for choosing the wrong bride.

His body felt so right, his mouth slanting across hers was something she'd dreamed of these last few nights alone.

Against her lips, he murmured, "I've missed ye, lass. Say ye've missed me, too."

She couldn't say the words—it wouldn't be fair. But she pressed kisses to his cheek, his chin, his throat, reveling in the feel of his hands sweeping her body, cupping her backside to pull him hard against her, against his erection. She shuddered at the feel of it, and then his other hand cupped her breast and kneaded it through the thin fabric of her nightclothes. Their kisses grew harsh and gasping, their hands frantic on each other. She felt feverish and dazed, her rational thoughts fading away.

She broke the kiss and whispered, "The rope. Use it. I don't trust myself."

She saw the triumph in his expression before he turned away, and regretted her words immediately. She was giving him exactly what he wanted— giving in to his seduction. Their roles had reversed, and she was the one leading him on now, leading him to believe she was closer and closer to being his wife. She should stop him—stop this disaster looming ever larger and larger in the near future. The closer they got, the more it would hurt when he at last had confirmation she was telling the truth. And that confirmation could come any day now—surely her uncle wouldn't take much longer to crow about his victory over the McCallums, and how Hugh had not lived up to the terms of their agreement.

But she said nothing—did nothing as he knelt at her feet and tied the rope around her ankles. She was trapped by her own neediness. What did she think could come of this, except her own despair, when she might be completely in love with him, and he had to reject her? But he wasn't rejecting her now—he picked her up and carried her to the bed, laid her down gently, then came over the top of her to kiss her again. She clung to him, hating herself for wanting his touch, hating that she felt betrayed by her own body. Desire had taken over, stripped her of caution and common sense.

When he slid his hand beneath her nightshift, she didn't stop him, only moaned and writhed like some kind of wild woman at each caress along her hot, sensitive skin. She shuddered with disappointment when he teased along the outside of her hips and then across her belly—until she realized what he was doing, sliding her nightshift ever higher. She felt the draft of air across her bare breasts only a moment before he bent his head. The first kiss on her nipple was delicate and moist, but it made her cry out with gladness. He swirled his tongue around her nipples before drawing each inside his mouth in turn. She arched, desperate for more, sounds coming from her throat she'd never imagined.

And at last he gave her what she wanted, sliding his fingers between her trembling thighs and into the wet depths of her. He knew just where to touch, just what to do. With his mouth at her breasts, and his fingers stroking and circling, she came apart in a climax more powerful than the one he'd given her just a few days before. She hadn't imagined such pleasure could increase, but it had. And he'd given this to her more than once now, never asking anything of her in return—except that she marry him.

He rolled onto his back, breathing harshly, hands fisted.

"Hugh?"

"Nay, 'tis all right. Go to sleep. I'll return to my own bed."

She told herself not to touch him, but she couldn't help it. She placed her hand over his erection where it pressed hard against his breeches.

He inhaled swiftly. "Riona, don't start what ye don't intend to finish."

"Are you going to your room to . . . finish?"

He didn't say anything.

"Let me help."

And without waiting for his answer, she pushed his shirt up and began to unbutton his breeches.

To her surprise, she thought she felt the briefest tremble, but he mastered himself. She folded back the flap and saw that he'd worn no drawers. In the shadows, she could see little except the dark silhouette of his penis. So she touched it, heard him gasp, felt the jump of his response. He was so very hard and hot and yet silky. She caressed him, exploring, until he spoke between gritted teeth.

"Like this."

He took her hand and fisted it around him and then showed her how to move. With her hand she pleasured him, with her mouth she kissed him, and it wasn't long before he spilled his seed across his stomach, his body jerking as hers had. She let go and stared at what she'd done, shocked now that the passion had ebbed, that she could so lose herself and forget her determination to resist. Or was it because he was leaving to go against another clan, where dangerous things could happen?

Dazed, she withdrew mentally when he stood up to clean himself. Turning her back, she felt unable to face him, to face that she'd let their relationship go another step further. He folded himself in behind her, his hips against hers, his arm around her waist. As he fell asleep, his hand cupped her breast as if it were the most natural thing possible.

And she bit her lip and tried not to shake with her crying.

CHAPTER 18

Hugh left before dawn for the raid on the Buchanans. He didn't wake her up, and Riona pretended she was asleep, which proved difficult when he gently touched her head before leaving.

Don't die, she thought with a prayer, *don't die!*

When he'd gone, she questioned herself. She hadn't been able to convince him that her denial of marriage was more than a foolish girl afraid of being married. So was she just accepting what happened to her, passively waiting until it was too late, until he hated himself—and her—for breaking the contract?

There was no one to help her make Hugh see the truth. Her last hope had been Dermot, but now she didn't know if she could trust him not to use this new knowledge against Hugh, have him ousted as the chief before he'd been formally inaugurated. Riona didn't know if she could live with such an outcome.

She bathed and dressed and tried to get through the day. The castle was abnormally quiet, a few servants going about their chores, but everyone seemed to be holding their breaths. It felt . . . oppressive and frightening. Every time she looked in on Lady McCallum, her head was bowed over her rosary beads, and after a while, her fear secreted its way into Riona. To clear her head, Riona took a walk outside, where tasks went on in the courtyard, but without the cheerful conversations or occasional hail across the yard.

She, Maggie, and Lady McCallum were just sitting down to dinner in a mostly deserted great hall when a clansman ran through the open double doors.

"Lady Riona, the watchmen have seen mounted men approaching. Samuel told me to tell ye."

Riona ran, Maggie behind her, practically stumbling down the outdoor stairs that led to the courtyard. Samuel waited there, arms folded across his chest, his normally cheerful expression replaced by one as immobile as stone.

Riona skidded to a stop next to him, then stared at the open gatehouse. "Do you . . . lower the portcullis, in case it isn't them?"

" 'Tis them," he said with cool assurance. "I could see our tartan."

She eyed him, not used to seeing Samuel like this. But he hadn't been able to watch over Hugh, his position these last ten years. He'd been left to sit with the women, and apparently, he hadn't appreciated it, though he'd let no clue show in front of Hugh, Riona remembered.

Mounted men suddenly thundered beneath the gatehouse, then into the upper courtyard, their horses tossing their heads with excitement. She caught flashes of grins, heard excited laughter, saw no barebacked horses absent a rider. She tried to calm herself, even as her heart was pounding so hard she felt a little weak.

Samuel stared down at the hand she'd put on his arm without realizing it.

She pulled away. "Forgive me," she called over the sound of men and horses.

He nodded, but didn't give her his usual grin, probably because Hugh had seen them. Hugh rode toward them, and Riona couldn't help her smile of welcome, even as she looked him over for injury, but saw none. His bare knees flashed beneath his plaid as he dismounted. He wore a bright blue coat, and with his black and red plaid, he looked as colorful as a king. But she hung back and let Samuel do the talking.

"It went well?" Samuel asked.

Hugh nodded. "Every cow accounted for and no one injured. The Buchanans fled like cowards before us."

Relief flooded through Riona, making her knees

tremble with weakness. Dermot and Alasdair dismounted behind Hugh, and she felt a little amazed to see the two of them smiling as they talked to each other. Nothing like a little dangerous warfare to make men lose their scowls.

Dermot clapped a hand on Hugh's shoulder. "We will celebrate your bravery tonight and inaugurate ye as chief. The men are already gathering over this victory—'twill be the perfect time."

Riona and Maggie exchanged wide-eyed glances.

"Your bravery?" Maggie said, her voice raised to be heard.

Alasdair swung an arm around Hugh's neck. "Did we not mention that your brother here crept into their camp alone and challenged the Buchanan tanist to single combat?"

Riona gave the appropriate womanly gasp, hoping to make Samuel smile, but his forehead only creased more.

" 'Twas my place to defend ye," Samuel said coldly. "If I'd have been there, ye wouldn't have been so reckless."

"I would have, old friend." Hugh put a hand on his shoulder. "It needed to be done to save lives. We crossed swords only a few times before the rest of the Buchanans began to flee, and without support, he soon surrendered."

"To you?" Riona looked past him. "Did you take him captive?"

"Nay, we let him return in defeat to his people," Dermot said. "Why waste our grain on him?"

For the first time since she'd known him, Dermot's expression was relaxed and confident, as if he was finally proud of his clan chief.

Her plan to have him stand at her side died. The truth might turn him against Hugh, just when Hugh had the support of all of his men. At last, she had to accept the realization that Hugh had become more important to her than her need to escape.

"Speaking of victory . . ." Hugh raised his arm along with his voice. "Let us begin the celebration of Clan McCallum!"

Men cheered and began to pour up the stairs to the great hall.

Maggie turned to Riona. "Should ye alert Mrs. Wallace?"

Riona put up both hands. "It's not my place. You're the sister of the chief and I have no official position here."

"Ye're the betrothed of the chief," Hugh said, staring at her with narrowed eyes.

Maggie looked between them hesitantly. "I'll make sure we have the best meal possible. I'm so proud of ye, Hugh!"

Maggie leaned up on tiptoes and kissed his cheek, but Riona felt the weight of Hugh's stare on her. Even Dermot and Alasdair made themselves scarce.

"Ye have no place here?" Hugh asked, his voice menacing by its very softness.

"I only meant that I am not the mistress of the household," she said.

"But ye will be."

She didn't answer. Her behavior in bed had probably confirmed the future in his mind, where, for her, it had made everything worse. "Let's not discuss this now, Hugh. This is a time to celebrate." She'd almost ended with "being a McCallum," but stopped herself. He would have taken that as even more proof that she'd marry him. "I should go to your mother. She was quite in fear for you. I don't think she ate anything today."

Hugh frowned, but then turned away when someone called his name. She hastened first toward the kitchen on the ground floor to see if they needed help, but Mrs. Wallace was in her element coordinating the household. Next, Riona visited Hugh's mother, who stood in her room looking out at the excitement of the courtyard.

"Lady McCallum, as you can see, Hugh's home unharmed," Riona said as she went to the window to stand shoulder-to-shoulder with the older woman.

Lady McCallum nodded, her eyes moist, but not openly crying. "Thank ye, Riona. Did they take back the cattle?"

Riona explained what had happened, then allowed a moment of silence to pass, before saying, "Surely ye'll come down tonight and celebrate his inauguration."

"If I do, I'll stay out of his sight," Lady McCallum said.

Though she sounded melodramatic, Riona didn't get the impression that it was deliberate. "You can't win back his good graces by avoiding him."

Lady McCallum's shoulders dropped with a sigh. "I cannot win them back regardless. He'll never forgive me."

"Forgive you for what?" Riona asked gently.

"For doing what I thought best ten years ago."

"Is this about Agnes?"

Lady McCallum stiffened, but didn't answer.

Riona knew that discovering the truth wasn't going to be that easy. "Whatever it was, holding a grudge for ten years is a long time. You can try to work things out."

"Then ye don't know my son very well," she said bitterly.

"No, I don't. And yet you, and everyone else, think I should marry him."

"Think?" Lady McCallum turned to meet her eyes at last. "I don't just think it. 'Tis your duty to marry him, to do as both of your fathers wished. Have ye not seen how lucky a lass ye are?"

"Did you think yourself lucky when you married his father?"

" 'Tis not the same at all."

"No? It feels it to me." When Lady McCallum looked as if she'd continue defending her son, Riona raised a hand. "I'm not here to argue with you. I just wanted to invite you to celebrate tonight."

"He doesn't want me there." Lady McCallum spoke with sad conviction.

"Maybe not, but no one can change that but you."

Those eyes, so like Hugh's, now met hers in fear. "What has he told ye?"

Riona frowned. "About what?"

Lady McCallum's gaze studied her face so intently that Riona almost felt touched.

"Never mind," the woman whispered. "I—I need to rest."

Riona saw herself out, but now she was even more puzzled than before. Whatever had happened between Lady McCallum and her son, it was certainly not a typical argument. Riona was still surprised by her own need to help Hugh come to peace with the past. But it was something she could do, and living among the enemy had taught her to take her small successes where she could.

But the chief's mother did come down for the ceremony that night, and Riona stood with the family in the crowded great hall. She was surprised and moved by the formal splendor of it, the robing of Hugh all in white, the granting of a white rod of lordship and the ancestral sword of his clan. The clan chaplain, from nearby Sula, gave a blessing. The entire hall processed out onto the torchlit courtyard, where Hugh stood above his people on the stone carved with the McCallum animal, a wolf, while a long oration began of the exploits of their ancestors, and a recitation of their names for generations. Riona was told all of this by Maggie, and even caught a few words here and there herself.

"Ye know, as Hugh's wife, ye'll have to learn the list of McCallums," Maggie told her, smiling.

Riona gave an exaggerated shudder. "In English, I hope."

But it might be Cat learning about the McCallums, not her. And she looked at Hugh and tried to imagine her cousin standing at his side, but couldn't.

They all returned to the great hall for a feast that lasted long into the night. Songs were sung in Hugh's honor, and Riona heard a few words calling him their "secured fortified rock," their "defensive shield," their "noble hawk." No wonder some chiefs considered themselves a god.

But not Hugh. He accepted the honor with utter gravity and solemnity, performing each part of the ritual with focus, standing at attention during all of the oration. Riona couldn't help being impressed by how seriously he took his part in the clan—but then she already knew what lengths he'd go to to ensure that his people thrived.

But he'd made a terrible error with her, and they would all find out someday soon. She swallowed back the feelings of grief and fear over what might happen. If Cat could be persuaded to continue the betrothal, all might yet be well. Perhaps that's who Riona should appeal to. Appealing to Aberfoyle himself, who'd deliberately tried to ruin the contract, might be the worst thing she could do.

And then she heard her thoughts, and realized she was thinking about appealing on behalf of the man who'd kidnapped and frightened her. But her feelings, everything, had changed . . .

It was almost dawn by the time Hugh entered his rooms, swaying and humming to himself. It was done—the clan approved of him and he was their official leader until he died. Dermot had organized everything himself, and it felt good to know that at last he'd won the man's approval.

But would he earn his betrothed's approval?

He went through both doors between their rooms and found her asleep, the bed curtains open as if she'd been anticipating his arrival. He laughed a bit in triumph, imagining being with her again. He lit a candle from the embers of the peat fire and brought it to the bed table to look upon her. Resting a hand for balance on the frame of her box-bed, he just stared at her, the way the candlelight seemed to shimmer through the golden strands of her hair.

He'd been so proud to have her at his side for the inauguration. She'd listened as intently as if she'd understood every word, although he'd seen his sister translating for her.

Better than Samuel doing it all the time, Hugh told himself. He didn't want people thinking his bodyguard coveted his betrothed—though he knew Samuel would never betray him. But would Riona use Samuel to get what she wanted?

He frowned down upon her, the sweet pinkness of her cheeks, her softly parted lips, the beauty of her curves, most of which he'd touched, and some of which he anticipated tasting at last. Every time with her was another lesson for them both. When he'd last enjoyed her bed, he'd been stunned at her need to share pleasure with him, grateful she'd wanted to touch him so intimately. Even a normal bride could have fears, but when one has been forcibly kidnapped—Riona could have been in fear of him forever.

Yet . . . when he'd returned from the cattle raid, she'd still said she had no official place in the household. She was the future bride of the chief, who willingly kissed him and pleasured him. Surely he'd won her over; it was time to plan the wedding.

He dropped a kiss on her head—he'd meant to be gentle about it, but almost fell over instead. She gasped and pushed until she realized who leaned over her in the dark.

" 'Tis me," he said. It was strange how numb his lips felt.

"Hugh." She said his name with relief.

"Who else would come to ye in the rooms of the chief?"

He sat down heavily beside her, and she rolled toward him as the mattress sagged.

Bracing a hand on his thigh, she said, "You sound extremely proud of yourself."

Was she teasing him or laughing *at* him? It was hard to tell the difference after all the whisky he'd consumed.

She glanced toward the window, where the sky had begun to lighten to gray. "A full night of celebration, I see."

He leaned down to nuzzle behind her ear. "We could celebrate more."

She coughed when he breathed on her.

"But we don't have the time," he said, slapping her backside.

She gasped. "Hugh!"

"Up, woman, we need to leave. My chieftains have invited us to travel our lands and be feted. I want ye to see what ye'll be a part of."

He saw the sadness that still lingered in her eyes when she thought he didn't notice. He might be drunk, but he wasn't stupid. He cupped her face in both hands. "Riona, Riona," he murmured, between kisses. He almost asked her to love him as a wife should a husband, but held back the words. He wasn't *that* mindless.

"We're going on a journey together?" she asked with hope in her voice.

"We are."

"Then we have much to prepare for. I suggest you get some sleep so you're refreshed."

"Don't need sleep." But her bed was very comfortable, and he lay down beside her.

She frowned. "*You* need to sleep, but I'm awake now. Why don't you let me out and—"

He shook his head, grinning.

"Hugh, a journey requires much preparation."

She started to climb across him, but the moment she put one leg across him, he pulled her down on top of him. Her thighs straddled his hips, and she was right where he wanted her to be.

She rolled her eyes. "Hugh, please, you've overindulged."

He ignored her, arching his hips to press his cock into the warmth between her thighs. He heard her quick intake of breath, saw the way her eyes seemed to lose focus.

"No ropes holding your legs together now," he murmured.

He let his hands wander up her torso, cupping her breasts, flicking her nipples with his thumbs, and enjoying the way she gave a tremble that he felt deep within. He cupped her face and pulled her low over him, so that she was forced to brace her hands on his shoulders or fall right into his kiss.

"I've got nothing on under my plaid," he said with satisfaction. "And ye've got nothing on under that nightshift." And then he kissed her.

CHAPTER 19

The whisky swam in Riona's head as if she'd drunk it herself. The taste of it was in Hugh's mouth and on his breath. With his hands holding her head to him, she had no choice but to accept the kiss—not that she could refuse. Just the touch of him, even drunk, was enough to reawaken her body to the pleasure they could share.

But this was dangerous, she knew. Little separated them from intercourse itself, certainly not ropes. If he decided to finish what they'd been working toward for weeks, she probably could not stop him. He rolled his hips up into hers, slowly, rhythmically, setting off the flutters she now knew would escalate into need.

She pressed against his shoulders and lifted her head. "Hugh, stop. If we're leaving today, you need to sleep."

His hands dropped to her hips and held her to

him, changing the angle until the pressure against her was so full of sweet pleasure that her head dropped back and her eyes closed. There was only the wool of his plaid that separated them, and suddenly it didn't seem like much. She saw the concentration on his face, the way he watched her, the way he wanted her. But when he reached for her breasts again, she used the moment to slide right off him where she practically sprawled onto the floor, her limbs momentarily too weak to carry her. Rising, she backed away, even as he came up on one elbow and reached a hand toward her.

"Riona, come back to me."

"No." She had to force herself not to laugh at the exaggerated sadness on his face. "Sleep, Hugh."

With a groan he sank back, and soon enough, his snores filled the room.

That had been close, she thought, hugging herself with relief. Though she was happy with the decision, her body wasn't, and it hummed with a state of arousal the whole time she was dressing for the day.

She spent several hours with Mrs. Wallace, learning what was involved in this kind of procession through the lands, including the ceremonial men who accompanied the chief. Riona wanted to understand all she could about the ways of Scotland, the country she'd long been denied. To her surprise, Maggie and her mother were both remaining behind, preferring to rest at the castle and await their return.

And then she thought about Brendan—should he be the groom who came along to help tend the horses? He and Hugh would spend more time together. To the marshal of horses, she implied that Hugh preferred having Brendan along, but in the end, by the time Hugh had awakened and come down to begin the journey at midday, the marshal asked his opinion about it anyway. She saw the marshal glance at her from across the courtyard, and then Hugh's gaze narrowed as he studied her. She sighed. Brendan wouldn't be coming, and she was going to hear about her decision to interfere. What did Hugh expect if he wouldn't tell her the truth?

But they never had a private moment alone, what with ceremonial men who accompanied them: his bodyguard, the bard to compose and tell clan history, the piper to accompany him, the spokesman to vocalize Hugh's messages, the quartermaster to arrange lodgings, the cup bearer who was supposed to taste the passed cup before Hugh, several ghillies to keep Hugh dry crossing a river or keep charge of his horse. Hugh seemed uncomfortable with the display of power, but Samuel explained to Riona that the clan expected their chief to behave like a prince. They journeyed west for several hours that day, to Alasdair's home, a two-story stone mansion built far more recently than Larig Castle, near the far end of Loch Voil, with pasture and farmland spread through the glen, and mountains towering above either side. That evening, they were feasted and entertained, and Riona thought for certain Hugh had forgotten the incident about Brendan that morning, until, during the singing, he pulled her outside into the garden.

They were alone beneath a summer moon, and though she didn't have a shawl or cloak, it wasn't terribly cold. With the mansion at her back and the formal gardens around her, she could almost believe she was back in England.

Hugh walked at her side down the winding path, hands joined behind his back, his expression serious.

"This is a beautiful home," she said to fill the tense silence.

"I don't wish to discuss the house. I need to make clear why ye cannot behave as ye did this morn, telling the marshal who to include in our company."

"You wouldn't care if it hadn't been Brendan," she pointed out, coming to a stop and forcing him to face her. Torches lined the gravel path, and she could see his annoyed expression well enough. "Didn't you just tell me that I had a place in your household as your future wife? I thought that meant I could make such decisions."

She could see his jaw clench, but he made no answer.

"Hugh, you have to tell me the truth," she said urgently. "Is he your son by Agnes, the girl you loved?"

"Nay, he's not," he finally said between gritted teeth.

She rolled her eyes. "Anyone with eyes can see he's your son. People have been watching the two of you together."

"Ye think I'm lying?" he demanded.

"You constantly accuse *me* of lying. Why should I believe you when I can see with my own eyes—"

"That he's related to me?" he scoffed. "Of course he is. He's my half brother, not my son."

Riona's mouth briefly sagged open. "What? Your brother?"

"My father raped Agnes."

The sadness in his voice made Riona shiver at the horror of his words. "Raped?" she whispered, hugging herself.

He nodded solemnly. "My father felt like he was a king of old, that he should have rights to whatever woman he wanted. A clan chief should be a father to his people, not an aggressor. But though he felt entitled, he always chose village girls with no power against him," he added bitterly. "Agnes wasn't the first he'd abused, but she became pregnant."

Everything she'd thought about Hugh when he was nineteen now rearranged itself in her head. "You weren't in love with her?"

"Nay, but I felt responsible. I was back from Sher-iffmuir; I felt like I was a man, and that as my fa-ther's tanist, I should protect the weak. But I didn't see what was happening, what he was doing to her. She worked in the kitchens, and sometimes I would see her weeding in the gardens. She was kind to me, concerned about my wound. We were friends."

She put a hand on his arm. "Oh, Hugh . . ."

He shrugged her off. "I found her crying. She didn't want to tell me what had happened, but I made her. In that moment, she was as frightened of me as of my father, and I hated him for it."

His words seemed to ring through the air with power.

"I offered to marry her," Hugh said at last. "I told my father to hell with the contract, that I was going to make this right."

Riona briefly covered her mouth before whisper-ing, "But he wouldn't let you."

"He laughed as he pointed out how trapped I was by the contract, that our clan would not only lose your dowry, but a land that was the source of our pride, the source of rare coin in the Highlands. I had to choose between Agnes and the clan."

She wanted to hold him, to comfort him, but he stood as remote as a tall mountain in a range of hills. A wash of painful emotion swept over her, and she knew it was too late, that she'd fallen in love with this stubborn, noble man who'd always put his clan first, and had spent his life agonizing over something that wasn't his fault. But loving him didn't mean she would ever be able to marry him.

"Agnes wouldn't have married me regardless," he continued bitterly. "She didn't want the clan to suffer for her. I made sure she had a new house in the village, promised her an annual sum for her and the child—but she died in childbirth, only knowing the shame, but never the joy of having a son."

Riona's eyes stung. "Brendan's grandmother has taken loving care of him, Hugh. He's a good boy."

"But then why is working as a groom?" he demanded. "Why is he opening up himself to hurt and shame? He was never to know about our father—our father made sure to tell his grandmother she'd lose everything from us if she told Brendan the truth."

"But he must have seen you, Hugh. He's not stupid. He sees the resemblance and knows what people are saying. He doesn't seem bitter, just curious. Sadly, in our world, many bastards know they can't ever be a part of their true family."

"I can't keep myself distant—that would be worse. I have to make a decision about telling him the truth."

She stopped herself from offering advice, knowing he could think through the ramifications himself. "Did your mother know?" she asked hesitantly.

His tone was grim as he said, "She knew."

"How horrible to discover that your husband is capable of something like that. Why do you hold it against her?"

His brows lowered. "She spent no time with my father, and wouldn't have suffered if she'd have spoken the truth."

"That you didn't impregnate a girl and leave her behind of your own volition?"

He brusquely nodded. "If we'd have gone against my father together, we could have explained everything. If she would have stood at my side instead of abandoning me, abandoning Agnes, things might have gone differently."

"If it's any consolation, she seems to deeply regret what happened." She wished to say more, but knew there was no point. Hugh knew his mother hadn't abused and abandoned the girl, but he could focus his anger on Lady McCallum as he'd never been able to with his father.

"Her conscience is full of guilt and I cannot absolve her of that," he said. "She has to find her own peace."

But Riona thought he'd never find his if he continued to blame his mother for her weakness.

OVER the next few days, Riona felt more like a consort's wife than a chief's betrothed. The chieftains and the gentlemen housed them in the same room as if the trial marriage were a real thing. During the day, Hugh held court, solving disputes at assemblies of the local people, even helping a newly widowed man find a wife. The law was in his hand, as was the sheriffship. He made fair rulings, and thank God, nothing was serious enough to be punishable by death. But even that was truly in his power.

People seemed intimidated before him, but later, when Hugh was distracted, she heard the rumblings of mistrust over his youthful transgressions, and of course the "bastard" that was now working in his stables.

She seldom had even a moment alone. The thought of fleeing sometimes seemed cowardly rather than an attempt to save herself. She needed to find a way to show the clan that when the contract fell apart, it was her uncle's manipulation at fault, not Hugh. She hadn't made the decision to abandon her escape plan lightly, but she couldn't leave Hugh to suffer. It was a decision she could freely make, and she'd learned to appreciate in a small way the things she could control.

On their final day away, he took her to the sacred glen of his people, leaving behind their retinue and following a path that seemed to lead into the mountain itself. But the path turned, went through a woodland, and before her spread out a broad glen that seemed carved out of the mountain itself. On the far side, stalks of barley seemed to wrap around the next mountain. A wet bog oozed across the floor of the glen, tufts of grasses rising from watery ground. He motioned to her and they followed a path that meandered along the base of the mountain, until they reached a cleft where water bubbled and overflowed from high above.

"Drink it," Hugh said. " 'Tis the best, purest water in all of Scotland—in all of the world."

She laughed and drank in her cupped hands, and the cold clarity of it was invigorating. "Delicious."

He looked out upon his land with pride. "When the malt taxes were revived a few years ago, there were riots in Scotland because we could no longer brew ale cheaply. Whisky took its place, and to avoid the taxes, it mostly went hidden. We're careful only to make a finite amount every year, and the Duffs went along with it, to conserve the water, peat, and barley necessary for distilling our whisky."

"And that keeps the price high," Riona said.

He grinned. "To keep what's ours from the excisemen, I've heard of whisky being hidden beneath altars and within coffins. 'Tis that important to us."

She took a deep, almost painful breath. The place was beautiful, bleak and forbidding, yet magical. She could see people in the distance, cutting deep bricks of peat and laying it across the ground to dry. Yet . . . the clan was close to losing it all, and there was nothing she could do.

But . . . she could do something to help Hugh, to bolster the respect of his people before things turned bad.

A storm followed them home, and though the entire party arrived drenched, frantic clansmen met them in the courtyard and Hugh went off to help rescue trapped and drowning calves.

Riona wasn't surprised. Hugh would do anything for his people. Admiration and sadness were twin flames inside her, but she had to keep moving, keep focusing on things she could control. She found Lady McCallum and Maggie sewing in the family's withdrawing room late in the morning, and while lightning flashed and wind roared, she tried to keep Lady McCallum calm by telling them about the trip, the people she'd met, the Gaelic words Hugh had been teaching her.

But through it all, she thought about Hugh's accusations against his mother, and she had to know more details. Dancing around the issue would take too much time, and Hugh could be home at any moment.

"Lady McCallum, I've been talking to Hugh about Agnes."

Maggie's head lifted from her sewing in surprise. Lady McCallum's pale face grew even whiter. The older woman gazed helplessly at Riona as if needing her silence.

The whole family had all been silent too long.

"The groom you met—Brendan?" Riona said. "She was his mother."

Maggie watched Riona cautiously. "The groom who looks like Hugh."

"He's not Hugh's son," Riona said. "Maggie, you know that Brendan is your brother. Hugh finally told me."

Maggie winced and glanced at Lady McCallum with worry.

"Your mother already knows," Riona explained. "Don't you, my lady?"

Lady McCallum's sewing dropped into her lap, and she put a trembling hand to her mouth.

"Mother—" Maggie began, then had to swallow. "Hugh told me never to speak of it, even to you. I'm so sorry that Father hurt ye this way."

"He hurt all of you," Riona said. "He let everyone believe Hugh was the boy's father, yet when Hugh wanted to marry Agnes, your father forbade it, because of me—because of the contract," she amended. Sometimes it seemed so real that *she* should be Hugh's bride.

Maggie lifted both hands. "What else could Hugh have done? He couldn't break the contract."

"Of course not. And Hugh feels guilty enough about that. But does he also have to bear the sins of his father, who let the entire clan think his son fostered a bastard on an innocent young girl rather than admit that he himself had raped her?"

Lady McCallum gave a little scream at that horrible word. Even Maggie blanched.

"And it's not ending," Riona continued. "This ugly secret could poison Hugh's relationship with the whole clan. Lady McCallum, your husband is dead now and can't hurt anyone else in the clan—including you. Can you not speak out in your son's defense? Agnes—and maybe other women—suffered, and we can't change that. But hasn't Hugh suffered long enough?"

Lady McCallum put her face into her hands and wept. Maggie wiped her own eyes, but didn't go to her mother, just stared at her, waiting, but Lady McCallum didn't speak.

"I heard other things I wasn't supposed to," Maggie finally said, her voice a hoarse whisper. "I wasn't here much, so people didn't know me, even forgot about me when I was near and spoke plainly. I heard . . . I heard a village girl hung herself because of my father."

Riona held her breath, and for a moment, all that could be heard were Lady McCallum's wrenching sobs. Maggie's strangely colored eyes glimmered in the candlelight, and outside the wind slammed a shutter somewhere in the castle below.

"I didn't want to believe it," Maggie added woodenly. "I knew he drank, that he could be loud and lose his temper, but I didn't know what—a man could do to a woman that would make her kill herself. I made myself stop thinking about it."

Riona reached to clasp Maggie's hand. "There was nothing you could have done."

"I can do something now. I just remembered— they said . . . they said she had a sister, too."

She didn't meet Riona's eyes as she said this, and Riona assumed it was out of misplaced guilt.

"I need to find this girl," Riona said, feeling renewed determination surge up inside her. "If she would speak up, we'd have proof of what your father was capable of. Then we could tell the truth about Agnes and the clan would surely believe us." If she could make just this part of Hugh's life better, she would feel some sort of solace when she was gone. "Do you know her name?"

Maggie shook her head.

"I do," said Lady McCallum, her eyes wide and stark with fear.

CHAPTER 20

After a day spent traveling, and then dealing with stubborn cattle in fear of their life, Hugh was grateful for a hot bath before supper. He could have wished for Riona to attend him, but since he still had to maneuver to make that happen, he hadn't been hopeful. He wasn't even certain where she was, since he'd seen his mother and Maggie in the great hall when he'd arrived, but not Riona.

Still, he felt satisfied with his progress with the clan. He'd renewed ties with a dozen chieftains and gentlemen who'd known him only by his youthful reputation. He felt he'd strengthened their confidence, and had known they'd been impressed with Riona. For a woman who was still reluctant to marry him, she presented only a dignified, sweet countenance to the world.

Just not to him. But that was all right—he preferred her fiery and stubborn.

When he came downstairs for supper, the great hall was more crowded than normal, which surprised him. His mother and sister sat at the dais with Dermot and Alasdair, but Riona was still absent. He went to talk to his sister about that, and realized that his mother looked positively ashen.

"Mother, are ye well?" he asked, frowning. "Perhaps ye should retire and a tray could be brought up."

She shook her head, bloodless lips pressed together. "I will be fine."

Hugh glanced at Maggie, and though she gave a little shrug, he thought her gaze darted away from his a little faster than necessary.

"I've not seen Riona all afternoon." He looked around. "Come to think of it, I've not seen Samuel either."

It didn't even occur to him that Riona might have run off. He no longer believed she could do it.

"Samuel accompanied Riona into the village," Maggie said.

"She went to see Mrs. Ross?" he asked.

"I—I'm not certain."

Again, she didn't meet his eyes.

"Maggie, what is going on?"

But then the double doors at the rear of the great hall opened, and Riona and Samuel appeared. They weren't alone. A young woman clutched Riona's arm in fright, then lifted her chin as she moved farther into the hall. The woman was familiar, but he'd been gone a long time, and couldn't quite place her.

His mother gasped and came to her feet as if she'd seen a ghost. But she turned away from the girl to grab Hugh's arm. "I need to speak. I need to speak to everyone."

As if people had suspected entertainment, heads turned toward the dais and conversations died to murmurs.

"Mother," Hugh began.

"Nay, I must speak."

With those words, her voice rang out, and the murmurs chilled to absolute silence. Riona, the woman, and Samuel froze on the far side of the hall and remained silent. Hugh saw Riona and Maggie exchange a confused glance, leading him to believe that even they didn't know what his mother was up to.

"I need the people of my clan to hear and believe the truth," Lady McCallum said in a loud voice.

Hugh tensed, ready to stop her and demand to hear in private what she planned before she said it. But Maggie grabbed his sleeve and shook her head.

"The late chief of the McCallums, my husband, was a cruel man. All of ye knew it, and many of ye suffered. There was little I could do."

Hugh fisted his hands. People were just starting to forget what had happened, to trust him as the man he'd become. And his mother was bringing it all up again.

"But he's dead now, and I can tell the truth without fear that the consequences will be visited upon my children. I took them away when they were young, I protected them, but I didn't protect your children."

Her voice broke, her head bowed, and Hugh saw a tear slide down Maggie's cheek.

After a moment, Lady McCallum continued. "My husband liked young women and made . . . advances. It was an ugly, cruel thing. I didn't know that he'd taken a fancy to Agnes McCallum until it was too late, and the girl was . . . with child."

Hugh felt the same shock that was mirrored in the faces of his clansmen. Why had his mother, who'd kept this ugly secret all these years, decided to speak up? And then he noticed again the woman Riona had brought, and realized why he knew her—her sister had killed herself several years ago, a rare tragedy. Just seeing her had made his mother speak the truth, publicly, for the first time. Had the dead woman been his father's victim as well? Had Riona discovered this and brought the sister here just to see what his mother would do?

And then Hugh saw Brendan standing at the back of the hall, eyes wide, mouth grim. Hugh didn't know whether he should interrupt and protect the boy from whatever Lady McCallum would reveal, or let him hear the truth at last.

"I was at that man's mercy," his mother said in a quiet voice that everyone strained to hear. "I was able to escape, to get my children away, but not far enough. I could never speak out for fear of what he might do to me or the children, but now—he's dead. My words are too little, too late, I know, but I needed the truth to be known. My husband fathered a bastard, young Brendan, and I hope ye'll be kind to him, for it's not his fault—nor is it the fault of my son, who begged to help Agnes by marrying her, but was forbidden."

Lady McCallum sank back into her chair as if her legs would no longer support her. She covered her face with her hands, and Maggie leaned to speak to her. But Hugh could only see Brendan, who now pushed past Riona and ran from the great hall. Everyone was speaking at once—Alasdair was trying to ask him something; Dermot leaned close as if he needed to be a part of it.

Hugh put up both hands. "I can't discuss this now. Brendan heard it all."

He left the dais and pushed through the crowd. People tried to talk to him, but he politely put them off. He reached Riona at the great double doors, where twilight had descended over the mountains like a purple curtain.

"Did ye see where he went?" Hugh asked.

"He's just reached the entrance to the lower courtyard," Riona said.

He briefly cupped her cheek. "Ye've had a hand in some of this, I believe?"

She blushed and nodded, then searched his gaze with worried eyes.

He gave her a faint smile and left the hall.

Riona hugged herself as she watched Hugh take the stairs two at a time and run across the courtyard. She'd hoped to influence Lady McCallum into speaking up on behalf of her son, but had never imagined the woman would be so kind as to spare Fiona, the sister of the woman who'd killed herself, the pain of having to relive in public what had been done to her sister.

Riona turned to Samuel. "I'm going to be with Hugh in case he needs me. Would you help Fiona find a meal and a place to rest?"

Samuel eyed her with interest, but only nodded.

Riona ran out into the evening, the chill mountain air seeping up beneath her skirts. She hurried across the courtyard, focused on following Hugh. More than one clansman stared at her as she went by, but she ignored them. When she reached the stables, breathing fast from her near-run, she stood outside the open door and peered in. Hugh squatted beside little Hamish the terrier, rubbing the overlong hair on top of his bobbing head. Brendan stood with his back to Hugh, his body tense, his hands fisted at his sides.

"Ye must have questions for me, lad," Hugh

said in the no-nonsense voice of a commander to a valued soldier.

Brendan turned around at last. There were no tears, but his face was set in lines of new knowledge and old pain. Riona's heart broke for the poor boy who was trying to be so brave.

Brendan took a deep breath. "My granny would never talk to me about my da. She said it only mattered how much my mum loved me, and how mum wanted me. But now, to hear she didn't want what was done to her . . ." His voice broke as it trailed away. After a moment to compose himself, he continued, "I'd hoped it was someone like you, that maybe ye loved her but couldn't be with a simple village girl."

Hugh continued to pet the dog. "We can't choose our parents, Brendan. And since we have the same father, I speak from experience."

Brendan shuddered. "'Twas ugly and wrong, what he did to her."

"It was. I tried to make it right for your mother. We didn't love each other, but we were friends."

"I bet it was you who made sure we have the nicest cottage in the village."

Hugh didn't say anything.

"I know my granny appreciates what ye tried to do. I do, too. I guess . . . 'tis all right that ye're my brother, not my da."

Hugh looked up at him and smiled, a smile that made Riona's heart near burst with love for him, for this man who tried so hard to make up for everything his father had done, and never felt he could do enough.

"Would you and your granny like to move into the castle?" Hugh asked. "We're brothers, after all."

Brendan shrugged his bony shoulders. "Thank ye, but I like where we live, and the friends who didn't care if I was your bastard or not. But can I still come here and work with the horses?"

Hugh rose to his feet and put a hand on his shoulder. "Of course. I look forward to teaching ye to hold more than a stick sword someday, too."

"I've been practicing already," Brendan said slyly.

Hugh laughed.

Riona crept away, leaving them in peace, knowing Hugh already possessed the strength and sensitivity he needed to deal with a confused boy.

WHEN Hugh returned to the great hall, he felt as if stones the size of the Grampian Mountains had been lifted from his shoulders. The truth of Brendan was out in the open, and he knew Riona had made that happen. After all this time, would his mother have come forward by herself, if not for Riona? Men who'd remained wary were now giving him respectful nods, but no one tried to stop him from returning to his meal.

He didn't see Riona, but Maggie still sat on the dais, eating with hungry attention.

When she saw him, she smiled. "I don't think I've eaten all day as I waited for this to happen."

He eyed her sharply. "Ye *knew* this was going to happen?"

"Not 'knew,'" she emphasized, "just knew."

Hugh sat down and spoke softly. "Riona says she knew, too."

"'Twas her idea."

"She got Mother to speak publicly about what she considered a private shame?"

"Surprisingly, Mother didn't need much prodding except the promise that Riona was going to find the sister of the girl who'd killed herself over Father's behavior."

"How did Riona find *that* out?"

Maggie's expression turned pensive. "From a dream I had long ago—but I didn't tell her that. I told her I heard rumors that Father was the reason this girl killed herself, and maybe the sister knew more."

"Ye knew the secrets of that girl's death?" Hugh asked gently. "Ye must have been young."

"Fourteen. I dreamed she was wearing death clothes, but since I didn't know who she was, I tried to forget about it."

Hugh put a hand on hers. "I'm sorry, Maggie."

She shrugged, and though she gave a wry smile, her voice trembled. "I tried not to pay attention to the things that happened in my dreams—I couldn't change anything, and I didn't want people to know what I was. They found the girl hanging the next morning." And then her expression seemed to crumble in on itself. "I didn't know it was because of our father."

Hugh brought her bowed head to his shoulder, and she clung to him and trembled as she mastered herself. He saw more than one person looking their way with sympathy, saw Mrs. Wallace wipe a tear away before hurrying from the hall.

"He's dead now, and his secrets are out in the light of day," Hugh said. "He can't hurt any of us again."

Maggie lifted her head and stared at him with wet eyes. "Brendan?"

"He's a braw lad. Shocked and sad, but he'll be fine. I'm going to teach him to sword fight."

Her smile trembled but grew wider. "Good. 'Tis rather strange to have a little brother. I hope he won't mind us watching over him."

Hugh nodded, then looked around. "Have ye seen Riona?"

"She went to console our mother in my place. She thought Mother might respond better to an outsider than her own daughter. And maybe she's right." Maggie sent him a secretive smile. "I like her, Hugh. How did ye get so lucky with a bride ye'd never even met?"

"She's not my bride yet," Hugh said, his own pleasure fading into worry.

Maggie touched his hand. "But she must love ye, Hugh. A woman doesn't do all this for no reason. Maybe she doesn't know that ye love her?"

He gave a start. "What?"

She laughed. "I've seen the way ye watch her. Your betrothal may be Father's doing, but ye're glad for it. Why don't ye go talk to her? I'll take her place with Mother and send Riona to you."

"Ye're a good sister."

She shrugged. "I've spent more time with Mother than you have. Everything that's happened these last couple days . . . well, it explains a lot of her behavior. She suffered being married to him."

"I know. Tell her I'll come see her in the morning. I have to be with Riona first."

WHEN Riona returned to her room, only a few candles lit the gloom. She was grateful to be alone, relieved that at last she'd been able to do something here at Larig Castle to help Hugh. No one could look at him anymore and see a man who'd abandoned a pregnant woman. The evil that was his father was at last revealed to the light, and she hoped the scrutiny would release the last bad memories.

She poured herself a glass of wine and drank it standing before the fire. Glancing at Hugh's door, she wondered if he was there, if he'd come to her. And then she heard a sound and turned swiftly, only to see Hugh lying in her box-bed, clothed in shirt and breeches rather than his plaid. And around his ankles, he'd tied the rope.

She burst out laughing, then covered her mouth.

He arched a brow. "I just can't trust myself with ye, lass."

When he reached a hand to her, she found herself running to the bed, and falling into his arms.

He hugged her hard for a moment, then said against the top of her head, "Maggie says ye made all that happen. Thank ye."

Smiling, she kept her face buried against his shirt, breathing in the precious scent of him. "I had help from both Maggie and your mother. How is Brendan?"

"He's glad to know the truth. I asked him to move here, but he'd rather have his old life."

"I understand that." With her ear on his chest, she listened to the solid, reliable thump of his heart. The wine had given her the courage to think of nothing beyond tonight.

"My Riona."

His voice was low with yearning, and he lifted her face until their eyes met and their smiles died. When he kissed her, Riona felt every last resistance fade away into some distant corner of her mind. They kissed and tasted with a growing urgency that she didn't question. Her hunger for him was insatiable, demanding. She came up on her knees over him and began to pull at the laces of her bodice, and then he was helping her. She'd never been undressed so swiftly in her life.

When she was standing, wearing only her chemise, she took the hem in her hands and met his suddenly narrowed eyes.

"Riona—"

She pulled it up and over her head, saw his indrawn breath as he took in her nudity by candlelight. He'd seen—or at least touched—her bare skin before, but there was something empowering about choosing to stand before him like this, unafraid.

And then he pulled off his own shirt and pulled her to him. The press of his hot skin along hers was wondrous. She clutched his shoulders and arched her back to be even closer to him. The hair on his chest teased her nipples, but that was nothing next to the feel of his hands sliding down to cup her backside. He separated her legs to straddle him where he sat on the edge of the bed, then arched her back so that he could take one breast into his mouth. She cried out and held him against her, unable to stop moving against his hips.

"Take me," she whispered. "Hugh, please, don't make me wait."

Her fingers fumbled between them for the buttons on his breeches. He reached to help her, and when his erection was free, she briefly took it in her hand as he'd shown her how to do. Her thighs were spread before him, and she moved forward as if to put him inside her.

And then she found herself on her back, Hugh bracing his hands on either side of her head.

He stared hard into her eyes, his breath coming fast. "Ye're sure ye want to do this."

"We're doing this," she answered with no hesitation. "I just don't know how best to—"

"Lift your knees," he said between clenched teeth.

When she did, he settled between her thighs.

"The first time—" he began.

"—might hurt," she finished. "I've been told. I don't care. Do that part quickly."

She felt the hard smoothness of him slide along her wet opening, and then he was deep inside her, filling her, the pain brief and fading compared to the incredible sensation of fullness and heat and dawning passion.

He kissed her then and she let her tongue invade his mouth as he was invading her body. For a long moment he didn't move his hips, just kissed her and caressed her breasts until passion heated her skin. She needed more and she began to squirm beneath him to make it happen.

And then he withdrew and slid deep inside her again, and she gasped.

"Oh. Oh!"

He laughed against her mouth, and they began the ancient dance of lovemaking, surging together and coming apart. Desire bubbled up ever higher, overcoming her, heating her, until all she could do was focus on the friction of their bodies, the wetness of his mouth on hers, the feel of his callused palm kneading her breast.

The culmination swept over her in a flash of brilliant awareness, as pleasure seemed to infuse and sensitize all the way to her fingers and toes. He continued to thrust into her faster and faster, and her pleasure went on until it was almost too much. And then he groaned and found his own release, crushing her into the mattress, but oh, it was good to be beneath him, to accept all of him at last.

"I love ye, Riona," he said quietly against her cheek.

And she burst into noisy tears.

CHAPTER 21

Hugh had never told a woman he loved her before, but he didn't think abject sobbing was the right response. "Riona?"

He propped himself up and tried to see her face, but she covered it with both hands and sobbed even harder.

"You can't love me," she cried between her fingers.

"Riona, talk to me."

He rose to his feet, and having totally forgotten about the rope around his ankles, not to mention his breeches, he almost fell over. But he had no time to deal with that. He sat down next to her, but she only curled into a ball away from him.

"Riona, I cannot help if we don't talk."

"Help?" She gave a harsh laugh that had nothing to do with amusement. "There is no help. I can't love you, Hugh—we're not supposed to be together.

You're my cousin's b-betrothed and I just—just seduced you!"

She shuddered and hugged herself, sobbing, while a terrible feeling of foreboding began in his chest and moved up to his brain. Why was she still saying this? She'd been happy—she'd helped his people, she'd helped *him*.

She sat up, pulled the counterpane around her shoulders with trembling fingers, then raised her face to his. Tearstains caught the candle and gleamed; her swollen eyes were full of sorrow. His foreboding became dread.

"I cannot have you," she whispered with despair. "I want you; I wish I could stay here and be your wife, but any time now the truth will catch up to us. I—I keep waiting for my uncle to arrive with glee as he keeps the McCallum land, and all the dowry money, for himself." Her head dropped and the sobs grew louder again.

Hugh felt almost light-headed with the sudden certainty that she'd been telling the truth all along, and he hadn't believed her. He wanted to pace, but the damned rope held him in place—the rope he'd used against her, to make her see that they belonged together. He felt like such a fool, and had no idea what to do first. Except untie the rope. He leaned down to do so.

"Hugh, you have to believe me," she pleaded. "But . . . no one needs to know what happened here.

You can let me go. I won't tell Cat. Some time will pass and I'll convince her to come meet you. You'll see, she's w-wonderful." She shuddered and cried some more. "And I've betrayed my cousin and slept with her betrothed."

Her last whisper was so agonized he felt as if she scratched him. He should touch her, but she was naked, and he'd seduced her—just like his father would have done. She'd been unwilling, and he'd relentlessly pursued her, even tied her into bed.

Guilt and shame washed over him. He yanked up and buttoned his breeches, then poured himself a large goblet of the wine and swallowed it all.

He'd thought he'd escaped the curse of his youth, the way he'd reacted to bad situations with recklessness. But when the betrothal hadn't gone his way, he'd simply told himself he was doing the right thing, and was just as reckless, if not more so. He'd stolen an innocent woman, humiliated her, and taken her virginity, ruining her for any other man. She could be with child.

He didn't know what to say to her. The words were caught so high up in his throat, it was like he was choking. He found himself on his knees before her.

"Riona." Her name was harsh in his mouth. "My God, what I've done to ye." He put his face on her bare knees. "I can't even ask for forgiveness. I deserve none."

He felt her trembling hand on his head, gently soothing back his hair. Now she was comforting *him*! He was so disgusted with himself that he wanted to fling himself away from her sweet presence. But she'd think he blamed her, and he couldn't do that.

"Hugh, you were not doing this for selfish reasons," she said at last. "You were acting on behalf of your people, when my uncle failed to follow through on his side of a good-faith bargain."

He sank back on his haunches to look up at her. "But if I'd have only believed ye, I could have returned ye immediately. But I was convinced that your father—your uncle—was trying to cheat me—"

"And he was," she said bitterly. "He was trying to ruin the contract and make it your fault. He planted me in that room to make sure you took the wrong woman. I—I don't know what he's said to Cat or my family about this. I've been gone over a month. My parents weren't due to come home until at least October, so they won't miss me. But Cat . . ." Her words trailed off, and her shoulders sagged.

Cat. There was another Catriona Duff in the world, the one he was supposed to marry. Not only had he ruined Riona, he'd dishonored her cousin. He sat down on the floor with his back against the bed.

Riona slipped down and sat beside him, the counterpane around her like a cloak. It covered her nudity, but it could not erase the images of her removing her clothes for him. She was being careful now not to touch him, but he didn't need to touch her to feel the heat of her presence, the call of his passion for her that even now wouldn't die.

"Why did ye let me . . ." And he couldn't finish the question.

"Why did I make love to you?" she asked, her voice hollow. "Because . . . I was tired of resisting myself."

The last word was not what he'd imagined she'd say.

"You thought I would be your wife," she said sadly. "And then you grew to desire me just for myself. And I couldn't resist. There was a part of me that pushed every doubt away. I just wanted to . . . feel, maybe to . . . pretend. I kept telling myself that before I left, I wanted you to know the peace of the truth about Brendan, and to begin to see your mother for the flawed woman she is, not the bearer of the guilt that should be your father's alone. I thought I could make up for what this"—she waved a hand between them—"was going to cost you. But all it did was make me see what a good man you are, how far you've come on behalf of your people."

"A good man?" He practically choked on the words. "I have hurt ye in ways I cannot even express. And tonight, the ultimate in pain. I took what was yours to grant your husband."

She leaned against his arm. "And tonight, I wanted to pretend that husband was you. It was my choice, Hugh, my decision. Being here, with you and your people, taught me to stand up for what I wanted even if I make a mistake. Don't blame yourself."

For endless minutes, they said nothing, just sat, barely touching each other, staring at the peat fire smoldering on the hearth.

"What should we do now?" she asked wearily.

He sighed. "Part of me thinks I should go after your uncle in revenge for what he allowed to happen to ye, for deliberately placing ye in the way of his enemy."

She stiffened. "Another war, Hugh? Because that's what it would be."

But focusing on that would distract him from thinking about losing Riona, because that's what had to happen. He'd spent weeks trying to make her fall in love with him and accept an arranged marriage, but—he was the one who'd fallen in love.

"Revenge is what my father would go after," he said at last. "I've already been proven enough like him tonight."

"Hugh—"

"Nay, your kindness after everything I've inflicted upon ye is only making this worse. Just because I don't think I should pursue revenge doesn't mean we don't deserve justice. Your uncle put ye into my hands, little caring what would happen to ye. I could have been a man like my father, for all your uncle knew or cared."

"All I ask is that we take our time before making a decision," she insisted. "No one here knows about this but you and me. I am not ready to let you abandon this marriage contract."

He flinched. "Ye think I should inflict myself upon your cousin?"

"I didn't say that. I can't even imagine it after how I've betrayed Cat."

He turned and took her by the shoulders, whispering fiercely, "This betrayal is my fault, Riona." The counterpane sagged, and he glimpsed the top of her breast, and wished he hadn't. He didn't want to desire her, but he still did. He always would. His traitorous body didn't care that he'd harmed her.

"You thought you were doing the right thing, Hugh. I knew better, and I still . . ."

And again they were silent.

"Riona, I need to give this serious thought. I don't want ye harmed by people finding out that a mistake has been made."

"Hugh, it's not about me but the clan—"

"Nay, for me, it's about you first. Promise me ye'll speak of this to no one except me. I'm going to send Samuel to the Duff castle and see if there's been word from your uncle."

She clutched his arm. "Won't that be dangerous for him?"

"Samuel thrives on danger," he assured her, feeling his attempt at lightness fall flat. "I won't make a decision until I ken what your uncle is up to. From what ye've said of your cousin, she won't let your disappearance be forgotten."

They continued to sit silently side by side for a long time, until Riona shivered.

"Into bed with ye," Hugh said, rising to his feet and reaching to help her. He tucked her in.

"Stay with me, please," she whispered, looking up at him with wet eyes.

He knew he shouldn't, but the worst had already happened. So he lay down on top of the counterpane and drew her against him. It was a long time before she slept, and each little shiver of sadness in her breathing cut him anew.

THREE days passed, and Riona couldn't take the awkwardness anymore, and confronted Hugh in his solar before dinner. It was the first time they'd allowed themselves to be alone since that night. He hadn't come to her bed, hadn't spent an evening talking privately. She missed him with an ache that only grew each day.

He stared at her as she shut the door. "Riona—"

"I know, I know, I shouldn't be here. But if Maggie asks me one more time what's wrong, I will simply scream."

"She is persistent," he said wryly.

He leaned back in his leather chair and stretched, making her think of how his body looked beneath his shirt and plaid. She shivered and tried to put aside the desire that always seemed to linger just beneath the surface when she saw him . . . when she thought of him . . . maybe just all the time. "I thought I saw Samuel at the stables."

"Ye did. We just spoke. Come sit with me."

She dragged a chair near his desk, but was surprised when he took her hand and drew her to sit on his lap. She perched there uncertainly.

"Just let me hold ye, lass." His voice was a low rumble in her ear. "I dream about us each night."

She closed her eyes on a sigh. "Oh, Hugh . . ."

She sank against his chest and huddled there, letting him caress her hair and back. He felt safe and warm—and still so forbidden. "Tell me about Samuel."

"Something unexpected has happened. Your uncle died of a fever several weeks ago and the news is only just now spreading through the Highlands."

She straightened in shock and the world suddenly seemed a different place. Her uncle had never shown anything but impatience with the women in his life, except for Cat. Perhaps her aunt would blossom now that she was no longer under his shadow. She met Hugh's somber gaze. "What does this mean for us?"

"Not much, I believe. The contract is binding regardless of your uncle's death."

Nodding, she frowned. "My aunt will be grief-stricken, but probably for show more than anything."

"She has come to the Highlands with his body, along with the new earl and his sister."

Riona gasped. "Cat? And Owen?"

He nodded. "I ken ye've missed your cousin."

"I have, but . . . she probably doesn't know I'm here."

"We don't know what Owen is aware of. But . . . have ye considered that soon word will spread that Owen's sister is with him, and not here with me? Perhaps . . . they'll think it's Bronwyn? I've mentioned a sister to more than one person."

Her stomach gave a twist of apprehension. "Oh, Hugh," she whispered. "I'm so sorry." He'd worked so hard to be a worthy chief to his people, and now they'd soon discover his dreadful mistake.

"Stop saying that," he ordered. "Ye've nothing to be sorry for. I've decided that we shall find a way to deal with this without revealing what we don't want revealed."

"But if you just explain everything, tell the clan you were deceived by my uncle—"

"And risk shaming you in public? Nay, I think I first need to meet with Owen."

A sudden pounding on the door startled them

both. Riona jumped to her feet as if being caught on Hugh's lap was the worst sin. Not compared to other things they'd done, she thought grimly.

Hugh came around his desk and went toward the door, but it opened before he got there and several people crowded in: Dermot and Alasdair, Maggie and Lady McCallum.

Samuel came in last, then closed the door and stood in front of it, arms folded over his chest, looking more intimidating than Riona had ever seen him.

Dermot led the charge. "We've heard news of the arrival of the new Earl of Aberfoyle—and his sister," he added, glowering at Riona. "I've made it my business to learn everything about Clan Duff. The new earl only has one sister."

Though her fingers twisted together before her, she tried to portray a calmness she was far from feeling.

"Aye, Samuel told me they'd arrived with their father's body," Hugh said.

"But I didn't tell anyone else," Samuel explained calmly. "Other travelers arrived today with the news."

"What have ye done, Hugh?" Alasdair asked, exasperated. "Ye always did act before thinking."

Hugh's jaw clenched and unclenched, and Riona could feel him keeping a rein on the worst of his temper.

"My uncle deceived Hugh," Riona said in a voice

that only wavered a little in the face of the angry men and confused women.

Hugh made a slashing motion with his hand. "What we discuss here goes no farther than this room, do ye understand? Dermot, have ye told anyone else how many sisters Owen has?"

Dermot hesitated, then shook his head.

"Then for now, Riona's true identity is secret. I will make the decision about the information the clan will have."

"Fine," Dermot said, then demanded, "Did ye ken she wasn't your betrothed? Or did the witch go along with her family to deceive ye?"

In two steps, Hugh had Dermot by the front of his coat and the room was in an uproar of raised voices. Lady McCallum gasped and covered her mouth, and Maggie looked like she wanted to jump between the men. Riona felt only despair that she was the cause of ruining Hugh's relationships with his friends after he'd just mended them.

"Don't ever speak about Riona like that again," Hugh ordered in a cold voice. "Everything that's happened is *my* fault, not hers. She is an innocent here."

Alasdair stared at her in frustration. "If ye're innocent, Riona, why did ye let us all believe ye were the earl's daughter?"

Hugh let go of Dermot, who didn't back away. "She told me the truth but was too frightened to tell any of ye. I thought she was lying, that her uncle was trying to back out of the contract and take the land from us. She has the same name as her cousin; she was the only young woman in the house when I stole her out of her room."

Maggie's mouth dropped open, but everyone else seemed to freeze.

"Hugh," his mother said in a trembling voice, "ye kidnapped Riona?"

She looked at her son as if her worst fears about him were confirmed, that he'd become like his father. Riona felt absolutely sick at heart, and wanted to fling herself between Hugh and all the disapproval and ugliness. But he wouldn't welcome her interference.

"I did," he said heavily, raking a hand through his dark hair. The queue came loose and his hair fell forward to brush his shoulders. "I thought I had the right after the earl tried to break the contract when we spoke. But I made a terrible mistake, and Riona has suffered for it—and the clan might suffer, too."

There was a long, tense silence, where everyone stared at Hugh and Riona. She knew what they were thinking—that she should have made Hugh see the truth. She wanted to curl into a ball and re-treat from them all back into her misery. But that would mean giving up, and she couldn't do that, not when Hugh needed her.

"Take her back," Dermot said. "Owen isn't the same man as his father."

"None of us know Owen well, do we?" Alasdair said bitterly. "He's a Scotsman who wanted to be English."

"That's not true," Maggie said.

Alasdair ignored her. "And we shouldn't give up the lass. We should fight over the wrong the old earl did to ye. A contract is just paper, but the land is our birthright."

"The land we could lose if he doesn't take Riona back," Dermot said.

"Do ye think brides are interchangeable?" Hugh demanded with bitterness. "I've dishonored both Riona and her cousin. I need to make this right. I will go to meet Owen."

"But that could be dangerous," Riona said. "Let me invite them here. Cat will want to see me." And she could introduce Cat and Hugh, and then quietly step aside. It would be better for everyone, even though her heart would break into a thousand pieces.

"And bring the devil into our midst?" Alasdair demanded.

"These are my cousins, not the devil," Riona insisted.

"Enough!" Hugh interrupted. "I will contact Owen and insist on a meeting. We will discuss this calmly and not like warriors demanding a battle that will only hurt both our clans and perhaps draw the attention of the British at Fort William."

Though Dermot and Alasdair exchanged skeptical glances, no one argued against Hugh, and Samuel opened the door for them.

"You were with him in England," Dermot said to Samuel furiously. "Why did ye not stop him?"

" 'Tis our place to support our laird, is it not?" Samuel asked.

Dermot swept past him, followed by Alasdair and then Samuel, who closed the door, leaving just the family.

Maggie looked at Hugh and Riona with concern. "How are ye both?"

Though Riona had worn a brave front these last days, to her embarrassment, tears brimmed in her eyes and fell down her cheeks.

"Oh, Riona!"

And then Maggie was hugging her, and Riona was so grateful for the support.

"I'll be fine," Riona said, straightening and stepping back. Hugh's expression was stark with grief and guilt, and she didn't want that. "We just need to make this work for the clan."

"What about the two of ye?" Lady McCallum asked. "How can we help ye?"

"Only we can take care of this, Mother," Hugh said grimly. "I'll have to see what Owen has to say."

"I want to be there," Riona said.

He eyed her. "That's not a wise idea. He'll be offended on your behalf, on his sister's behalf—and furious with me."

Frustrated, Riona began, "But Hugh—"

"Nay, I'll handle this as I see fit."

He left the solar with a confident stride, and Lady McCallum hurried after him.

Maggie and Riona stared at each other for a long minute, until Riona felt uncomfortable, wondering what Maggie must be thinking about her strange relationship with Hugh.

"I'm so sorry ye had to go through this alone," Maggie said.

Riona gave her a weak smile. "I survived. I even fell in love, much good it will do me."

"And he loves ye," Maggie said softly.

The grief twisted her throat, but Riona forced words out. "He told me. I almost wish he hadn't, for it is so much to bear, knowing that we can never be together."

Maggie gripped Riona's upper arms. "Don't say that! I refuse to believe Hugh can't make it happen."

"I could never do that to your clan, Maggie," Riona insisted. "My dowry is far smaller than my cousin's, but worse than that is losing the land both clans have been sharing."

"I still insist that we not lose hope. Is Owen the same man he once was?"

"I have no reason to believe otherwise," Riona

said, "but we've had little to do with each other these last years. He's a practical man, not given to Society's entertainments. And if I wasn't with Cat, I was closeted away with Bronwyn."

"I believe dealing with Owen is the right thing. I can just . . . feel it."

Riona eyed her suspiciously. Maggie's strangely colored eyes seemed focused far away . . .

HUGH had simply wanted to escape all the accusing eyes, but if he needed to write to Owen, he should have stayed in the solar and kicked everyone else out. Instead, he went up to his bedroom, where there was a smaller writing desk. As he was about to shut the door, he saw his mother hurrying down the corridor toward him.

He sighed and awaited her. "Mother, I don't need another lecture on my mistakes."

"Ye won't hear that from me," she said softly. "Allow me to come in, please."

He opened the door wide, and she went past him. After closing it, he turned to see her standing still in the room, staring around her as if she'd never been there before.

"Mother?" he said curiously.

She shook her head, then met his gaze with embarrassment. "I have not been in this room in many years. The memories are not pleasant, and I'm glad ye'll be making new, happier memories here."

He gritted his teeth and said nothing, just moved past her.

"Hugh, I know things seem bleak right now, but . . . I believe in ye. Ye'll make this work."

At the desk, he found paper and opened the ink bottle as he sat down. "Thank ye for your encouragement, Mother, but I don't ken how ye can feel positive about that. I've spent my life trying to be different than my father, and apparently, that's impossible." He heard his own bitterness, but didn't bother to hide it.

"Ye're nothing like him," Lady McCallum said fiercely.

Hugh looked up from his paper in surprise.

"Never, ever think that of yourself. Ye may have been an impulsive young man, angry that your plans for the future were so rigidly defined for ye—but ye tried to help Agnes, whereas your father only brutalized her. Ye've tried to help your clan—"

"And took advantage of an innocent woman. Not so different than him."

"Regardless of your mistake, ye treated Riona with such kindness that she's fallen in love with ye!"

He flinched. "She doesn't love me, Mother. I have ruined her for a good marriage. She has no choice but to see if I can salvage this disaster, because my actions *ensured* she had no choice. And she's come to appreciate our clan, and doesn't want to see innocent people harmed by my mistake."

"Don't be so foolish, my son. She loves *you*, and wants to help *you* help your clan."

He stared at her, keeping his bleakness buried inside because he couldn't imagine a future without Riona. "Mother, I appreciate the kind words, but I have to write a letter to the new Earl of Aberfoyle right now."

She nodded, and to his surprise, she briefly touched his arm.

"I have faith in ye, Hugh. Don't lose faith in yourself."

CHAPTER 22

For two days after Hugh sent the letter to Owen, Riona lived on tenterhooks. She remained mostly with Maggie and Lady McCallum, both of whom spoke cheerfully about everything from thread to rain. Riona had a hard time achieving any sort of cheerfulness. Hugh was avoiding her in private, and she could not blame him. Every time he saw her, he must be reminded that the well-being of his clan was now in jeopardy. So far, Hugh'd been right, that the average person didn't seem to know or care that the earl had returned with a sister who wasn't Riona.

At night, Hugh slept in his own bed, and more than once she found herself creeping through the dressing room on sleepless nights to put her ear against the door, wanting just to hear him breathe. The words "I love you, Riona," had begun to seem like a dream that she'd awakened from into a nightmare.

On the third morning, she was startled out of sleep by Maggie shaking her.

"Riona, wake up!"

With a gasp, Riona bolted upright. "What's wrong?"

"Hugh left to meet Owen without us! Get up, get dressed, I have a gown laid out for ye."

"But—but—"

It was hard to talk when Maggie was yanking stays over her head and nightshift.

As Maggie tugged on the laces, Riona asked, "Did you overhear Hugh's plans?"

"Nay. But I was informed by someone sympathetic to us. No need to concern yourself with whom." Maggie pulled a petticoat over Riona's head and tied it at her waist, then did the same with her skirt.

"Maggie, but who—"

"Never ye mind."

Frustrated, Riona helped Maggie slide the masculine waistcoat of her new riding habit up her arms and laced it in front. There was no doubt Maggie was frantic to follow Hugh. And Riona was fine with that. She grunted as Maggie shoved a stomacher down behind the laces.

"Sorry," Maggie said. "Here are your coat and boots." She tapped her toe while Riona donned them. "Let's go!"

They had no problem taking horses from the

stables. Brendan loved being able to help his new sister. It wasn't until they were outside the curtain wall that Riona felt able to speak freely.

"Maggie, were you told where Hugh is going? I can't see him, and even if we could, he'd see us."

Maggie stared out over McCallum land. Mist hovered above the surface of Loch Voil down below them, and curled up the path. The sun wasn't yet visible, but the sky was golden in the east as if the mountains wore halos.

"The whisky land," Maggie said with conviction. "That's where I was told Owen wanted to meet him."

"But . . . what if we catch up to Hugh?"

"We won't. There's more than one path, and I'll take a different one."

Riona opened her mouth, then shut it again. She'd already gone along with Maggie's plan; there was no point in quibbling. Maggie's gaze was fixed on the rising path before them with determination.

Several hours later, Riona began to recognize the land, and knew they were near. The path narrowed through a copse of trees, then opened up to the vast bog that crossed the glen. And not fifty yards ahead of them, Hugh and Owen faced each other, and the tension in the lines of their bodies was a visible thing.

Maggie caught Riona's reins and whispered, "Let's stay within the trees and listen."

They both dismounted but weren't noticed, because the two men were focused on each other.
Owen was a tall, lean man, who wore his sandy-
colored hair pulled back in a queue rather than
hidden beneath a wig. He was not dressed as a
Highlander, but wore elegant breeches and coat,
with a waistcoat, fine shirt, and cravat beneath,
very much an earl.

Riona glanced at Maggie, who seemed to absorb
Owen with her focused gaze.

"Your father told me I could not have Catriona
to wife," Hugh was saying heatedly. "I could not
permit him to break the contract that was promised
to my clan."

"So you kidnapped my cousin?" Owen said lev-
elly, but with indignation in his voice.

"Your father put her in Cat's room—and I was
fool enough to fall into his trap. Did he even tell ye
about Riona being missing?"

Owen's lips thinned, but he didn't answer.

"He wanted me to take her, to save your sister. If
ye think I do not regret my actions," Hugh added,
"then ye'd be thinking wrong. I regret putting
Riona, an innocent woman, in the middle of this
feud the contract was supposed to heal. Do ye want
this feud to continue, Owen?"

Owen stiffened. "I cannot overlook the injury
done to my cousin, regardless of the circumstances,
nor can I forget the dishonor to my sister, who was

supposed to be your bride. The contract states that should the conditions not be met, you forfeit this land and Cat's dowry. And surely Riona is ready to return home."

"Riona's home is with me," Hugh said coldly.

Though used in an ugly argument between two men important to her, those words thrilled Riona. Hugh wanted her, was doing this for her, too, and not just the clan.

"You violated her, McCallum. There's nothing else to discuss."

"Then let us do what our ancestors would have done, and place the fate of our clans on our own shoulders. I challenge ye to combat by sword, and the winner will rewrite the contract in his own terms and all will abide by it."

Riona felt a chill, then opened her mouth to protest.

"Nay!" Maggie screamed before she could.

Both men whirled, hands on their swords and pistols.

Maggie ran down the slope of the hill, Riona on her heels.

"Riona!" screamed another woman's voice, and out of the trees closer to Owen, raced Cat.

Riona gave an excited cry and ran to fling her arms around her cousin, as beloved to her as her sister.

Cat was sobbing, her brown hair falling out of its

chignon. "I—I didn't know what had happened to you!" Cat said, hiccupping on the words. "F-Father tried to tell me you'd decided to set up your own household, but I didn't believe it, especially when he wouldn't tell me where. Oh, Riona, I was so frightened!"

They hugged again, hard, then turned to face the men.

Owen was staring at Maggie, eyes narrowed but unreadable. With her hands on her hips, Maggie met his gaze defiantly.

But Owen didn't speak to her, instead said to his sister, "You *followed* me, Cat? At least those two"—he gestured at Riona and Maggie—"had each other on such a journey."

"I have a groom," Cat sniffed. "He's with the horses."

Then her expression sobered, and she darted a glance past Riona's shoulder at Hugh, who stood in his black and red belted plaid, massive arms crossed over his chest, and glowered at the women.

"Owen told me I'd been betrothed since child-hood," Cat said, "and Father never told me. Riona, this is he, the villain who *kidnapped* you?"

"Ye're speaking about my brother!" Maggie said with indignation.

She eyed Owen uncertainly, while he boldly looked her up and down.

"Yes, he kidnapped me," Riona said. "Th-this is

the man you are to marry, Cat, Hugh McCallum."
To her horror, her voice was shaking and tears
stung her eyes.

Cat put a hand on her arm. "I'm sorry it's been so
terrible for you. Surely, it's better that the contract is
broken after his terrible behavior."

And still Hugh said nothing to defend himself.

"It was only frightening at the beginning," Riona
insisted, "and Hugh never harmed me. He just
wouldn't let me go, because he honestly believed
I was the woman he was to marry. He treated me
with honor."

Hugh's frown grew more ferocious, and she
knew what he was remembering. She just hoped he
kept quiet about the ropes.

"But ye're not that woman, Riona," Owen said
coldly. "And I refuse to allow my sister to marry
such a man."

Cat stared at Hugh, little bothering to hide her
fear at the merest thought.

"Cat, this contract is so important," Riona insisted. "We have to find a way—and not armed
combat!—to come to some kind of agreement."

"I cannot in all honor marry you, Lady Catriona," Hugh said. "I love your cousin, and I've already taken her to wife in the time-honored way of
our people."

Riona groaned. "Hugh!"

Owen drew his sword with a metallic swish. The

sun, peeking through clouds, glinted along it with menace. "Then any discussion is over. I accept your challenge, McCallum, and this just won't be to first blood, but to the death."

"Owen!" Cat cried. "I thought you wanted to be a man of science! I won't allow this. No one is going to die! If Laird McCallum loves Riona—" And then she gazed at Riona with trepidation. "But do you love *him*?"

Hugh's gaze burned into Riona's, but he did not beg her for her favor.

Riona covered her mouth with both hands as her tears spilled at last. "I feel so ashamed."

Cat's expression mellowed into tenderness. "Don't cry, Riona. Don't be ashamed. None of this was your fault. And I'm not betrayed—I don't even know him!"

For a moment, there was no further sound but the wind. Riona and Hugh simply looked at each other, and in his gaze, at last she saw love and anguish and guilt, and a terrible farewell that seemed to crush her chest. He would honestly fight to the death to make this right?

"I won't stand for this!" Maggie cried. "There has to be another way."

For a long, tense moment, the silence was unbroken. Hugh glared at Owen, and although Owen gave him back equal menace, at last his gaze turned to Maggie and stayed there. He wasn't hiding his emotions now, Riona saw. There was speculation in his knitted brow, and then his forehead cleared with a momentary wide-eyed look of realization and then deep satisfaction. It all flashed by quickly, and Riona wasn't certain what she'd seen.

But then Owen spoke. "I have another proposal, McCallum. I will marry your sister and seal the peace between our clans once and for all."

Riona gasped. Maggie went still, but she made no protest.

Hugh glanced between them frowning. "My sister? What connection is there between ye?"

"You were in England half the year, she was in Edinburgh," Owen said. "We have spent time together once or twice, have we not, Maggie?"

Her chin came up even as a revealing blush washed across her cheeks. But still she did not protest the idea of marriage between them.

Hugh gave his sister a baffled stare. "Maggie, ignore his ridiculous idea. Ye don't need to marry him. This is my disaster, and I will fix it."

"A marriage between our clans is all that's necessary to make things right," Owen said. "I will be satisfied with Maggie as my bride."

Now it was Cat's turn to give her own brother a frown. "What is going on? You two knew each other *that* well?"

Maggie didn't answer.

A knowing smile curved Owen's lips, even as Hugh's eyebrows lowered in an ominous frown.

"Maggie, say yes," Owen said, his voice rough at the edges. "You alone know what happened between us. Together, we can make a new contract, and our people can share this land again. Your brother and my cousin can be together; my sister need never fear marrying a man she's never met. Of course, her dowry will be held for her future husband," he said to Hugh in warning.

"I have my own dowry, though it isn't as large as Cat's," Riona added, and risked a glance at Hugh. For the first time, she felt a touch of hope.

She could see he was torn between protecting his sister, and the chance that their love—and the contract—might be saved. But Riona could never be happy if she felt that Maggie was reluctant.

Maggie was studying Owen as if he were a strange plant whose use she was trying to ascertain. Owen let her look her fill, confidence in his straight shoulders and the curve of one eyebrow as he awaited her decision.

"I will marry you, Owen," Maggie finally said, her voice cool, almost detached.

Owen sheathed his sword with finality and even triumph. Riona wondered if he'd come here already prepared with this plan. Her cousin was a smart man. But he was also an earl, who could have married into another titled family.

"There will be no marriage if I forbid it," Hugh said angrily. He strode to his sister, taking her shoulders. "Maggie—"

Maggie put her fingers against his mouth, and Riona could have sworn they trembled.

"Hugh, I want to do this," she said with quiet resolve. "Owen's right—this will solve all the problems between our clans. I may not know him well, but I do know him. And for me to be able to bring about a peace that's been absent for generations? I will feel such pride, Hugh." She lowered her voice and spoke with even more solemnity. "And this *feels* right to me."

She emphasized the word "feels" in a way that seemed to relax Hugh.

He cupped her face in one hand. "Ye're sure."

At last, she allowed a small smile. "I'm sure. Let me do this, Hugh. I think Owen is right—it's meant to be."

Owen's smile faded a bit as he stared at Maggie, but he said nothing.

Riona's hope tried to soar, but she held it furled, fearful. "Maggie, are you certain?"

Maggie turned, and her strange eyes glittered. "I'm certain. I've been waiting for my destiny to reveal itself—and now it has."

Owen rolled his eyes. "Enough of this nonsense, Maggie. I won't hear any more of it."

"Oh, we will be discussing things," Maggie said.

Then she turned to her brother. "Hugh, may I have your permission to accept Owen's romantic proposal?"

Cat didn't bother to hide her laughter.

"Was I not romantic enough for you?" Owen asked, his triumphant smile returning. He took a step toward her as if he meant to prove his intentions.

Riona saw Hugh stiffen, knew he held himself back.

Maggie kissed her brother's cheek. "This is what I want, Hugh," she said in a low voice. "Let me have it."

Hugh nodded, but he didn't look happy about it. "Ye have my permission," he said quietly, enfolding her in a quick hug. "But if these negotiations don't work out, he and I will have another discussion."

Maggie gave a small smile. "They'll work out."

"Come here and speak with me, Maggie," Owen said, turning his back and striding toward the edge of the bog.

She followed him with an elegant, confident stride that said she was prepared to have her way, now that she'd accepted.

Hugh turned to Cat and bowed. "Lady Catriona, I apologize for the wrong I've done ye, the dishonor I've brought to ye."

Cat eyed him speculatively. "I can feel no offense for something I didn't even know about—

something I didn't want. Riona and I always talked about choosing our own husbands. If Riona willingly chooses you, then I am content, for I, too, will have the man of my own choice."

Riona thought her heart would burst with love and gratitude. She hugged her cousin hard. "I've missed you so! I thought I'd ruined everything between us."

"Oh, Riona, in some ways I envy you." Cat broke the hug, then quickly added, "For your relationship, of course, not the man himself. But I do believe he is waiting to claim you."

Suddenly, Riona didn't seem to be able to take a deep enough breath. Was this really happening? Could she have her own happiness?

Hugh, Riona, and Cat waited silently as Maggie and Owen spoke privately. Owen practically stood over Maggie, he was so close. They didn't touch or betray a yearning, but there was something there between them, something that must have been simmering a long time.

Hugh seemed distracted by worry for his sister, and Riona understood. She still felt dazed herself. He didn't bring up their marriage or their future.

Only when Maggie at last turned away from Owen did Hugh say stiffly, " 'Tis time to return to Larig Castle. We can discuss your wedding there."

Not our *wedding*, Riona realized with a start. But she knew he loved her—she could be patient.

"Wait," Maggie said. "Hugh, what will ye say to the clan about how we've changed the contract?"

Without hesitation, he answered, "I will explain what happened, of course."

"No, you will not," Riona said sharply.

Everyone turned to look at her.

"You may be their chief, Hugh, but they are only just beginning to know and trust you. You made mistakes in your youth, and I alone know how much you've changed." As that came out of her mouth, she thought Maggie might protest, but the woman said nothing. "Since the clan does not yet know you as I and your family do, they don't need to know the truth of what went on between us, as long as it solves the problems between the McCallums and the Duffs."

"Ye're suggesting I lie?" Hugh asked stiffly.

"How is it a lie that we want to be married, that we want a future together?" she asked with quiet certainty. "Why do they need to know the private details of how we came together?"

"I never want my actions to make ye publicly shamed by what happened to ye," Hugh admitted hoarsely.

"It's not about me, but the ability to lead your clan!"

"Enough with the self-sacrificing attitude on both your parts," Owen said with disgust. "Tell us the story and we shall all swear to it. We've all worked hard to make right what our fathers did. It needs to be finished."

Owen looked pointedly at Maggie, and though she met his eyes, she said nothing.

"We can say part of the truth," Hugh said quietly. "That the moment I saw you by the light of day, I was struck by your beauty and your courage."

She knew immediately the moment of which he spoke, when she'd emerged out of the coach by daylight and seen him for the first time, too. He had changed her entire life—for the better—but she hadn't known the truth that day. It was strange, yet gratifying, to know that the moment had changed him as well.

"I had to have you for my own and I wouldn't let the contract stand in the way," he continued with fervor.

Maggie smiled at her brother, tears in her eyes. "And that's the truth, isn't it? And between all of us, the best results have happened."

Riona answered Maggie's smile with one of her own. "Just say that you knew who I was from the beginning—after all, I'd told you the truth, remember?"

Hugh grimaced, and Owen shook his head.

" 'Tis done," Hugh said. "I don't care about myself, but I never want to shame ye again after everything I've put ye through."

"It was worth it," Riona said quietly. She thought

for a moment that Hugh would say more, but was disappointed when he turned away to the horses.

As they all approached Larig in mid afternoon, Riona stared upward at the magnificent castle with a new perspective. This was her home now— would be her home forever. Her eyes stung and she blinked them, not wanting to distract Hugh, who'd seemed overly sober and silent during the journey back. This didn't make her nervous, as it once might have done. He'd confessed his love to her, and she trusted him.

But she'd never told him of her own love, she realized. Was he concerned about her true feelings, now that they would be married? But she needed privacy to discuss this, and didn't know when they'd have it.

The guards didn't recognize the new Earl of Aberfoyle, and Hugh announced him in a ringing voice. "You shall all show your respect and care for the earl," he continued, "and treat him as my new relation."

The guards sent glances toward each other, but all bowed as they passed. Word seemed to spread from behind them and outward around the upper courtyard, where ghillies and gentlemen alike emerged from the barracks to stare. Owen rode straight in the saddle, unconcerned with anyone but Maggie. Riona caught him glancing at her frequently, but except for offering her water and oat-cakes on the journey, they'd spoken little.

Maggie's usual cheerful expression was absent, as if she was mulling what she'd agreed to. But Riona knew the McCallums and honor, and knew Maggie had meant everything she said. Riona now understood what it was like to think you had to marry a stranger, and she could only hope that Maggie and Owen shared more of a history than Riona knew of.

After handing over their horses to grooms—including Brendan, to whom Hugh gave his first smile of the day—they all ascended the stairs to the great hall on the first floor of the main tower-house. Word must have already spread inside, for Mrs. Wallace was waiting there, and she stared at Owen with wide eyes, as if the devil himself had come to visit.

Riona slid her arm within Cat's, who looked nervous, and murmured, "Don't worry, everyone here is wonderful and will treat you with respect."

Cat only nodded.

"Is it strange to know you should have been mistress here?" Riona asked knowingly.

Cat's eyes widened. "You always did understand me too well."

They both chuckled, and the tension eased.

"Mrs. Wallace," Riona said, "please see to accommodations for the Earl of Aberfoyle and his sister."

Mrs. Wallace's usual smile blossomed. "Of course. Lady Riona, would ye wish to accompany us?"

Cat glanced at Riona in surprise at the honorific, then bit her lip to hide a smile. Riona looked to Hugh uncertainly.

He nodded. "Go with them, Riona. Mrs. Wallace, when the ladies are settled, please return to speak with me. I have instructions for our feast this night." He arched a brow at Riona. "Rest, my lady. I will take care of everything."

She felt that knot in her throat again, the exultation of being loved, being cared for. But . . . she wanted to go to him, beg him to tell her it would be all right, that he could get past the sacrifices they'd all made to end the feud between their clans.

That evening, she chose her favorite new gown, a deep blue that parted down the front to reveal an embroidered stomacher and the lace of her petticoat. Mary stared at her with awe, and even Cat and Maggie, who came to be with her, seemed impressed.

"I think you must be in love because you're even more beautiful," Cat said.

Her voice had a wistfulness that surprised Riona. Her cousin had always been so independent, wanting to do as she pleased before having to settle into a man's home. Riona only hoped that she could make Cat see that marriage wasn't such a bad thing . . . if one could overlook the kidnapping part.

The three women descended to the great hall, and Riona inhaled with shock. She'd never seen the large room decorated for such a feast, with colorful tapestries and banners on the wall, every torch lit, and at least a hundred people gathered. How had Hugh reached so many people in so little time? They'd all come for him, their chief.

Hugh was standing with Owen on the dais, and they looked anything but at ease with each other. But the earl seemed to relax upon seeing Maggie, as if he'd been worried she might change her mind. He guided her to a seat beside him, and she gave him a polite smile. With a sigh, Riona turned away from them, knowing that she would help her future sister-in-law all she could.

Hugh was looking down upon her with such seriousness that she felt a pang of worry. But the frown faded from his brow, and he bent over her hand.

"Do ye trust me?" he whispered.

He stared up at her with those gray eyes she'd once thought of as winter cold, but she now understood the thaw as if it were springtime between them, a time of beginnings.

"I trust you with all my heart," she answered quietly.

And then he straightened, and still holding her hand, called for attention in a voice that wasn't overly loud, but rang with command. Everyone went silent, as if they'd been waiting for this moment. Riona felt as if even breathing would disturb the pregnant stillness.

"I'd like to introduce ye to my wife, Riona Duff."

There was a cheer, but it died away in confusion.

"Aye, ye knew her as my betrothed, but I've taken her to wife in the ways of our ancestors, but this will be no trial marriage. We'll have it blessed before the priest."

At last he smiled at Riona, and she gave him a tremulous smile in return. Whatever he said next, she knew it would be for the best.

"But I tell ye this because Riona was not the bride I'd been promised since childhood. Her cousin Lady Catriona was."

He gestured to Cat, who blushed to the roots of her hair, but kept her chin high. Owen's face was a mask of impassivity, but his eyes blazed as he stared at Hugh.

In the hall, the dead silence had returned, along with sidelong looks of uneasiness. Riona knew that they were remembering the terms of the contract, and what its sundering would mean to them.

Hugh took both her hands, and though he spoke to the hall, he looked only at her. "From the moment I saw Riona, I knew I had to have her to wife," he said, his voice rough. "I felt a passion and a destiny that I could not deny. I did not forget the contract between our clans, but I knew that I would find a way to come to terms with Aberfoyle. While I did this, I kept the truth a secret from everyone, and I regret that it was necessary. Fear not, for the contract remains between our families. Lady Catriona will have her pick of husbands, a decision she welcomes making on her own."

Cat gave a real smile to Hugh for the first time, and Riona felt the last of her tension fade away.

Hugh continued, "My sister, Maggie, will become the earl's bride, and both of our marriages will heal the rift begun hundreds of years ago between McCallum and Duff."

The cheer at those words was deafening, and even Owen looked surprised. He glanced at Maggie, who met his gaze, and it held for so long, Riona had to look away, feeling as embarrassed as if she'd seen them kissing. She knew there wasn't love there yet, but they had . . . something.

Hugh lifted the *cuach* up high. "This whisky, the water of life, has also helped heal the past." He took a long sip, then passed it to Owen, who didn't hesitate to drink it.

When the cup passed her, Riona took hold of it, to Hugh's obvious surprise.

"Ye don't have to drink it, lass," he murmured. "I remember how it tasted to ye."

"I'm your wife, Hugh McCallum, and I'll do as I please."

Laughter spread out around her, and she took a

sip—a tiny one—of the whisky. She nodded, holding her breath, trying not to cough as it burned down her throat.

"That is good," she said hoarsely, and passed it to Maggie.

Hugh grinned and took her hand. "Come with me, Riona."

The redness from the whisky turned into a hot blush. "Hugh, we can't leave yet," she whispered.

He chuckled. "Then come stand outside with me."

He led her through the crowd, and people briefly clasped her hand or wished them well. At last they were outside on the landing, where torches lit the castle, but the stairs still seemed to go down into darkness.

But Hugh didn't descend, only looked at her with searching eyes as the wind ruffled his dark hair.

And then he dropped to one knee and reached for her hand. "Riona Duff, I did not properly ask ye to marry me yet. If ye would, accept my hand in marriage, and accept a place in my castle, and in my heart."

She didn't believe she had more tears, but they came.

He pressed his lips to her hand, then met her gaze. "I love ye, Riona, yet I don't feel worthy of ye. I doubted your word though ye only ever spoke the truth. I focused on the needs of my clan rather than what I was doing to ye. I almost lost ye." His voice grew husky. "That would have meant unbearable sadness to me. Ye've become the light in my heart, Riona, a love I never thought I could have, after my father took away all my choices. Say ye'll marry me." He paused, and his next words were hoarse. "Say ye love me, lass."

"Oh Hugh," she whispered. "I've loved you longer than I even knew. I was so afraid we could never be together, that I wouldn't let myself believe in our love, nor trust in it. Even now, it still seems almost unreal. But I love you!"

She flung her arms around his neck, and he caught her and rose to his feet, holding her off the ground.

"Of course I'll marry you, Hugh. But remember, though you may have named me your wife, that doesn't excuse you from helping to plan our official wedding."

He laughed and set her on her feet. "As ye can see from our feast tonight, I'll be good at that."

"You'll be a most excellent husband, Hugh, and every day I'll thank God that I was the one you kidnapped."

He grinned, then held her by the hand and led her back into the hall, back into the embrace of their clan.

Letter to the Reader

Dear Reader,

Thank you so much for reading *The Wrong Bride*, my first foray into books set in Scotland. I hope you enjoyed the story of Riona and Hugh falling in love, even with all their misunderstandings.

And I bet you thought things were pretty settled at the end. Maggie seemed a bit . . . reluctant to marry Owen, the Earl of Aberfoyle, and there's a reason for that. As you'll discover in my next book, *The Groom Wore Plaid*, Maggie and Owen had not parted on good terms when they were teenagers. And now he wants to marry her to end the feud between their clans. She's willing to see if he's changed, even hopeful that they can forge a life together that's more than just an arranged marriage. But then she has a dream of Owen terribly injured on their wedding day. She vows that they will not marry if it means his death. Owen, of course, has other plans, and sets about convincing her . . .

If you'd like to read an excerpt of *The Groom Wore Plaid*, please visit my website at www.GayleCallen.com. Look for the book in your favorite bookstore in March 2016.

Happy Reading!
Gayle